THE SANCTUARY

Charlotte Duckworth started her career as an interiors and lifestyle journalist. She is the bestselling author of *The Rival*, *Unfollow Me* and *The Perfect Father*. She lives in Surrey with her partner and their daughter. You can find out more on her website: charlotteduckworth.com.

NO LONGER PROPERTY
OF ANYTHINK
RANGEVIEW LIBRARY
DISTRICT

Also by Charlotte Duckworth

The Rival
Unfollow Me
The Perfect Father

THE SANCTUARY

CHARLOTTE DUCKWORTH

QUERCUS

First published in Great Britain in 2021 by Quercus
This paperback edition first published in 2022 by

QUERCUS

Quercus Editions Ltd
Carmelite House
50 Victoria Embankment
London EC4Y 0DZ

An Hachette UK company

Copyright © 2021 Charlotte Duckworth

The moral right of Charlotte Duckworth to be
identified as the author of this work has been
asserted in accordance with the Copyright,
Designs and Patents Act, 1988.

All rights reserved. No part of this publication
may be reproduced or transmitted in any form
or by any means, electronic or mechanical,
including photocopy, recording, or any
information storage and retrieval system,
without permission in writing from the publisher.

A CIP catalogue record for this book is available
from the British Library

PB ISBN 978 1 52941 866 8
EB ISBN 978 1 52941 867 5

This book is a work of fiction. Names, characters,
businesses, organizations, places and events are
either the product of the author's imagination
or used fictitiously. Any resemblance to
actual persons, living or dead, events or
locales is entirely coincidental.

10 9 8 7 6 5 4 3 2 1

Typeset by CC Book Production
Printed and bound in Great Britain by Clays Ltd, Elcograf S.p.A.

Papers used by Quercus are from well-managed forests and other responsible sources.

NO LONGER PROPERTY
OF ANYTHINK
RANGEVIEW LIBRARY
DISTRICT

Did you know the number 1 cause of death in pregnant women is murder?

Yes, that's right.

The number 1 cause of death. Not complications with the pregnancy, or the delivery of the baby.

No.

Murder.

Allow yourself a few moments to let that sink in.

As a pregnant woman, you are intensely vulnerable. More likely to be the victim of violent trauma than if you weren't pregnant. And twice as likely to die from it.

Now, I know what you're thinking – you're thinking that they're talking about jealous husbands, reluctant fathers . . . sociopaths who see the baby as an inconvenience, a problem to get rid of.

But there are other ways to murder people, aren't there? Neglect. Negligence.

Let's examine that phrase, 'violent trauma'.

Think about that for a minute too.

It fits, doesn't it?

So, tell me now. Deep down, in your heart of hearts.

Do you think what you did was murder?

Because I do.

THE JOURNEY

NICKY

Right now, I can't think of anything I want to do less than go on a yoga retreat. Even worse, a prenatal yoga retreat.

'It'll be good for you,' Jon grins. 'Cheer up.'

'Did I say that out loud?' I say, staring down at my suitcase. 'I really am losing my mind.'

At that moment, my youngest, Seb, comes screaming into the bedroom and jumps on the bed.

He. Never. Stops. Three years old and he's hit peak toddler-energy. I don't even get the respite of a lunchtime nap any more. It's pure torture.

Sorry, I mustn't think things like that. It's pure joy, of course, being his mother. Pure *agonising* joy.

Seb starts bouncing as Jon grins at him. My head pounds. The contents of my suitcase spring out and onto the bed with every jump.

'Sebby, not now,' I say. 'Seriously. Not now.'

'Mummy, I brought your toothbrush and toothpaste!' Benjamin comes rushing into the room.

'Ah, sweetie, thank you,' I say, leaning down and stroking his cheek. 'That's very kind of you. Oh . . .'

The lid of the toothpaste isn't on properly, and as Benjamin handed it to me, giving it a good squeeze for luck, it covered my hands in sticky paste.

'Are you *sure* you don't want to get away?' Jon says, passing me a baby wipe. He wraps his arms around Seb.

I laugh. Perhaps he's right.

'I just feel bad leaving you to cope with these ruffians alone!'

'I'm sorry, Mummy,' Ben says, taking the wipe from me and putting it in the bin.

'Oh, sweetie, that's OK, it was an accident. And talking of accidents . . .' I turn to Jon. 'There's another reason I'm slightly dreading this trip. Three whole nights of Auntie Bonnie. I'm not sure I can bear it. I can't begin to imagine how she's got herself into this situation. You don't understand, Jon. You don't know what she's like.'

'She's your sister, and I've known her her whole life. I bloody well do know what she's like.'

Seb squeaks with laughter, clapping a hand over his mouth.

'Naughty word, Daddy!' Ben says. 'Go sit on the naughty step!'

I laugh at my, *yes*, adorable son and smile at my lovely, supportive, kind husband. I have nothing to complain about.

I'm exhausted, but what pregnant mother of two children under eight isn't? Nothing unusual about that.

Perhaps Jon is right. Perhaps this break is what I need. It'll help me get my head together, sort out my feelings once and for all. And Bonnie's not always difficult. I haven't seen her for a while. Perhaps pregnancy isn't the worst thing that could have happened to her. Perhaps the yoga retreat will actually work wonders on us both. Perhaps I'll get some actual sleep.

Perhaps she'll finally tell me who the father of her baby is. I should stop being so cynical.

'It looks great, you know,' Jon says, as Seb tries to koala-climb over his back. 'The views over the valley are incredible. Rolling fields, grazing sheep, the lot. I'm quite jealous. Did you know they were featured in *Grand Designs* magazine last year? Eco-build of the year?'

'Yes, yes, Bonnie told me,' I say. I know I should be impressed by all that stuff, but really, I don't have the energy any more. I'm trying to think what would impress me these days. I reckon a night of uninterrupted sleep is the only thing that would do it. But somehow, I don't think sleeping in a tent in the Devon countryside is going to offer me that either.

Oh God, when did I become such a grump?

'I looked it up last night,' Jon says. 'When you went to bed.'

'Oh,' I say, looking back at him.

'Sorry, I didn't think you'd want to see it. You know, it'd ruin the surprise.'

'No, you're right,' I reply. 'But tell me – please tell me there are baths and proper toilets?'

Jon grins again. It's endearing, how happy he is with his lot. And I know we are incredibly lucky: plenty of money, a nice house, no health worries, two gorgeous sons, and a bun in the oven.

But . . . it wasn't meant to be there, this new bun. It was never meant to be.

One anniversary night of passion, and here I am. Pregnant at forty-two with a baby that was never in the life plan.

I was *so* looking forward to going back to work this year.

7

When I found out I was pregnant I sobbed for hours, but no one seemed to understand. I confided in my only friend with three children, Sarah, hoping she'd get it. But she just told me how wonderful it was to have three.

'The third really is the icing on the cake. And just think – another year of maternity leave!' she said, winking.

She didn't get it. I loved my children, but I missed my job.

And the hardest thing of all is that Jon and I are on completely different pages. He's so happy about it.

'There are definitely proper toilets,' he says, sensing my stress. 'I don't think there are baths though. Sorry, Nicks.'

'No baths! Mummy, you are going to be really smelly!' Ben says, with fascinated glee.

'I'm only going for three nights,' I reply. 'Mummy will be just fine. Right, you lot, are you going to help me get my luggage to the car?'

BONNIE

'You're really going through with this then?' Jeremy says, spooning cereal into his mouth.

'Yes,' I say. 'I am.'

'How are you even paying for it?' he says. A line of milk trickles down his chin and he wipes it away on the back of his hand. I roll my eyes. As flatmates go, Jeremy's not bad, but his table manners leave a lot to be desired. 'I looked it up and it's crazy money.'

'I told you, my sister's husband is paying,' I reply. 'It's the least he can do . . .'

Jeremy's eyes sparkle.

'Oooh, goss?'

'Oh God, nothing, just the usual middle-class angst,' I say, zipping my bag shut. 'Nicky was very excited about going back to work. She's a bit disappointed about having to put that on hold again thanks to baby number three coming along uninvited. That's all. I guess he feels bad, so this is his way of treating her. Throw some cash at the problem. It's easy for the men, isn't it? They get to be parents without having to do any of the hard stuff.'

'I wouldn't know and I don't want to find out,' Jeremy says, standing up and putting the now-empty cereal bowl down on the one patch of my chest of drawers that isn't cluttered with stuff.

How the hell am I going to have a baby, living here? How am I actually going to do it? There isn't even enough room for my own things.

There's so much riding on this weekend. It has to work out. It just has to. Otherwise I'll have to see if I can rent somewhere else. Somewhere on my own.

The thought of that is overwhelming.

'I'm off, boo. I've got a dance class. Have a good . . . trip.'

I look up at Jeremy and he smiles.

'Be careful, you crazy idiot,' he says. 'Love you.'

'Love you too,' I say, and he slips out of the room before I have time to offer him any similarly patronising advice. Like: 'Take your bloody cereal bowl with you, you lazy bastard!'

I stare down at my rucksack. The woman running The Sanctuary sent over an extensive list of 'suggested items' we might like to bring when we booked our place. I read it over again:

- Clothes suitable for yoga
- Wellies or walking boots
- Waterproof clothing for walks in the woods (long trousers are advised as there are stinging nettles and brambles)
- Slippers or other indoor shoes
- Comfortable clothes for mealtimes

- Yoga mats are provided but you can of course bring your own
- Please be sure to bring enough layers appropriate for the time of year
- Luxury white robes, towels and linens are provided

Waterproof clothing? Walking boots? Who has all this stuff anyway?

If I've forgotten anything then Nicky will lend me whatever it is, I'm sure. She thinks I'm so useless, she's probably packed two toothbrushes just in case.

Knocked up at twenty-two, during my final year of catering college. That's how she sees me and my pregnancy. As the literal *worst* thing that could have happened.

I get it, though. From the outside, my life looks like a mess. After all, at the moment I'm living in a shared student house, one bathroom between four of us. I've got the biggest bedroom – the main, at the front of this run-down '30s terrace – but even so, it'd be a squeeze to fit a cot in here and all the paraphernalia I know comes with babies.

I've seen it – the way baby stuff just spreads and spreads until it takes over every available surface, from floor to ceiling. I remember how house-proud Nicky was on the family WhatsApp when Benjamin was first born, telling us all how painstakingly she and Jon tidied away his toys every night, reclaiming their 'adult time'.

'It's important we maintain our identity as a couple, not just as mum and dad,' she'd declared. Dad had no idea what to make of it, but to me it felt as though she was protesting just a bit too much.

She kept telling us how Benjamin was the perfect baby – the one who did everything by the book – and boy, were they smug about it. And then Seb was born. Ha bloody ha. And now look at them. The last time I went to theirs, the place was a tip. She told me she barely had the energy to tidy up her own crap these days.

I shift over to the mirror, regard my reflection. I'm wearing a loose tie-dye kaftan over some patterned leggings, my ankles skinny against my Buffalo trainers. I'm only thirteen weeks pregnant, and given how scrawny I've always been, there's absolutely no way you'd be able to tell yet, if I'm wearing loose clothes. If anything, I've lost weight. I haven't actually been sick, but I've been so worried about how it will turn out that I've lost my appetite.

Nicky's the opposite, eating everything in sight. We couldn't be more different really. She takes after her mum, I take after mine. But she's all right, considering she's twenty years older than me and the only thing we really share is a father. As older sisters go, things could have been a lot worse.

And even though it wasn't really my intention, this weekend is going to be a good opportunity for us to bond. Spend some more time together.

I smile at my reflection. I've been waiting for this weekend for what feels like an eternity, and now it's finally here.

It's going to be an interesting few days for sure.

I turn around, shove the last of my things into my rucksack and zip it up, hauling it over my shoulders. Time to go.

Clear eyes, full heart, can't lose.

GEORGIA

I'm busy contemplating whether or not to take a bikini, and indeed, whether any even still fit me, when I hear the FaceTime ringtone calling from the living room.

Brett.

I rush through and catch his call just in time. I feel my heart juddering and a strange nervous sickness as the screen fills with the image of his handsome face.

'Hello, baby,' he says, his sharp eyes slightly bloodshot. 'How's my favourite girl? Did you manage to get back to sleep?'

'A little bit, thank you,' I say. He only left for the airport a few hours ago yet it feels as though he's been away for months. We have grown so used to being together. It's all been so quick. 'I miss you already though. Flight on time?'

'So far,' he says. 'Looks pretty quiet too. I'm just in the lounge. Had some breakfast and managed to get a bit of work done.'

He rubs his eyes.

'I hope you get some sleep on the plane or you'll be so tired in your meetings.'

'Ha. You know me, I don't do tired. You're so sweet to worry about me when it's you who we need to be worrying about.

13

You and the jellybean,' he says, glancing around as though checking no one else can see, and then blowing me a kiss.

I feel a surge of longing, an ache at the lack of his physical presence. We've not even been together for a year yet, but we've barely left each other's sides since we met.

This is the first time he has had to travel for work, and it's as hideous as I imagined. When he left earlier this morning, I vomited for the first time since I was about four months gone.

'We're fine,' I say. 'Missing you.' Tears spring to my eyes. When did I get so needy? This pregnancy has seemingly obliterated my old personality. Confident, polished, self-assured. The sort of woman who surprised her boyfriend by turning up for dinner dates without any knickers on.

But now. Now I'm pathetic. Snivelling and needy on the end of the phone, hoping he won't go off me now I'm fat and miserable.

Where has that confidence gone? It's the most bizarre experience.

I stroke my bump. I want this baby more than anything. But still, I never expected my personality to change along with my body.

'When do you leave for your spa break?' he says.

'It's not a spa break!' I say, suddenly panicked. The anxiety claws at me: *He didn't listen to a word you said about it. He doesn't love you. He's going to leave you.* 'I told you! It's a prenatal yoga retreat.'

'Honey, I was joking,' he says, smiling, an edge to his voice. I exhale. Is he cross with me? I can't tell. 'I know it's a prenatal yoga retreat. I even know that it's at a place called The

14

Sanctuary. And that it's two miles outside Okehampton in Devon. And that it's going to take four and a half hours to get to from your flat in Notting Hill.'

'What?' I say, open-mouthed. 'How did you . . .'

He grins. His perfect American smile. My mother is obsessed with the whiteness of his teeth. Sometimes, I think she's more in love with him than I am. She can't believe my luck.

I suppose I can't either.

'You ordered an Uber to take you there, honey. On my account. You do know you're going to have to change cabs in Bristol though? Only you would try to book an Uber all the way to Devon!'

'Oh,' I say, feeling stupid. He's smiling, but kindly. 'Yes, of course. The app told me when I booked.'

'But I knew the name of it anyway,' he says. 'I looked it up last week when you told me about it. There's lots of pictures of it online. The renovation. What an awesome project. And views to kill for. I'd love to do something like that one day. Get out of the city.'

'Yes,' I reply. 'I can't wait for some proper country air.'

'It looks amazing,' Brett says. 'Although the woman running it sounded a bit nuts in the article. No, what do you Brits say? *Intense*.'

'Well, she was really nice to me when I booked my place,' I say defensively. 'I told you – she offered it to me for free, without any obligation to feature it in the paper.'

'Ha! That's what she says but . . .'

'I know,' I reply. 'Well, if it's good, I'll feature it. If it's not, I won't.'

15

'Sounds fair.'

'I'm a journalist beyond reproach, don't you know! Listen, the baby hasn't been moving much this morning,' I say, staring at the corner of the phone screen. 'Only a little bit. Not like the normal rolling about . . .'

'Honey,' he says, smiling at me. 'It'll be fine.'

He looks tired. I shouldn't dump this on him. *Transference*, that's what they call it. I know the real reason I'm worried, but I can't be honest about it, so I pin it on something else.

'Sorry, I know.'

'The woman running the place is some kind of childbirth expert, you couldn't be in safer hands . . .' he says.

'She's a qualified midwife,' I say.

He laughs.

'That's it. We don't really have them so much in the US. But she'll put your mind at ease, I'm sure.'

'I know, I know,' I say, sighing. Brett is always so endlessly rational. But my anxiety isn't rational. I know that. Doesn't mean it's any less real.

'I miss you,' I say, looking him directly in the eyes. He looks exhausted now. I don't want to add to his load. It's a big deal, this trip. He's been up late every night this week preparing for it. 'Sorry, baby. I'm excited about it, honestly.'

'I want you to send me pictures of your tent as soon as you get there.' He smiles, and again, I wish he was in the room with me, to put his arms around me and protect me from the world.

Gah, what have I become?!

A notification flashes up on my phone, briefly obscuring his forehead.

16

'Oh,' I say. 'My Uber is going to be here in ten. I'd better go, sweetie. I haven't even finished packing yet.'

Brett rolls his eyes.

'Oh God, the poor guy'll be waiting ages.'

'Ha ha, very funny,' I say.

There's a pause and he gazes at me through the screen. My lovely, lovely boyfriend. Who sees me as perfect. His perfect English girlfriend.

If only he knew.

'Good luck with your meetings,' I say, my voice suddenly stiff. 'I miss you.'

'I miss you too, honey,' he says. 'Have an amazing time.'

The emotion builds inside me until I feel I might explode. I can't keep this secret any longer. Suddenly the distance between us feels like a threat, a sign that I need to come clean, because what if I don't and something happens and . . .

'Wait . . .' I say, but he doesn't hear me. He simply blows me a kiss and hangs up.

I stare back at the suitcase, a single tear making its way down my face.

POPPY

It's the first time Poppy has missed having a car since she broke up with Ant.

She had completely forgotten about the car. It's the little things like this that keep surprising her.

The journey to Devon takes just over two hours, then at Exeter St David's she waits for a bus to Okehampton. From there, she will have to catch a taxi from the town centre to The Sanctuary.

It seems crazy that it should take that long to get there, when it's really not that far at all. But the car, like so many other things, was something she left behind, without thinking about, when she walked out on their marriage.

Not that she had any choice.

She gazes out of the window as the train hurtles through Bridgwater. They'll be going through Taunton next. Despite her frustration at how long the journey takes, it feels good to be on this high-speed train. To be speeding away from everything, and towards . . . well, who knows?

Towards something. The hope of an end to the pain, at the very least.

But it's going to be strange for her, to be in Exeter again, no matter how briefly.

It's crazy, in fact, to think that she'll never go back to their house. That it's not even their house any more. It's sold. No longer even 'subject to contract'. But properly *sold*, to Mr and Mrs Shaw and their two daughters, aged two and four.

They will settle in nicely, of course. After all, who couldn't love it? Poppy and Ant had done it up to the nines. The Shaws were the first family to view it, and they put an offer in two hours later.

Ant said they should have asked for more money, was angry with the estate agent for pricing it too low. It was just another sign of how wrong everything had become – that those were his priorities, that that was where he chose to focus his energy.

Poppy hopes the house brings the Shaws more luck than it brought them.

Her hand rests on her bump. It's always a surprise when she feels it there. Sixteen weeks gone – or is it seventeen? She can never remember. She ought to write it down.

She pulls out the book that she brought for the journey, but she can't concentrate and the type swims before her eyes as she tries to read. She's not interested in these fictional people with their fictional problems. Not when she has so many of her own real-life ones to confront.

She takes a deep breath. It's going to be OK. This weekend couldn't have come at a better time.

She smiles and takes another look out of the window. It's drizzling, typical Somerset weather. But it's what makes the countryside so lush and green, so who is she to complain? And anyway, the forecast for Devon is bright sunshine. She likes that idea – that she is leaving the rain behind.

Her phone buzzes in her lap.

It's Ant.

Are you OK? Called your mum's when you didn't pick up but she said you've gone away for the weekend? Where? She was cagey. Hope you're all right. I'm finding it hard. Love you x

She takes a sharp intake of breath. *Love you?* What right does he have to say such things to her? He doesn't love her, not really. If he did, they'd still be together. He would have coped. He would have supported her. Been the husband she needed.

Tears spring to her eyes and she lets them trickle down until they reach her lips. The lady sitting opposite her on the train glances up, sees she is crying, furrows her brow. Poppy tries to reassure her with a weak smile – the last thing she wants is anyone asking if she's OK – but the woman looks away. So Poppy turns her head back towards the rain instead, and tries not to think of Ant. Of the mess they got themselves into. How they couldn't survive the wreckage, despite how strong they once were.

Just over a year ago, everything was so different. The extension was almost finished, the new bedroom beautifully decorated with vintage Laura Ashley wallpaper – fit for a princess about to celebrate her first birthday. But she never even got to spend a single night in it.

Poppy told the woman running the retreat – Selina – about her situation when she booked her place. She hadn't gone into details, just told her the bare bones.

Selina had taken a day to reply.

I'm terribly, terribly sorry to hear what you've been through, she wrote. *But how wonderful that you are expecting again. I'm sure you and your husband must be very concerned. But we will do everything we can to ensure we work on your anxiety and set you up for the best possible outcome in this pregnancy. As a midwife, I have extensive experience working with prenatal mums and many tried and tested techniques . . .*

The message went on and on. Poppy was quite amazed that Selina had turned an email that was meant to be full of condolence and sympathy into a way of boasting about her achievements.

Poppy inhales, exhales, closes her eyes and tries to find some kind of inner peace. But that's not what's inside her. Not yet anyway.

The woman opposite gazes at her again, then her eyes rest on Poppy's bump.

Pregnancy is often one of the most anxious times in a woman's life.

Well, yes, indeed.

Let's hope this weekend can fix her.

Otherwise who knows what she might do.

SELINA

I'm in the last yurt, making sure everything is 'just so' when Will comes to find me. The guests are paying a lot for this weekend. Everything has to be perfect.

'Your hands are shaking,' he says, but it's more in irritation than concern. 'What's the matter?'

'Everything has to be just right,' I say, smoothing out the duvet again. 'We can't afford for anything to go wrong.'

He stares at me.

'It was your idea to invite the journalist to stay for free! She'll have stayed at the best of the best. But more than that, she'll know people. Important people. And if she has a great time and decides to review us properly . . .'

Will sighs.

'Calm down,' he says. 'It's all going to be fine.'

'I just can't believe we had a cancellation. It's going to be such a small group. No atmosphere . . .' I stutter. Before I know it, the tears are streaming. 'And we aren't even able to keep the deposit.'

If only Will had taken more of an interest, helped me out with the booking process, he might have pointed out that we should have a refund policy in place. But no, it was all on me.

I had to set up everything. He was too grumpy that we weren't running a cooking retreat, as he'd wanted. But they're ten a penny round here. I wanted to do something unique.

He takes a step closer towards me. He doesn't put his arm around me though. Doesn't make any attempt to comfort me at all.

What has happened to us? What has happened to our relationship? He loved me so much once. And now . . . everything we've worked so hard to build . . .

'Selina,' he says slowly. I can see the effort it's taking him. How hard it is for him to feel warmth towards me. 'It's all fine. The tent looks magnificent. We have four guests arriving and they are going to have an amazing time. This is what you've – we've – worked so hard for, for so long. You have nothing to be upset about.'

'But why did there have to be a cancellation? It was all going to be perfect!'

'Selina! You said the poor woman had a miscarriage; you can't exactly blame her for cancelling.'

'Oh God, I know. I wasn't . . . I didn't mean to be callous. I know, it's terrible for her. It's not that I don't feel sorry for her, it's just . . .'

He gives a tiny, almost imperceptible snort.

'Of course I do,' I continue. 'I just mean . . . *why* did she have to have a miscarriage? Why do I always have such bad luck?'

He sighs.

'I think she's the one that really had the bad luck,' Will says coldly. And there it is again: that curdle of disgust. The way he really feels about me. I'm sick to my stomach. How

23

can I get him back? It's been months now, and nothing has worked. 'Let's just concentrate on getting through the next few days and making them as good as possible for our guests. Especially the journalist. We need this to work, remember?'

'Yes, thank you,' I reply. 'I'm aware of that.'

'Well then.'

'What happens if someone else pulls out?'

'No one else is going to pull out,' Will says firmly. 'It's going to be absolutely fine. And the tent looks incredible.'

'I'm exhausted and they're not even here yet. Some yoga teacher I'm going to be.'

'You'll pull it out of the bag. You're good at . . . what you do,' Will says. His voice is softer, but it still feels as though he's humouring me. Playing a role.

I sniff. I can't face the battle. He needs to accept the way things are now. He has to forgive me.

'At least the weather is good,' I say. 'Record-breaking for May. The valley's never looked more beautiful. I mean, they can't help but be impressed by that, can they?'

'Do you want some more good news?' Will says, ignoring me.

'More than some,' I say.

'Badger's agreed to do the wildflower meadow tour on Sunday.'

'Oh. That's good.'

'It is. Right, well, if you've finally stopped fussing, then I'll get back to the kitchen and start prepping the lunch.'

He leaves without giving me a chance to thank him.

Fussing! I stand back a little, looking around the tent. I've put my heart and soul into this place and it's impeccable.

The finest bed linen, Moroccan kilims on the floor, a wood-burning stove in one corner perfectly laid with logs and kindling so that all our guests have to do is strike a match and sit back and enjoy the flames. Plentiful fluffy white towels stacked on the bed. Bottles of mineral water from the local spring, complete with recycled glasses – the same type they have at Soho Farmhouse. I got a bargain set on eBay. They're seconds but no one will notice.

There's an oil diffuser and a selection of essential oils for them to pick their favourite. I've even filled a little vase on the bedside table with wildflowers picked this morning. Outside the tent, there are brand new wellies available for our guests to wear if the field is muddy.

It's all so much nicer than the things I've lived with my whole life, but to get the money, we have to go upmarket.

A little shiver of excitement flows through me. My mood has turned, finally. I can't wait for them to arrive. OK, there are only four of them coming now, and we shelled out for five eye-wateringly expensive bell tents, but even so, it's a good trial run. Our first paying guests.

And OK, one of them isn't actually paying because Will had the admittedly genius idea of offering her the space for free, in the hope that she writes up a review for her paper. But even so, she was *prepared* to pay, so that shows we've got something people want. I've worked on the yoga schedule painstakingly, ensuring it provides everything a pregnant woman could need and want from a prenatal retreat.

There's just one thing clouding it all.

Kai.

But hopefully he won't be a problem. Not this weekend. He knows how important it is to me, to all of us. I told him it was for his own good to stay out of the way, to do as he's told, to trust me. I'm hopeful he'll manage to keep himself together.

But he's been so delicate lately . . . prone to bursting into tears at the drop of a hat, vacillating between anger and misery. If one of them just looks at him the wrong way, then who knows what he'll do, or what he'll say.

I shake my head. I'm not going to let my worries about Kai ruin this. This moment of perfection. We are on the cusp of something life-changing, I can feel it.

If you work hard enough, you will be rewarded.

It's high time I was rewarded.

I hear the crunch of car wheels against gravel and I feel a flutter of excitement. I smooth down my top.

It's happening. Finally.

The first guest has arrived.

THE ARRIVAL

On a day like today, when the sky is clear, this place is beautiful. Like nowhere on earth.

When it's grey and drizzly, it feels like a symbol of all the despair in the world.

Even so, I can see why someone might live here.

Remote enough to be private. But not completely cut off from civilisation. There's the neighbouring farm, of course, just an eight-minute stroll away, with their fresh eggs left by the roadside daily.

To get back to the rest of the world, the soul-dragging convenience of Co-op and Boots, all you have to do is hop in the car and in ten minutes you're in Okehampton, with its typical Devonshire market-town charms.

Or lack of.

But here, you are tucked away from the world, nestled in a tight valley and surrounded by woodland.

The track down to the farm is hidden and, if you do find it, unforgiving. No rambler who stumbles across it would choose to wander down its windy, uneven path. The trees bend overhead and meet in the middle as though the weight of the world presses down on their branches.

The only sign that The Sanctuary even exists is a small hand-painted wedge of wood propped up against the hedgerow by the turning.

It's clear that unexpected visitors are not welcome here. Invitation only.

Twelve acres of land all to yourself.

The perfect place to commit a crime, eh?

The perfect place to bury a secret.

NICKY

As I make my way out of our small village and join the motorway, something strange happens.

I begin to relax.

I can't remember the last time I drove somewhere just for me. All the car journeys I make these days seem to involve ferrying the boys around, or driving to my mum's to drop off supplies, or to the supermarket or somewhere equally mundane.

The sat nav tells me it's going to take just under two hours to get to The Sanctuary. I can't remember the last time I had two hours of peace and quiet. Two hours to myself, even if I am stuck in the car.

A memory from my university years hits me. Driving myself up to Newcastle from my mum's house in Woburn. I'd scrimped and saved from my part-time job in the supermarket and finally managed to buy myself a car. An old Rover Metro, with 90,000 miles on the clock and a load of rust on the undersides that I tried to ignore.

I loved that car. Oh, how I loved it! And what it represented: my freedom.

It was such a liberation to be able to hop in it at any given point and drive, well, anywhere. Without having to ask permission or a favour. I particularly loved those long drives up north, back to uni, Jon, to fun and happiness, a welcome relief after a weekend spent trying to cheer up my lonely mum. I'd burn a CD of songs, make a bacon sandwich and grab a bottle of water, then set myself up in the driver's seat with everything I could ever want within easy reach and . . . just . . . drive.

I particularly enjoyed the motorway. The relentless, hypnotic nature of it. Two hours on the M1 just driving, driving, driving.

And thinking. About everything. About the future. About getting back to Jon. The man I couldn't keep my hands off. Jon, who, I somehow knew from the second we met, was going to be the man I'd marry and have kids with, even though no one expects their university relationships to last. And I'd think about my career. My determination to become a schoolteacher, and eventually, a head teacher.

Those long drives should have been a chore, but they were like therapy, back then. Just me and the open road, no distractions.

Freedom.

That was how I used to feel, driving back to Jon.

Like a rock landing in my lap, all the levity I've been feeling disappears. I've forgotten again.

I've forgotten what's happening. What's looming large on the horizon.

I put my hand over my bloated stomach. Too early to tell what it might be. I just look out of shape, like a mother who's let herself go.

Suddenly it's as though the atmosphere in the car has changed, even though I'm the only one in it.

I think of the way Jon reached for me in bed last night, his hand snaking under my nightdress, and how, even though it was the last thing I wanted, even though I was utterly exhausted . . .

How despite all that I lay back on the bed and I let him do what he wanted, because what did it matter now anyway, it was all too late, and I kissed him afterwards and told him I loved him and I cried a little as he buried his head in my neck and said he'd miss me this weekend because I knew, deep down, that I wouldn't miss him.

That, if anything, I couldn't wait to be away from him.

This pregnancy. I was just getting back on track. Why did it have to happen? Why?

I am so ashamed of myself for thinking these thoughts, but they persist.

I've had friends over the years who've been desperate to have children. They've waited months, if not years, have had to resort to expensive treatments to finally get that pink line. And then there are the ones for whom it hasn't happened at all. It should have happened for them. Not me. Not me and our once-a-month night of watered-down sex.

I'm angry on their behalf. How dare I not want this baby?

But I'm forty-two years old, for Christ's sake. What are the chances?

Jon loved it when I told him, of course. Made jokes about how fertile he was. He didn't seem to notice that I was crying. Not to begin with, anyway.

When he did finally notice how distraught I was, he tried his best to be supportive. To persuade me that it would be OK.

He tries his best.

I sniff, wiping my eyes with the back of my hand. The speed restrictions ease off, and I put my foot down. I think again of my old car, how if you went over 65 mph it'd start to shake, how I lived in fear that things would start to fall off, but how it only added to the thrill. That feeling of being young, alive and free. It's so alien to everything I feel now.

I take a deep breath. The memory of Sebby and Benj this morning comes to my mind. My gorgeous, wonderful boys.

It'll be OK. It might even be a girl. Not that I particularly mind. But perhaps it would be nice. It'd bring a different dynamic to the house. Jon would love it, too. He's got three brothers, has always said he'd love a daughter.

The clouds ahead of me part, and a shard of bright sunlight strikes the motorway ahead. I think of what awaits: The Sanctuary, the chance to have some time truly to myself, to relax and take the pressure off. The chance to sleep in, with no one interrupting me or demanding anything of my time.

And there are counselling sessions included. Perhaps the woman running the place can help me come to terms with my situation better.

The thought lifts me.

It'll be OK with the new baby. Of course it will. I'm just tired, and I need a break. I'm overwhelmed right now but the truth is it's just an unexpected turn in the road. But that's life.

And I've got a stronger car now. I'll be able to get through it.

BONNIE

We arranged for Nicky to pick me up outside the Dartmoor museum in the centre of Okehampton but she's late which must mean she's lost.

I was planning on getting a bus here but I missed the ten past and in the end couldn't be arsed with waiting around for the next one so I decided to walk. It's absolutely boiling and of course I forgot to bring a hat, but it felt good to burn off some of the nervous energy. It's been making me feel sick to my stomach.

I'm lucky that the baby hasn't made me feel sick yet, but women in our family seem to have it quite easy with pregnancies.

I feel a little bit smug about the fact that being pregnant at my age is actually best for both me and the baby. It's the optimum time, your early twenties.

Obviously, Nicky was beyond shocked when I told her I was pregnant. She never mentioned the 'abortion' word, but I could tell it was hovering there, at the back of her mind. She's always been so ambitious, has never been able to understand my desire to drift through life, letting the wind take me where it wanted.

'But you're so smart, Bon,' she used to say. 'You could literally be or do anything.'

'*Anyone* can be or do anything,' I replied. 'That's the point of life. It's called free will.'

'See what I mean? Even your pathetic arguments are smart. Why don't you want to channel that smartness into—'

'Something that'll make me rich?' I replied. 'I don't know. I guess I just don't see life the same way as you do.'

I couldn't tell her the truth. That secretly, this was all I had ever wanted. To be a mother. To have a family of my own.

I have felt lonely my whole life. I know I'm technically not an only child, but Nicky is so much older than me – more like another mother than a sister. I grew up craving the company of other children, determined to have five or six kids one day.

I don't care that it's unfashionable to want children in your twenties. I don't have some burning desire to carve out a career just for the sake of it. I want to be at home, cooking for my husband and playing with my kids. And if that makes me a disappointment to feminism, then . . . feminism can go fuck itself.

I linger on the pavement, wishing I could have a cigarette, thinking about the father of my unborn child. It sounds so serious, so *real*, when you put it like that, and I smile. I pull out my phone, but as usual, the battery is dead, so I can't even check if he's sent me a text message. I kick at the pavement with the toe of my trainer, hoping Nicky finds me.

She's never come to visit me here in Devon. I know she's busy with the boys but it still feels lame. I haven't actually seen her since Boxing Day last year. We would have met for an

Easter lunch at my mum and dad's, but Dad had flu and Nicky tried and failed to hide her relief at having a reason to get out of it. She still doesn't like my mum much, even though, really, my mum is the most inoffensive person you could meet. Her only bad quality is that she's a bit, well, bland.

Nicky and I are not as close as we were, but something about being pregnant, and in a slightly, well, *precarious* (read: messed up) situation, makes me want to connect with her more. It makes me want to pull all the threads of our family together and tie them in one humungous knot.

I take a seat on a low wall outside the museum, and then, finally, I see a dark blue car drive past me and pull up. It looks kind of sporty at the front but the back has 'practical family car' written all over it.

That just about sums Jon up.

I walk towards it and open the passenger door.

'Hello,' I say. 'You found me then?'

'Well, it wasn't easy. Why the hell is your phone switched off?' Nicky says.

'I forgot to charge it. Sorry.'

'Jesus, Bonnie. Never mind. Do you want to put your bag in the back?'

'No, don't worry, I'll keep it on my lap.'

She's pissed off with me already. I climb in the car. The seats are leather, and there's a kind of weird chrome trim around everything on the dashboard.

'Nice car,' I say, because somehow I think this will please her.

'Thanks, it's new,' she says. 'Jon loves it.'

I smile to myself.

'How are you anyway?' she asks. 'Beautiful day.'

I glance sideways at her. Her thick brown hair is pulled back into a surprisingly perky ponytail. It makes her look younger than usual.

'It's a stunner,' I say. 'Did you see that the tents have got log-burners in them? Guess we won't be needing those.'

She nods.

'Probably for the best. Knowing me I would have burnt mine down,' I say.

'Yeah, you would.'

She laughs and turns to me with a full smile. I feel strangely irritated with her for agreeing with me.

'Are the kids devastated you're leaving them? Guess Jon is going to have his hands full. He won't know what's hit him.'

'He'll be fine,' she says. 'He's always helping out with them.'

I sit back in the seat, a flash of guilt running through me. I shouldn't needle her. After all, I haven't been entirely honest about my reasons for suggesting this weekend away. Nicky has no idea what she's letting herself in for.

'Well, thanks for picking me up,' I say. 'And I really hope that you have a good time at this place.'

'It's fine,' she says. 'It'll be great for us to spend some time together! Who would have thought we'd be here now, both pregnant at the same time . . .'

'Insanity,' I say, helping myself to the packet of chewing gum wedged in the drink holder. 'It's amazing where life takes you . . .'

I tail off.

Because life didn't take me this way. *I* took me this way.

What Nicky doesn't know is that this pregnancy was deliberate, very much planned. The story that it was totally unexpected – an 'accident' – is one I've constructed just to make it more acceptable to others.

There's a pause. I wait for Nicky to fill it but the sound she makes, when it comes, is not what I expected to hear at all.

I stare at her.

She is crying, the tears free-falling down her cheeks.

'What?' I say. 'Are you OK? What's the matter?'

'I . . . nothing . . . I . . .'

'Nicky, it's OK! What is it?'

I feel alarmed. I don't think I've ever seen her cry in front of me. But then again, this is what I wanted. This is what I've been hoping for – for her to show some actual vulnerability for once, to drop the facade of perfect mother and perfect wife that she's so attached to.

She gives a great sniff, wiping the tears on the sleeve of her hoodie.

'God. Sorry. Nothing,' she says eventually. 'It's just pregnancy. You know. It makes me emotional, I guess. And I'm exhausted.'

I frown.

'Is there something you're not telling me?' I ask, my heart suddenly pounding in my chest.

'What?' she says. Her tears have dried away to nothing, but her nose is still red. 'No, nothing like that. Listen, I'm honestly just knackered. Shall we put the radio on for the last bit of the drive?'

I give a tight smile.

'Sure,' I say, staring out of the windscreen.

Let her have her moment of peace.

There's plenty of drama to come this weekend, after all. And she doesn't deserve any of it.

GEORGIA

I fall asleep in the Uber. When I wake up, my neck is in excruciating pain, and there's a line of dried dribble on one side of my chin.

'Oh God,' I murmur, wiping my face with my hand. I feel my cheeks redden, but the driver is staring straight ahead at the road, listening to something on the radio, and doesn't even notice me.

'Are we nearly there?' I say, taking a look through the window. I can make out hedgerows and passing places at the side of the road. We're definitely not in London any more.

'Ten minutes to go,' the taxi driver replies.

'Oh, wow, thanks,' I say, but he doesn't reply.

I pull out my phone but there's nothing from Brett. He'll be on the plane now, and I'm not sure if he'll have access to Wi-Fi.

I tap on the app for my emails and pull up the one that Selina, the lady who runs The Sanctuary, sent this morning. She requested that we don't arrive before midday, but it's nearly 2pm. Does that mean I'm technically late? She mentioned that there would be a healthy buffet available for us to have when we first arrive, but didn't specify a time.

I should have checked.

Will all the other women have met each other already? I feel nerves creeping over me, then try to force myself to stay calm. It's stupid. It's not the first day of school. We don't have to be best friends.

I don't even have to talk to these women if I don't want to.

I lay a hand on my bump. I know why I'm out of sorts, of course. It's guilt. Pure and simple.

It's pressing on me so much that sometimes, in the evening, I hide in the bathroom and Google 'What to do when you feel guilty', but the answers always seem to be for people who are feeling guilty for no good reason.

I've never had that problem. I've always been very happy to let myself off the hook, to take care of my own needs. Until now, anyway.

I scan the email again. Selina's added a section where she offers the chance for one-on-one 'therapy' sessions with her.

Talking Sessions

As a mother and as a midwife, I have extensive experience working with pregnant women . . .

She hasn't provided any details, but I bet she has some stories to tell.

. . . I have also had many years of therapy myself, including the time when I lived in LA and was fortunate enough to attend several sessions of therapy with the renowned Spike Barnett. And I am more than happy to spend an hour each day to talk to you one to one, and discuss any specific, private worries you may have about your pregnancy, or any other elements of your life. These sessions are entirely voluntary, and there's no requirement to take me up on this offer! Just know that I am here for you, that this is your weekend, and that I will do all I can to

ensure you leave The Sanctuary as an empowered mother, confident in
your natural abilities to be the best possible mother to your new baby.

'Here we are,' the Uber driver says, swinging right, down what looks like a dirt track. His tongue clucks in irritation. The taxi trundles along, accompanied by the rattle of stones hitting its sides and the sensation that we are being thrown around in a bumper car.

'Gosh,' I say. 'Sorry, it's a bit rough.'

'Are there no proper roads in Devon?' he jokes.

'It's private land,' I say, but he doesn't respond. 'I mean . . . I guess they should tarmac it . . .'

But I look out of the window and think, no, of course they shouldn't. How ugly would that be? The countryside is breathtaking, proper old-school rolling hills and far-reaching views.

Compared to my tiny Notting Hill flat, where cars sit bumper to bumper outside the living room window day and night, it's paradise. I grew up in a market town in Somerset, and this place reminds of my roots.

The driver turns a corner and suddenly there it is. The Sanctuary, looking more beautiful in real life than it did in the pictures on the website. I clearly left the clouds behind in London, as the sky is bright, bright blue. The sun is shining onto the roof of the main barn, as though bestowing it with a blessing from the heavens. It's surrounded by greenery on all sides.

No wonder it's called The Sanctuary. It looks so calm and serene – the opposite of the frenetic London street we live on.

'Oh wow,' I say, my mouth falling open a little. 'It's beautiful.'

I grab my phone and put the window down to take a photo.

'I have no signal here,' the driver says, tapping at the phone secured to his windscreen. 'I'll have to sort payment when I get back into 4G. It'll be expensive.'

'Yes, sure,' I say. 'I know, it's a long way. That's fine. Thank you.'

He lifts his head and nods. His eyes rest on my huge stomach.

'You want help with your bag?'

'No,' I say, reaching over to where my suitcase sits on the seat next to me. 'I'm fine. Thank you, thank you so much.'

I shut the taxi door behind me and trudge up the shingle pathway to what I presume is the front door. Beside the path is a beautifully landscaped lawn, surrounded by white hydrangeas and lavender coming into bloom. They've clearly spent a lot of money on this place.

Selina and her partner live in the barn. I think there was a farmhouse here too once, but I'm not sure what happened to it. We'll be staying in the bell tents on their field, but she promised luxury and it looks as though this place is going to live up to her word.

Off in the distance, beyond a field bursting with flowers, I spot another, smaller barn, and then a row of stone outbuildings next to it, their doors painted a muted sage green. Perhaps more guest accommodation?

It's like a scene from a pastoral novel, except for the great expanse of glass in the front of the main barn.

The property is huge. In a way it's good I didn't do too much research before I got here – I didn't want to know what I was letting myself in for. It would have been too easy to talk myself out of coming.

I found The Sanctuary website after Googling 'pregnancy anxiety' late one night when Brett was holed up in his study working. I was meant to be working too, but I couldn't concentrate.

It felt as though everything I had been aiming for, the life I had been building, was falling apart. Which made no sense, because meeting Brett was all I could have dreamt of and more, and yet . . . since his arrival, nothing has gone the way I intended it to.

That's life though. You can't make plans. Life laughs in the face of your plans, as my mate Lou always says.

Anyway, I scanned the website, saw that there was a retreat happening in just two weeks – 'We're so excited to be able to open FINALLY!' – and it seemed like a sign from someone, or something. I booked my place straight away, without even asking Brett.

And then Selina replied, saying she had noted my job title in my email signature, and that she would be happy to offer me a place for free, as this is their first retreat. *No pressure to review, of course, but as an expert on all things lifestyle, we would really value your opinion!*

I hardly ever take freebies, but she was so nice about it, I felt I couldn't refuse.

And now, here I am.

There are two cars parked already in the driveway – an old Land Rover and a shiny new Prius. Top of the range.

But of course the other women here must have money. This weekend is costing them more than a grand each. Not exactly small change.

I take a deep breath and walk up to the front door. Through the wall of glass I can see inside. There's a spiral concrete staircase, lots of greenery, the walls painted a soothing off-white.

There's an old-fashioned bell-pull hanging down and I yank it, swallowing my nerves.

After a few seconds, one of the doors inside the hall opens, and out walks a tall, willowy woman with freckled skin and long dark hair. Her eyes are huge and lined with kohl. She's wearing animal-print leggings and her legs are as thin as pencils.

She smiles at me through the glass then opens the front door.

'Hello and welcome,' she says. She speaks softly and I feel instantly at ease. There's a hint of something transatlantic in her accent, and it reminds me of Brett. 'You must be Georgia! So lovely to have you. Please do come in.'

'Thank you,' I say, hefting my suitcase over the threshold.

'Come and get a drink – you can leave your bag there. My partner will take it over to your yurt in a little bit. The others are here already. How was your journey? We're very happy to see you.'

She's talking very slowly, as though taking great care over every choice of word. She seems so self-assured, so confident.

'Thanks,' I say again. 'It was a long journey.'

'You live in Notting Hill, is that right?' she says. 'Did you drive?'

She's still smiling, looking up at me, her chin pulled in slightly towards her chest. Her teeth are as white and straight as Brett's.

'No, I mean, yes. I got a cab. Well, two cabs actually . . . turns out Uber have a four-hour limit.'

I laugh, feeling stupidly nervous. She pauses, her hand on the door that leads off the hallway.

'Oh,' she says, looking surprised. 'A taxi all the way from London? Wow. That must have been . . .'

Expensive. That's what she's thinking. Perhaps she's regretting giving me my place for free.

'I don't drive,' I say, smiling. 'Never have done.'

'I'm not much of a fan of driving myself,' she says. 'Especially with the roads round here! Do come in and meet everyone.'

We enter an enormous kitchen, with a double-height, beamed ceiling. Along one wall is an expansive run of stainless-steel kitchen units, the type you'd find in a professional kitchen, contrasting dramatically with the battered farmhouse table opposite.

It's eclectic but charming. And the sense of space is breathtaking. I can't imagine having a kitchen this big.

Around the large table sit three women.

I plaster my biggest smile on my face, try to imagine the emancipation I'll feel when this weekend is over. Despite having just met her, I feel sure, somehow, that Selina is going to make me feel better about everything.

'Hello!' I say. 'Lovely to meet you all. I'm Georgia.'

POPPY

When she arrives at The Sanctuary, what makes Poppy most angry is the size of the place. Which is irrational, really. What does that matter in the grand scheme of things? But still. How lovely for them to be living like this, in all their acres of land with their breathtaking views. How absolutely *lovely*.

Perhaps it's because she's still upset about the fact that they had to sell their house. Coming here, to this absolutely beautiful haven of a home, is such a slap in the face.

Or perhaps deep down Ant's message has affected her more than she'd like to admit.

Love you. Why would he say that?

Whatever the reason, Poppy finds herself struggling to get a grip as she sits around the large, weathered table in this humungous kitchen, and listens to Selina talk.

Selina's delivery is smooth and unhurried, her voice so gentle that at times Poppy has to strain to hear her. Her accent is unusual – as though she's talking in a 'telephone voice' – but underneath, Poppy can hear the sharp tang of an American accent creeping through.

Selina seems confident, but there are mannerisms – the

way her fingers keep digging into the back of her hair, the occasional hand flap – that belie her nerves.

Poppy can't tell exactly what it is Selina is nervous about though. It's not what she's saying. Perhaps it's how it's being received.

Poppy wraps her hands round the glazed pottery mug as she listens. In it swirls a mesh pyramid filled with apple and cinnamon 'tea'.

She wishes, briefly, that she could throw the tea into Selina's face to shut her up. She imagines Selina's skin peeling off as it scalds, leaving just the rotten truth of her underneath.

She gasps at herself. No. She would never do something like that. She's not capable of violence like that.

Is she?

Selina has already made a big fuss about the wildflower-tea-brewing session on Sunday. They'll be able to pick their own herbs and flowers and then come back here to blend their own infusions.

Poppy could kill for a cup of coffee, but this a caffeine- and alcohol-free retreat.

'Can't take any risks with these things,' Selina said when Poppy asked for a cappuccino. 'Clean body, clean mind!'

'I want this weekend to be all about you,' Selina is saying now. 'Your needs, your desires. I've printed you a mini-schedule, but of course everything on this list is optional. I've designed it specifically to ensure you get the most out of your weekend, but – as I always like to say – *you do you*.'

She gives an awkward laugh. Laughing doesn't come naturally to her, apparently. Across the table from Poppy, the last one to arrive – Georgia? – smiles. Her eyes wrinkle at the corners and Poppy wonders if she's older than she looks. She's very, very attractive and polished in her cashmere sweater.

The other two – Bonnie and Nicky – are sisters, though they look more like mother and daughter. Bonnie is beautiful. A real natural beauty. And not a scrap of make-up on her face.

Poppy considers them all. Her hands rest on her bump. It's a shame they will be caught in the crossfire, but it can't be helped.

'Now the theme of this weekend, as you know, is The Intuitive Mother,' Selina continues. Her eyes widen whenever she tries to emphasise her point, but her voice remains the same muted level throughout, as though she's whispering at a baby's bedside. 'And intuition is something you are going to hear me talking a lot about over our time together. I feel very passionately that you, and you alone, know what's best for you and your baby. But with the joy that is the internet, and the wisdom from friends who are trying to help but don't realise how damaging their input can be, it's very easy to find your inner voice being drowned out. By the time you leave The Sanctuary, I want you to feel transformed. Completely. It's not an exaggeration to say that you will feel like a completely different person.'

Poppy makes a choking sound into her cup.

'Are you all right?' Selina says, snapping her wide eyes on Poppy and giving a confused smile.

'Sorry,' she replies, embarrassed. She needs to be more careful. She doesn't want to draw attention to herself just yet. 'Yes, it's just my tea. Went down the wrong way.'

'Oh dear,' Selina says, blinking. 'So, anyway, as I was saying . . . I'm glad there's just a small group of us, as it means that I can give each and every one of you as much help and support as possible. My door is always open, so please, do make use of me, even in the free time. I'm always around – pottering in the garden or whatever. Just come and find me . . . So, shall we take a brief look at the schedule . . .'

Dutifully, they all lean over the piece of card in front of them.

When Selina handed them out earlier, she told them they were printed on seed paper, so that they can take them home afterwards and plant them in their gardens.

But I don't have a garden any more! Poppy wanted to shout. She doesn't even have a window box.

She bit her tongue.

'OK, so, starting today, we will be going on a guided country walk at four pm – but this is optional, so if you don't feel up to it, then you are welcome to rest in your yurt. Then we'll have our first session of restorative yoga at six pm. This session will last forty-five minutes and is absolutely brilliant for recharging batteries. We'll have dinner at seven thirty pm, followed by a short journaling session, where I encourage you to write down all your anxieties and concerns about your pregnancy. We can then work on harnessing your own intuition to address these over the weekend. Then tomorrow we start the day bright and early with breakfast served any time from six am . . .'

The young one – Bonnie – is twitching in her seat, her head bent low over her bowl of tea. Poppy looks across at her. She's very thin, almost to the point of looking unhealthy – as though she doesn't treat her body with the respect it deserves.

Poppy remembers those days though. That curious combination of feelings: a mixture of insecurity and invincibility.

Poppy is surprised at how few of them there are – she always thought yoga retreats had at least twelve people on them.

It's disappointing. She was hoping for a bigger audience.

'Just four of you,' Selina said earlier, when Georgia took a seat at the table. 'There was meant to be another lady joining us, but unfortunately . . . she had to pull out at the last minute. But I'm really pleased it's just the five of us in total. It'll be lovely to have such a select group and hopefully we'll all get to know each other really well.'

Georgia nodded.

Now, Georgia's staring down at the little schedule in front of her. Poppy feels a strange instinctive pull towards her – as though she wants to give her a hug.

The door opens, and they all look up. In walks a man.

This must be Selina's partner, Will.

He has a full beard and a mop of dark hair, but despite his hirsute face somewhat obscuring his features, Poppy can see how pleasingly symmetrical his jawline is. He's wearing a loosely knitted dark green jumper over a lumberjack shirt. Suitably farmer-like.

Poppy knows a lot about Will. He's slightly older than Selina. They've been together for four years.

'This is Will,' Selina says, her eyes darting from him back to the women. Her voice is still calm and soft, but she shifts on her feet slightly. He stares at her, standing stiffly in the centre of the kitchen, like some kind of exhibit. A nerve twitches in his jaw.

What a peculiar couple they make.

'He'll be cooking all your food,' Selina says. 'We only serve seasonal food, and the produce has all come from farms within a twenty-five-mile radius of The Sanctuary. Of course, a lot of it comes from our own kitchen garden, and we'll give you a little tour of that tomorrow. We have a volunteer here, Badger, who's been working tirelessly on the gardens and wildflower meadow. I'll introduce you to him too. We're absolutely passionate about reducing food waste and being as sustainable as possible – at some point Will'll talk you through everything we've been doing here to reduce our impact, I'm sure.'

They all nod. Will takes a step forward towards the table, lifting his head up to properly look at them, and then, all of a sudden, he stops short, for just a second.

He flashes them an immaculate smile.

'Lovely to see you all, ladies,' he says. 'And thank you for bringing the beautiful weather with you too! I trust you all had good journeys here.'

So he's a charmer then, Poppy thinks. Posh too. Despite his smooth demeanour, she notices his neck is slightly flushed.

Poppy glances at Selina. A frown is attempting to escape through the mask-like expression on Selina's face.

Poppy sits back in her chair, her fingers still wrapped around her mug. There is obviously more to this situation than meets the eye. Coming here was the right thing to do. She just knew it.

SELINA

I've sent all the guests back to their yurts to freshen up before the guided country walk. I'm just going to take them over the Nine Acres, round the stream and back through the chalk grassland, carefully avoiding the bluebell meadow, but now I'm wondering whether I should talk to them as we go. I hadn't really planned this part of the weekend too much – I've been so focused on the yoga.

I'm in our living room at the other end of the barn – this part of the building is off limits to guests. It's cramped in here. Functional but unloved.

We wanted the kitchen to be as big and welcoming as possible, with its vaulted double-height ceiling and huge doors out onto the garden and then the higher field, around which the bell tents are dotted in a semicircle. As a result, we had to squeeze our accommodation into the other side of the barn. Two bedrooms – one for us and one for Kai – a bathroom and a tiny living room. It reminds me of the flat above the pub where my father lived before he died. A home, but also, somehow, *not* a home.

But then I have never had the same attachment to the concept of home as others. I've been nomadic all my life.

Until I met Will. My hero.

He is sitting on the sofa, his back to me, staring out of the narrow window at the fields beyond. He seemed a bit distracted in the kitchen earlier but I don't have time to probe it further now. I have to focus on this weekend, on making it a success.

I linger in the doorway, looking at him.

'Hopefully they'll settle in OK,' I say, and he startles, turning around.

'Oh,' he says. 'I didn't see you there.'

'No,' I say, and there's part of me – maybe ten per cent – that wants to ask him what's on his mind, and if he's all right, but a bigger part of me is too scared of the answer.

I've been let down by so many men in the past. They have exhausted me. My whole life, all men have done is exhaust me. And now my son, a grown man himself, is exhausting me too.

'Do you think they'll get on? Did you sense a strange atmosphere among them?' I ask, walking over and sitting on the sofa next to him. He shifts further away from me.

'What?' he says. 'No, not really. I was only in there five minutes. They looked perfectly normal to me.'

'Hmm.'

Something is bothering him. I think about the way he froze in the doorway as he came in, and then quickly turned on the charm.

'What's on your mind?' I ask.

'What?'

'I can tell there's something bothering you.'

'Oh . . . I said I'd call Ed. I hadn't realised the time.'

'Right.'

Ed, his brother, is going through a divorce at the moment, and is apparently traumatised by the whole thing. One of his hobbies is shooting rabbits with an air rifle, so I've found it hard to muster up much sympathy.

But somehow, I know Will is lying.

'I'm just tired,' he snaps, 'and worried about him.'

'Perhaps we should invite him to stay for a bit?' I say. Not one single part of me wants to extend this particular olive branch, but I do it anyway. For the greater good.

Ed thinks I'm weird. He's jealous too, that we took on the farm when their father died, even though we had no choice really.

After all, back then he wasn't about to uproot his perfect family from Bristol and drag them down here to live in the middle of nowhere. It's not our fault that he now wishes he had, that he might still be married if he'd only taken Melanie away from the city and all those chances to meet someone who wasn't an arsehole.

But perhaps the time has come to build some bridges. Perhaps if I start to concede a little, it will help fix things between Will and me.

'You hate Ed,' Will says.

'Will, I don't hate anyone. We've just never given each other a fair chance before . . .'

He stares at me.

'Anyway, we have the room now. Once the guests have gone, he can come and stay in one of the tents. You two can go fishing and have manly chats and do whatever it is that you need to do. I'll stay out of your way.'

Will looks unconvinced.

'Maybe,' he says. 'I'll see how he feels.'

He won't look me in the eye now and turns to stare out of the window.

'Listen, I need to get some air. I'm going for a walk.'

He stands up and lets himself out of the side door.

I linger for a while, watching the door, half expecting Will to come back in. The anger starts to rise.

How dare he behave so strangely today of all days?

But closely following my anger's tail is fear. Fear that he won't come back. Fear that one day he'll just up and leave and I'll never see him again.

I shake my head.

But he can't do that. He knows he can't. And he won't.

I take a deep breath, stretch my arms high above my head and do an eagle and then a tree pose, trying to bring my focus to the present, and the strong, stable earth beneath my feet. There is so much energy in the air at the moment, and most of it is chaotic. I need to focus on the present moment – the only thing that exists – and embrace its stillness.

Once I feel calmer, I collect my wellies from the rack, and take them through to the kitchen.

It's time for our guided walk.

THE WALK

If you go down to the woods today . . .

Does it ever worry you? That people might find out what you're hiding here?

The brazenness of it all . . . letting people come and stay, letting them roam around your home unguarded, letting them explore the land, knowing what you know. Knowing what's hidden there.

Do you really think taking them on a 'guided walk' will stop them from wandering off of their own accord?

Of course you do. Because you're arrogant.

You think your secrets are safe. You think the others won't tell.

But what do you know about your guests' secrets? What if theirs are even worse than yours?

What if they know more than you realise?

What if they start digging?

What if they decide to explore just that little bit further?

What if they start to push the boundaries? In more ways than one . . .

NICKY

Georgia and I have swapped tents.

She thought I might like to be in the one next to Bonnie. I couldn't think of a way of turning the offer down that wouldn't have offended either or both of them. And it was a thoughtful gesture.

The inside of the bell tent is a thousand times nicer than my bedroom at home. I sit down on the bed, pushing the mattress slightly with my palm to test it. Firm and thick.

I swing my legs round and lie down flat on my back, staring up at the tent's roof. I can hear the sound of bells tinkling in the breeze outside. Wind chimes. I close my eyes, letting my fingers run over the sateen duvet cover.

Instantly, a sense of peace washes over me.

We've been meaning to get a new mattress for months now, but it's one of those jobs we never get around to. The thought of trying out mattresses with two young kids in tow, bouncing on all the beds in the showroom, is exhausting.

So instead we've just been making do with the mattress we bought when we first got married. Now stained and saggy, like me.

I should ask Selina where she got this one, because it's absolutely perfect.

With an effort, I sit back up, realising that if I don't get moving I'll fall asleep. On the bedside table there are sprigs of wildflowers in a tubular vase. One of them is a deep purple, the exact same colour as my bridesmaids' dresses, and I reach out and finger the petals, before leaning down to sniff it. But I'm disappointed to find it doesn't have a fragrance.

I never have fresh flowers in the house. It's little things like this that seem so daft but that in fact lift your spirits. I resolve to buy myself more flowers when I get home.

Bonnie marches into my tent unannounced as I'm changing into my waterproof trousers. I bought them last year when Jon started suggesting we go on a weekly walk through the countryside around our village.

It was lovely in the summer, of course, but I can't say I particularly enjoyed this new family tradition in the bitter cold in February.

The truth is I find it very difficult to do things that don't have a specific purpose these days. Call it the mother's curse, but it feels as though every waking moment must be used as productively as possible. And wandering for hours across muddy woodland doesn't really feel like productivity to me. Not when there's always washing and cleaning waiting for me back at home.

I take a deep breath.

This kind of thinking is the reason I'm on this break.

'What the hell are they?' Bonnie laughs, flopping onto

my bed and pointing to my legs. 'Are they made of kagoul material?'

'They're waterproof trousers.'

'They have elasticated ankles!' she shrieks. Her laugh is too loud. It feels forced, somehow.

I look at her. Her cheeks are bright red. She's wearing the same clothes she was wearing when I picked her up outside the museum. My eyes rest on her bare ankles.

'Apparently there are loads of ticks in the woodland,' I say. 'Selina said. And they can jump really high.'

'Scary,' she says, widening her eyes in sarcasm.

'Your ankles are bare. You can't wear those trainers.'

'Why not?'

'They've got a platform heel! You'll trip over and break your leg. Plus they'll get ruined.'

'Fine,' she sighs, 'I'll put the wellies on.'

'You're in a good mood,' I say, tying the waistband cord of my trousers.

She shrugs.

I glance out of the flap of the tent that Bonnie left open. The sky is still full of glorious sunshine, but you never know – it could easily turn to rain. I'm probably best off in my waterproof jacket too.

It's a slightly different shade of blue from the trousers though, so they look terrible together.

I pull it on. Bonnie looks down, but I can tell she's smiling.

'You won't need that,' she says. 'It's boiling out there.'

'All right, fine,' I say, taking it off. 'What are you smirking about?'

I feel suddenly young again, like we are two teenage friends gossiping.

'Nothing,' she says, looking up again. 'I'm just happy, I guess. A change is as good as a rest. It's nice to be away from my shitshow of a house share.'

'How's your course going?'

'It's fiiine,' she says, dragging the word out. 'I dunno. People have it worse. It's OK. My tutor's pretty great.'

'How are the other people in your class? Do you get on?'

'Of course!'

'Do they know about . . . your situation . . .'

'You sound about eighty.' She rolls her eyes. 'Some of them do, yes. They're not particularly interested. Half of them are mature students anyway.'

'Hmm. But still, the . . . father, he's happy about it, yes?'

'Nicky! You promised not to ask. He's not on my course anyway.'

'I don't understand what the point of all the secrecy is. You should just tell me what's going on. I'm not going to judge. Christ, and no offence, but I really, *really* don't care, you know. You're a grown-up, and it's your life.'

'I am and it is.'

'So long as you're all right.'

'I'm absolutely fine. I'll go and change into my wellies and come straight back. Did you see they've left crystals on our pillows? Mine was a moonstone – apparently helps to balance hormones and relieve stress. What did you get?'

'I don't know,' I say, turning round to the bed. I lean forward and pick up the small mesh bag on the throw pillow, opening it and pulling out the rock inside. It's pink and smooth, and beautifully cool under my fingertips. 'Oh. It's rose quartz.'

'Classic,' Bonnie says. 'Do you remember, when I was a kid, I had a bracelet made out of rose quartz? But the elastic got all saggy and one day it fell off at school. Never found it. Anyway, I'll be back soon.'

She leaves the tent and I stand there rolling the rose quartz around in my hand. It starts to warm up against my skin.

I read the little card inside the bag.

Rose quartz is protective during pregnancy and with childbirth. Its loving, nurturing energy is powerful in times of stress and healing to mother and child. The healing properties of the stone may aid fertility, conception, pregnancy and childbirth. The ultimate gemstone for love.

I take some deep breaths and try to appreciate the space, the silence, the fact that I don't have anyone asking me for anything right now.

It's so wonderful here that I'm slightly worried I won't ever want to leave.

BONNIE

The wellies are brand new, but they're a bit too big, and as I walk they loosen and then flop back against my ankles, making a ridiculous noise that's not too dissimilar to a fart. It's pretty funny. But also embarrassing.

When I get back to Nicky's tent she's waiting outside. Thankfully she's abandoned her fifty-shades-of-blue-kagoul combo. But still, the trousers!

'You look like you're about to go on *Celebrity SAS* or something,' I say and then I look up at the sky.

'Shut up,' Nicky replies, pouting. She doesn't mind me taking the mickey out of her. She's got a good sense of humour – something we get from our dad. Whatever the situation, he always finds a way to laugh about it. As a kid I always thought it was a bit insensitive, but now, I can see it's just his way of coping.

'My wellies are too big. They keep making fart noises.'

She grins.

'Thanks for making me come,' she says, taking a deep breath and stretching her arms above her head. She closes her eyes as the sunlight falls on her face. 'It's good to be here. It really is.'

I feel my cheeks flush. I hate that I'm the kind of person who needs loads of praise, but I've looked up to Nicky my whole life, and whenever she says anything nice to me, I feel about six years old again.

'Well, thanks to Jon the grade A husband for paying for us both. Your broke-ass little sister could never have afforded it.'

'Broke-ass?' she says, her top lip twisting. 'What are you, fifteen?'

We walk up the gravel path that snakes its way around the bell tents and up towards the main barn, slicing the lawn in half.

'What was that?' Nicky says, pulling on my arm.

I stop short.

'What?'

'That sound?'

'I didn't hear anything,' I say.

'It sounded like a baby crying,' she says, screwing up her nose. 'Weird.'

'Oh,' I reply. 'I didn't . . . I didn't hear it. Probably an animal in the woods.'

Nicky nods, but she looks puzzled.

'It was definitely a baby.'

I shrug. There are no babies here. Not yet, anyway. We continue our walk towards the others, who are lingering by the patio area behind the barn. This part of the garden is covered in gravel, with an enormous metal fire pit in the centre. It looks like a witch's cauldron.

Selina appears, sliding the barn door shut behind her.

'Hello, ladies,' she says, in her soft drawl. 'Shall we set off?

It's about a forty-minute round trip. Hope you'll all be able to manage?'

Selina's eyes fall on Georgia's massive bump.

'Will you be all right walking that far, Georgia?'

'Oh yes,' Georgia says. Her cheeks flush. 'I . . . I seem to be having a big baby. I know I've got a huge bump but I've always kept myself really active and I've been determined not to let pregnancy affect that.'

I glance at her legs. She's wearing leggings with her walking boots and I can see the outline of her calf muscles through the material. I hope I look that fit when I'm her age.

'Good for you,' Selina says. 'That's a wonderful example of trusting your body. You and only you know what it's capable of. So often in life we don't listen to our bodies, to what they are able to do. We don't trust those instincts. But it's funda-mentally important that we learn to block out all the "noise" from the experts, and learn to listen to the noise that comes from within. Our gut is constantly telling us what's right. When we suppress that voice, it allows stress to run riot within our body, which manifests in all kinds of unpleasant ways.'

'Our gut?' Poppy says.

I turn to look at Poppy. She's hardly said a word since we all arrived.

'Yes,' Selina says, and she flashes her whiter-than-white teeth at Poppy. Her head is cocked to one side, her eyes wide and unblinking. 'The vagus nerve directly connects our gut to our brain. It's why you often get an upset stomach when you're stressed.'

Poppy doesn't respond. There's an awkward silence.

'Anyway,' Selina says. 'It's wonderful that you're all up for a walk. One of the biggest misconceptions in pregnancy is that you should lie around all day taking it easy. If only! It's very important to stay active, to keep your blood flowing and oxygen circulating to all parts of your body.'

'Surely you shouldn't overdo it though?' Poppy says. 'Surely there are risks?'

'Well, yes, of course,' Selina replies. She gives a short cough, then smiles. 'But you know, there are risks throughout life. Avoidance of all risk is impossible.'

We start to walk across the field behind the barn, five astride, as though we are old friends. In the distance I spot a man in a grey T-shirt, hunched over the earth, raking it over.

'So how do you judge which risks to take?' Poppy continues. It occurs to me that Poppy has an agenda of some kind, but I can't work out what she's angling at.

'That's where listening to your gut is imperative,' Selina says, striding through the long grass. As she walks, she lifts her knees up high and tosses her long hair over her shoulders.

Her hair is almost as long as mine, but it's thin and straggly. Her face is a patchwork of freckles and lines, but her posture is incredible. I push my shoulders back and straighten my neck.

'But how do you know what your gut is telling you? And what is just what you've been conditioned to know?' Poppy says. The grass is longer at this end of the field, and damp too. My wellies continue to squelch and fart as I walk.

Selina turns to her directly and smiles.

'Don't worry, this is exactly what we will cover this weekend,' she says. 'Thank you for bringing it up. It's a fundamental question. Quieting our minds, listening to our bodies. Did you know that your mind is really just another organ, exactly the same as your arm or leg? You are ultimately in complete control of it. What it says, does and thinks.'

'But that makes no sense,' Poppy says. 'If it's the same as our arms and legs, then surely our gut must be too, and that means we're in control of that as well? So which bit are we meant to listen to, and which bit are we in control of?'

Nicky starts to tense up next to me. She hates this kind of thing. An atmosphere.

I make eye contact with her and she widens her eyes in mock fear. I suppress the urge to giggle. I glance sideways at Georgia who's pulling an impressive poker face.

'Oh, look over there at the bluebells!' Nicky says, pointing ahead at a wooded area, carpeted in blue and white. 'So beautiful – are we going that way?'

'What?' Selina says shortly. 'Er, no. Not today. It's very easy to get lost in those woods. It'd be safer if you stayed out of them, if that's all right.'

She turns back to Poppy.

'You clearly have a lot on your mind,' Selina says, dropping her voice and reaching out an arm. Her tanned fingers wrap around the sleeve of Poppy's coat, giving it a squeeze.

'I understand why,' she says, quieter still. 'Please, just trust that all will become clear over the course of the weekend.'

That shuts Poppy up for now, but the tranquillity of this countryside moment seems spoilt somehow.

As though it's started to rain, even though it hasn't.

GEORGIA

I hope I didn't come across as showing off. But I've completed two marathons. A little countryside walk isn't going to do me any harm.

I know Selina was trying to be kind, and after all, I am the most pregnant of all of them. Just gone eight months, to be precise. But they don't know that.

I told Selina I was five and a half months pregnant when I booked my place. I was worried they wouldn't let me come, that they'd think I was too far into the third trimester. That there was a risk I'd go into labour.

I shudder. Imagine going into labour here. There's nothing and nobody for miles.

Thankfully, my bump is actually quite small for my gestation so it's easy to pretend I'm not as far along as I really am. It began to worry me a few weeks ago, but we went to Harley Street for a private scan and everything was fine. It was something to do with the baby's positioning, plus the fact that I haven't put on much weight. Also, I have a long torso, so there's more space for the baby to spread out.

I have been trying to eat healthily. I can't afford for anything to go wrong with this pregnancy. I'm thirty-nine – the mere fact that I fell pregnant feels like a miracle in itself.

We trudge through the grass, and I take in deep lungfuls of country air. I can smell the faint scent of manure, carried on the breeze. It smells like my childhood and even though it's warm, the air feels crisp. Invigorating.

I am glad I came.

In the distance, the sky is darker, whereas above our heads it's the brightest blue. It's amazing how quickly the weather can change in this part of the world. I glance up. There's a threatening mass of black cloud looming right ahead.

At first, I was grateful that we didn't have to do an awkward 'meet and greet' session or go round the table and give a potted speech about who we are and where we came from. I wanted this weekend to be about me, about what I'm going through.

But now I'm deeply curious about these other women. What their stories are. I don't even know if any of them have had other children. I assumed, like an NCT group, that we would all be first-time mums, but Nicky, the tallest one, has a kind of world-weary look that I recognise in all my friends with kids. Bonnie is clearly a live wire.

And as for Poppy . . . after that peculiar interrogation of Selina, she intrigues me most of all.

A frisson of excitement takes over me. This weekend feels like the beginning of a whole new chapter in my life. Perhaps we'll all end up friends for life? Who knows?

After all, I would never have imagined that my chance meeting with Brett would change literally everything about my life, but look what happened.

'It's beautiful here,' I say, meaning it. Ahead of us stretches nothing but field. 'Do you own this land too? How long have you been here?'

'No, this is our neighbour's land,' Selina says. She speaks slowly, as though considering every word with utmost care. 'We've been here three years now. For the first two we were just living in a caravan on site while we refurbished the main barn.'

'That must have been tough,' I reply.

'You have no idea.' Selina laughs. 'At times I really questioned my own sanity. The winters were particularly challenging. It was absolutely freezing. But I've lived in worse places, and we knew it would work out in the end.'

'How did you find the land?' Bonnie asks.

'Oh, it was . . . well, it belonged to Will's family actually,' Selina says, flushing slightly. It's the first time I've heard her stumble over her words. 'His father died a few years ago, and his mother had to go into residential care. His brother lives in Bristol with his family and wasn't interested in coming to look after the farm, so we took over . . .'

'Wow, that was lucky,' Poppy says. Although she's smiling, her tone is mocking. 'Imagine, meeting the man of your dreams, and he just so happens to come with acres of land for you to build on! Nice.'

'Actually,' Selina says, 'it was Will's idea to convert the barn. Not mine. He'd always wanted to do it, but when we met we came up with the plan together. I guess you could call it fate! We divided the plot and sold the farmhouse separately, and Will's brother got the proceeds from that.'

74

'It's a beautiful place to live,' I say. Selina is strange – with her ethereal, other-worldly tone of voice – and I can't quite figure her out, but it's not particularly kind of Poppy to start implying she's just a shameless freeloader. 'I grew up in Somerset, so I feel very passionate about this part of the world.'

'What about you, Selina?' Bonnie says. 'Have you always lived here?'

'Oh no,' she replies. 'I've lived all over really. I was in the States for a long time.'

'I thought you had a bit of a twang to your voice. My partner Brett is American,' I say. 'Whereabouts did you live?'

'I moved to LA when I was seventeen,' she replies. 'I was there for twenty years in the end.'

Something about the way she says it tells me she doesn't want to elaborate further. We fall into silence and continue our march across the open fields. As we climb to the top of a hill, I realise I can smell something in the air.

Smoke.

'Oh, can you smell that? I love the smell of bonfires,' Nicky says. 'Is that weird?'

'Who would have a bonfire in *this* weather?' Bonnie says.

Selina's forehead wrinkles.

We reach the top of the hill and pause for a few seconds looking down into the valley. The sky is suddenly very dark, which makes what's in front of us stand out even more.

In the valley below is a shape that makes no sense.

The wind carries the smell of acrid burning towards us, but it's the flames that now have our attention.

'Shit! Is that . . .' Bonnie says, her voice a shriek. 'Is that a person? On fire?!'

Selina runs forward down the hill and we all follow, stumbling through the long grass towards the burning shape below.

'Oh my God,' I say, as I hurry towards it as quickly as I can, one arm wrapped round my bump. 'It can't be . . .'

It certainly looks like a person, standing in the middle of the field, arms outstretched, but they are completely engulfed in thick orange flames.

Selina reaches it first.

She turns back, waving her arms in the air.

'It's OK!' she calls to us. 'It's just a scarecrow! It's not a person, it's a scarecrow!'

My heart is thundering in my chest. I feel sick, and winded from the run. I rest my hands on my bump, feeling the thump of my own pulse.

My back spasms. I shouldn't have run so fast.

'Thank God,' I say. 'Thank God for that.'

'Don't get too close,' Nicky says, but Selina either ignores her or can't hear. She takes off her hoodie and tries to smother the flames. But they're dying back anyway now, the straw from inside the scarecrow smouldering and smoking. My eyes start to sting.

Nicky pulls on my arm.

'You don't want to inhale the smoke. Stay back.'

'Is there anywhere nearby we can get some water to put it out?' Poppy asks.

We're surrounded by vast open field on all sides.

I look at Selina. She gives the scarecrow an aggressive kick at the bottom and the whole thing collapses to the ground. I'm impressed by her courage. She continues to smother the remaining flames with her hoodie.

Then, the dark clouds I spotted earlier live up to their threat. It starts to spit, just a little at first, but it's only a matter of time before it pours down.

We stand around the smouldering scarecrow. Thankfully the grass in the field is soon wet through and doesn't catch light. The rain continues to fall, getting heavier, as we stand watching. It's such a dramatic contrast to the bright sunshine only minutes earlier.

Soon, the fire is completely extinguished. All that's left of the scarecrow are parts of the frame, some scraps of fabric and, most unpleasantly, its hat and shoes.

'God, it's like *The Wicker Man* or something,' Bonnie says, and then she starts laughing. 'What a way to start our retreat!'

I've pulled the hood of my jacket over my head. The water runs down the front and drips onto my nose. I think of Brett; how he would like this, what a fan he is of 'typical British weather'. He grew up in Florida, just outside Tampa, where the weather sets in for weeks.

'How did it catch fire?' I say, looking around. 'It's so strange. There's no one here . . .'

'Lightning?' Nicky asks.

We all stare at her.

'But it was hardly even raining before,' I say.

I turn to look at Selina. She's panting, her eyes wide with shock. This is the least composed she's looked since we arrived.

'I'm sorry, ladies,' she says. 'This is very . . . unfortunate. I do apologise if you had a fright.'

'Why would there even be a scarecrow in this field?' Bonnie asks. 'There's nothing growing here. It's just pasture.'

It's a good question. I shudder.

'Just kids, I expect,' says Selina. 'Some stupid joke. That's the problem with young kids round here, there's not enough for them to do, they get bored . . .'

I don't like it. Now the sun has gone in, it feels so much colder.

'I'm sorry,' I say, 'but I feel a bit sick. I might turn back. With the rain too. If that's OK? It's just the smoke . . . the smell is very strong. I had quite bad nausea in the early days and still find certain smells difficult . . .'

Selina looks at me.

'Of course,' she says. I feel guilty for spoiling her plans. 'I'm so very sorry. How about the rest of you? What would you like to do?'

'I'm happy to go back on my own,' I say quickly. 'I don't want to ruin anyone's walk. I'm sorry to be a pain.'

'You're not being a pain,' Nicky says. 'I'm happy to head back too . . . To be honest, the rain looks like it's setting in.'

Poppy and Bonnie nod their heads.

'I'm easy,' Bonnie says. Her hair is completely drenched. She flicks some of the long tangles out of her eyes. 'Guess there's plenty of time for walking the rest of the weekend.'

'Well, if you're sure,' Selina says, but I can tell she's frustrated at how things have worked out.

'I'm sorry,' I say. 'I've ruined everyone's plans.'

'Don't be silly,' Selina says, reaching out to squeeze my arm. 'It's fine. If you're all sure, we'll go back.'

I nod. Something about the charred scarecrow remains in front of us has put me right off. I've been so tired this week. Even the long journey getting here seems to have worn me out – perhaps it's true what they say about third-trimester energy levels. I just want to go back to my tent with a cup of hot chocolate and rest for a bit.

'Are you going to leave it there?' Poppy says, pointing down at the scarecrow.

'I'll let Will know what's happened when we get back. He can come down later to clear it up.'

We begin to walk back up the hill.

'So weird,' I say. 'What a horrible practical joke.'

'I can't think what kind of person would want to do something like that,' Poppy says. 'It's like an effigy or something.'

'I told you, it'll just be the local youth,' Selina says. 'It's a good example of what happens when you don't channel your cosmic energy into something positive. The kids who did this are bored, but instead of focusing on something productive, they choose to make their own . . . entertainment. It's sad, but what can we do? I don't want it to upset you. But perhaps it would be helpful to discuss this later, at our journaling session. I can give you some good tips on how to empower yourselves to be able to deal with unwanted things like this in the future.'

'Sounds great,' Nicky says.

'Yes, it'll be very useful for when we next encounter a . . . burning scarecrow,' Bonnie says, under her breath. She rolls her eyes at me.

I try not to laugh. Poor Selina.

She strides forward confidently, but I couldn't help noticing the waver in her voice. As though she's as freaked out as the rest of us.

'Come on,' she says, gesturing to us. Though she's trying to hide it, I can tell she's really upset. 'Let's get out of this awful rain.'

POPPY

Poppy is hiding behind the door to the private part of the barn, listening to Selina tell Will about the scarecrow.

The others have all gone back to their tents.

'It was wearing my clothes! Christ, Will! What the hell?'

Poppy raises an eyebrow at the swearing.

'What clothes?' Will says.

'Some old leggings, and one of my jumpers . . .'

'Are you sure? They could be anyone's. I thought you said they were burnt to a crisp anyway?'

'I could see. In between the flames. The pattern of the fabric!' Selina shrieks. 'They were mine, definitely mine! For fuck's sake. Who could have done that?'

It's as though Selina's mask has been wrenched off, and underneath there's a completely different woman.

The woman Poppy knows all about.

It makes Poppy wish she could reach out, from here, and wrap her hands around Selina's neck.

'Don't be ridiculous,' he replies. 'I'm sure it's just kids.'

'It's gone,' Selina says triumphantly. Poppy strains her eyes to try to make out what she's doing. Selina is rummaging through a chest of drawers by the side of the bed.

'That jumper, it's one I got last year on that yoga workshop. It's gone, it's not in here! I knew it. I could tell straight away. Someone's taken that scarecrow out of our kitchen garden, and dressed it in my clothes, and set fucking fire to it in the field by our house.'

Her language is so surprising. Such a contrast to the wax-work statue of a woman who's been playing hostess.

Poppy peers again through the tiny gap in the woodwork round the door. She can just make out Selina, her head in her hands, as she slumps onto their bed.

Will is standing awkwardly next to her. He doesn't move to comfort her. There's something peculiar about this pair. Their whole relationship.

Poppy wonders how Selina convinced him to take her on. What he ever saw in her. Why they are still together when there's clearly so little love or affection between them. She's not even that attractive.

It makes Poppy feel a bit better, knowing that Selina's relationship, at the very least, appears to be a mess.

'Don't get upset. Whoever did this – that's what they want. It'll just be a joke,' he says.

'Someone's been in our bedroom, Will, and taken out my clothes.' Selina's voice is more muted now. Every word perfectly pronounced and evenly spaced. The diction of an actress.

Poppy blinks. Her eyes are sore from peering through the crack. She steps back slightly and rubs them. But then she hears something else – sobbing.

She forces her eye back to the gap. Selina is still sitting on the bed, but now her chest is heaving; great, dramatic sobs pouring out of her.

It's a distasteful show.

'Oh, come on now,' Will says. 'Don't cry about it, for Christ's sake. Pull yourself together.'

But she doesn't respond. She just sits there crying. They are the strangest couple Poppy has ever seen. Nothing about their relationship feels right. It's almost as though they are brother and sister.

But no, not just that. A brother and sister who secretly hate each other.

Poppy takes a step back again and checks her watch. It's nearly 5.30pm. They're meant to be having their first yoga session at 6.00pm. How will Selina manage to compose herself before then?

Something tells Poppy that somehow she will. She can almost feel how important this weekend is to Selina; how much she's staked on its success.

Poppy leaves her spyhole, a secret smile on her face, and goes back to her bell tent. It's still raining. She assumes the others are all resting in their tents – she can see smoke rising from one of them.

She goes inside her own and sits on the bed. She's tired, but her head is thrumming with the adrenaline of being here, of finally being so close to Selina, of seeing her personal life so intimately.

She isn't exactly sure how she expected to feel but it wasn't like this. She doesn't even feel that angry any more. Instead, she feels drained. Selina's presence is like a poison, polluting the air.

Poppy rummages around in her backpack and unearths her phone. She rereads Ant's message, telling her he loves her. Suddenly she has a strong compulsion to phone him, to confess all, to tell him where she is. To ask him to come and get her, and to rewind the last year of their lives, to go back to a time when everything was simpler. When they were so arrogant – and ignorant – to think that bad things would never happen to their perfect family.

But she didn't reply earlier, and now she can't, even if she wanted to, because her phone has no signal. Not a great surprise – they are in the middle of nowhere, after all. In the welcome pack, which Selina thoughtfully left on the bed, there's the Wi-Fi password so she should be able to use WhatsApp, but she's not completely sure she wants to be connected to the outside world right now anyway.

It'd just throw her off course.

No, she has to remember what she came here for, what she came here to do, and she must not allow herself to become distracted or dissuaded in any way.

She looks around her tent. The earlier rain has lowered the temperature, and so she goes over to the log-burner in the corner and opens the heavy metal door.

It's all brand new – so new that you can tell it's never even hosted a fire. The glass on the front of the door is clean and shiny. Inside, two chunky logs have been laid on top of a pile of kindling and newspaper. She takes a match and strikes it, holding it against the paper until it's almost burnt to nothing. Then she drops it right before it singes her fingers.

For a few moments, she sits on the rush flooring in front

of the log-burner, allowing the warmth from the fire to heat her face, poking it at intervals and inhaling the smell of the smoke.

It reminds her of the scarecrow, of the fright in Selina's face as she pushed it over and smothered the flames.

There was no hesitation when she did that.

Selina is brave, then. Strong. The type to act first, think later.

It is all so interesting. Selina is not exactly what she was expecting.

There's a small mesh bag on Poppy's pillow. She picks it up and teases open the drawstring. Inside is a bright orange stone. The colour is vulgar, surprising.

She takes out the piece of paper that was folded up inside the bag, and reads it.

Orange Calcite

Promotes positive thinking and clears feelings of stress, fear and tension. May be helpful in energetically healing the reproductive system.

The fury builds up inside her. In her insensitive way, this is clearly Selina's idea of helping. Or attempting to empathise.

Whatever it is, it is completely off-key. Insensitive. Unfeeling. Ridiculous.

But why on earth had she expected anything else?

Poppy takes the crystal and walks towards the fire. She rolls it over a few times in her hand, feeling its sharp, jagged edges, and before she has the chance to think any more about it, throws it into the flames.

SELINA

I have ten minutes to get ready for my first yoga session. I've pulled myself together, of course. I've had to. I'm the only person keeping this place going. It's all on me.

I don't know what to wear for yoga now. The leggings the scarecrow was wearing were old, but they were my favourites. My lucky ones. It seems so stupid, but it feels like a warning, or some kind of bad omen.

And then, of course, there's the small matter of who would have thought this was an amusing joke to play. I recognised the scarecrow, of course, despite his fire-damaged appearance. He's the one Will and I built together a couple of years ago, to put in the kitchen garden after the birds kept eating all our raspberries. We even gave him a name: Brian.

I can deny it to myself all I want to, but the truth is staring me in the face.

It can only be Kai that's done this. His way of trying to sabotage the weekend.

Only Kai would have known how much I liked those leggings. Only Kai would have been able to come into our room and take them, unnoticed.

But at the same time, it doesn't feel like something he

86

would do. He's depressed, not vindictive. And especially not today, when he should have his hands full for once.

I also don't know how, logistically, he was able to get the scarecrow to the field and set fire to it without anyone seeing.

I frown, shake my head. It doesn't matter. Will's right – whoever did it *wants* me to have this reaction. I'm giving them all the power and satisfaction by responding this way. I refuse. I refuse to be riled.

I take out my second-favourite pair of leggings and pull them on, then take my top off. I'm standing there, naked from the waist up, when I hear Will come in the room.

'Sorry,' he says, turning away. 'I didn't know you were getting changed.'

'It's fine,' I say, picking up my sports bra and pulling it down over my head. He doesn't even want to look at me any more. I can't bear it.

'Just wanted to say I've sorted the scarecrow,' he says. 'What's left of him is on the bonfire for the next time we have one.'

'Thanks. Perhaps we should save it for Guy Fawkes night.'

I grin, and our eyes lock. He turns away without meeting my smile, and I remember how blown away I was when I first met him. How handsome I thought he was, how drawn I was to him. It was a meeting of souls, even before it was a meeting of minds.

I couldn't imagine what he would see in me though. He was from an old-school farming family. That kind of posh that's also rather scruffy; all gum boots, Barbour jackets and big dogs. The sort of man who would only ever consider dating someone from a similar background.

But it turned out that Will was the black sheep of the family. His parents had tried to pair him off with various girls from Roedean and Badminton and he'd rejected them all. It turned out he quite liked the idea of dating a hippy, yoga-loving free spirit, who'd run away from home to live in California.

I knew why. I made him feel braver than he was.

It was probably just to annoy his parents, but I wasn't complaining when he asked me out for a drink, or when he suggested I move in with him after three months, when I told him the council flat Kai and I were stuck in was getting me down.

Turns out that posh farmers like the idea of being white knights once in a while. And then I found out about the land, and everything fell into place. It was all meant to be.

But that was years ago.

'How are you feeling now?' he asks.

There's not a huge amount of warmth to his voice but the fact that he's asked is something.

'Better, thank you,' I say. 'I don't know why I got so upset. I think I'm just exhausted.'

'Well,' says Will wearily. 'It's a big weekend.'

'And I'm worried,' I say, dropping my voice to a whisper. 'What if it's something to do with her? What if she has friends, and they've found out what happened . . .'

'You're being paranoid,' Will snaps. 'Nobody knows.'

I nod but I'm not convinced.

He doesn't know that I don't even trust my son. Not completely.

'I'd like to do some meditation before the class,' I say. 'Just to clear my head.'

'Of course,' he replies, turning to leave.

'Oh, I forgot,' I say. 'Have you seen Kai? I know I asked him to stay away, but at the same time I . . . well, I didn't expect him to listen.'

'No. I expect he's still in the pigsty,' he says, but as he leaves I hear him muttering something under his breath.

I let it go.

No doubt he's stressed too – he's got to cook dinner for everyone soon.

I sit on the rug at the end of our bed, cross my legs and bring my hands to heart centre.

And then I close my eyes, trying to block out the vision of her that pops up to torment me whenever I start to become overwhelmed.

I push her ghost away, using the words I've rehearsed over and over.

You are at peace now, so leave me be.

THE EVENING

The Intuitive Mother.

That's an interesting name for the theme of this weekend.

There's nothing intuitive about your mothering, that's for sure.

But it's an easy sell, isn't it? 'Trust your intuition.' You can chuck that phrase around like it's something profound.

Like it's something original and groundbreaking. We all know the truth though, don't we?

Smoke and mirrors.

I've been watching the way you work.

Pregnant women are like vulnerable sponges. Sucking up advice left, right and centre, from any source. They're frightened, even if they don't quite know it yet.

Anyone who sounds confident and reassuring – LISTEN TO ME, I HAVE ALL THE ANSWERS – will draw them right in.

Listen to ME!

Oops, no, I mean YOUR INTUITION! It will guide you!

Emperor's new clothes.

Because the whole point is that these women don't have any intuition about this stuff yet. And so instead, you take them and you brainwash them with your opinions and convince them that – abracadabra – it's their intuition talking to them, not you!

And they fall for it. And they're so grateful, so pathetically grateful to you for providing all the answers.

People like you are the cancer of the information-overloaded world we live in.

NICKY

Our yoga session is held in a glass cube of a building set back from the main barn. I never did yoga when I was pregnant with the boys, and now I wish I had done.

Clearly, Selina has worked hard to create a tranquil space, and when the yoga is over and she hands us all eye masks and blankets, telling us to lie down in whichever position is most comfortable, I find myself falling asleep to her incantations.

Suddenly, her cultivated, melodic voice makes perfect sense. She must have learnt to speak like that during her training.

'When you are ready, please roll yourself into a comfortable seated position,' she says.

The room is hushed and still. Underneath my beaded eye mask I can smell traces of smoky incense. Selina said she would usually burn it throughout the class, but as we're all pregnant, she wouldn't, in case any of us were particularly sensitive to smells at the moment.

Very sensible, given Georgia's reaction to the scarecrow burning. She practically turned green.

I place a hand on my bump. I'm so lucky. I've never struggled with sickness in pregnancy. I have so much to be grateful for.

And yet . . .

I roll myself back up to sitting and take the eye mask off and blink. The others are all gazing around too, through bleary eyes.

'That was amazing,' says Georgia drowsily.

Selina smiles.

'I'm so glad,' she says.

I glance over at Bonnie. Her slight face is pale and neutral, her hair a messy mane around her shoulders. I wish she'd brush it once in a while.

'So,' Selina continues in that same breathy voice. 'We have forty-five minutes before dinner. If you'd like to go back to your yurts for some more rest then of course please do so—'

'Tents,' Poppy interrupts.

Selina blinks at her.

'Sorry?'

'They're tents,' she says. 'You keep calling them yurts. Yurts are semi-permanent structures held up by wooden poles. Tents are held in place by ropes and stakes.'

'You know what,' Selina says, flashing her a broad smile, 'you are absolutely right. It's my silly mistake. They are bell tents, not yurts.'

She pauses.

'The most expensive and luxurious bell tents on the market, in fact.'

That last bit comes over more defensively than I think she would have liked.

Poppy just stares at her.

'Um, so, as I was saying,' Selina says. 'You can either enjoy

96

some time in your . . . *bell tents* . . . or you're welcome to join us in the kitchen. Will does enjoy explaining his cooking processes so will be very . . . happy to have an audience!'

She doesn't look too sure about that.

'I don't know if I explained to you that as well as being a chef, he's also a qualified chef instructor. Anyway, if you're at all interested in cooking then do come along and watch him – it's really quite a mesmerising experience. And you might pick up some tips.'

We all get to our feet – Georgia more slowly than the rest of us – and gather by the doorway, sipping our lemon water.

Georgia does look extremely pregnant. It'd be rude to ask her how far along she is though.

Bonnie takes a long drink.

'Ahhh,' she says, putting the glass down. 'That was nice. Did you enjoy the yoga? Told you it would be good!'

'Yes,' I say. 'It was amazing. I can't remember the last time I felt this . . . relaxed.'

Suddenly I want to text Jon and tell him. And thank him, really, for stumping up the money to send us on this weekend, and for insisting I go even when I protested that I couldn't leave the boys.

'It was just what I needed,' I continue. 'And dinner sounds great. I didn't realise Selina's husband was a professional chef. Do you want to go and watch him cook? Maybe you'd find it useful?'

Bonnie is an amazing cook. She can look in a fridge, pluck out five ingredients and throw something delicious together without even trying. It took some persuading – and in the end our dad was the one who actually put her application in for the course – but we were all so pleased for her when she got her place at Le Saffron Chef's Academy. It's incredibly difficult to get into, and chefs that leave go on to work in some of the most exciting restaurants across the country. It's the first thing she's ever stuck to, and we were all so impressed.

But then she got pregnant, and even though babies are a blessing, I'm worried that she won't be able to finish her training now.

'Maybe,' she replies. 'I'll see how I feel. I'm going to go back to the room and get changed first. I feel like getting dressed up a bit.'

'Oh, OK,' I say. 'Fair enough. But as it's all veggie food this weekend, I might go. Jon's been on at me to try Meat Free Mondays.'

'Sure,' she says. 'I'll see you in a little bit for dinner then. I'm absolutely starving! It better be good.'

She turns on her heel and leaves. Georgia and Selina have already disappeared, but I notice Poppy is still sitting on her yoga mat, staring into space. I don't want to leave her here on her own.

'Are you OK?' I say, taking a few steps towards her.

'What?' she says. Her head snaps up and she looks at me. Her eyes are tear-stained.

'Gosh. What's the matter?' I say. I sit down on the floor beside her.

'I lost my baby last year,' she says, quietly. 'Well, she wasn't even a baby. She was eleven and a half months old. She had just begun to walk.'

My hand flies to my face; that familiar tightening in my chest. The absolute agony of it. Of the very idea of losing one of my babies.

'Oh my goodness, Poppy,' I say, swallowing. 'I'm so very sorry.'

'Everyone says that,' she says, looking down. She sniffs. 'I'm sorry too. But it doesn't do any good. It doesn't make any difference. It doesn't bring her back.'

'No,' I say. 'Of course not.'

I try to put my arms around her but the way she is holding herself – bolt upright, in the same position she ended the yoga session in – makes it awkward. In the end I just rest a hand on her leg.

It seems inadequate as a gesture.

'Are you worried?' I say. 'That it might happen again? Is that why you came this weekend?'

She laughs. A harsh, brittle sound. I frown.

'Something like that,' she says, looking away. 'Something like that.'

She stands up, wiping the remnants of the tears from under her eyes.

'Well, I suppose we should get ready for dinner,' she says. I wince. Have I said the wrong thing? Have I offended her somehow?

'I don't know what to say,' I say, standing and opening my hands out to her. 'Other than that I'm so terribly sorry, and if there's anything I can—'

'You have kids already, don't you?' she says.

'Yes, two boys.'

'And you're expecting your third.'

I look down guiltily at my stomach.

'It wasn't planned,' I say.

Why is it that having two children is the culturally expected thing, the 'right' thing to do, but having three makes you seem strange somehow? Why do we insist on judging everyone for their life choices?

'I feel too old and tired to have another baby, if I'm honest. To start it all again. Sorry. I don't want to be insensitive. I just find it hard to—'

'It's a privilege, being a mother,' she says. 'And you're not too old. You got pregnant. That's nature's way of telling you you're not too old.'

'That sounds like something Selina would say,' I say, but she doesn't smile.

'See you at dinner,' she says, picking up her jumper.

I linger in the yoga studio for a few more minutes, staring at my reflection in the mirror that spans the width of the back wall. I look completely exhausted. My hair is still damp and frizzy from this afternoon's walk; the meagre scrap of make-up I applied this morning before I left home now completely gone.

The dark circles under my eyes are still there though. My ever-present companions.

I walk slowly back to my tent, thinking about Poppy. What it must have felt like to have lost a child like that. Poor, poor Poppy. I can't even bear to imagine.

I am so lucky. There is a lesson there, in the pain on Poppy's face.

I will try harder, I think, as I take a baby wipe out of my bag and rub it over my entire face.

I will try harder to be grateful for this baby, to appreciate what I have.

BONNIE

The pissing rain has stopped again, finally. It definitely wasn't forecast. It feels a *bit* like the weather is trying to tell me something. Or perhaps I'm being paranoid.

After the yoga session ends, I decide to take a stroll around the grounds. The place is massive. Sprawling. To the right of the main barn there's a kind of allotment area – Selina referred to it as the 'kitchen garden' which sounded pretty pretentious to me – behind which lies an overgrown patch bursting with wildflowers.

I stand watching them for a while. The sheer colour and variety of blooms is pretty mesmerising. I imagine myself painting them one day. How hilariously bourgeois would that be?

Behind the main barn, there's a small patch of roses and other shrubs in a border. There's also a greenhouse that looks like it cost an absolute bomb. Someone has obviously put their heart and soul into making this place beautiful.

I keep walking until I reach the woodland that Nicky wanted to explore earlier, ignoring Selina's warning to keep out of it. It's a shock going from the bright light of an open field into the dark shadiness of the woods. The ground is completely covered in bluebells. I pick my way carefully through them, trying not to trample on any, until I come to a clearing.

There are no bluebells here. I glance up. The branches above form a protective canopy over my head – if it started to rain again, I'd stay completely dry.

Nature is so cool.

There's a patch of dark earth beneath one tree, just ahead of me. Like someone has recently raked over the ground. As I walk closer, I spot a collection of white pebbles next to the trunk.

The same white pebbles from outside the barn, where the fire pit is.

I crouch down. The pebbles have been disturbed by something, but even so, I can just about make out the first letter they once formed. J.

The other stones are too scattered to make the letters out clearly. It's almost like a jigsaw puzzle. The second letter might have been an O, or maybe an A.

I try to rearrange them, but it's too difficult to work out what they once said, so in the end I just make a heart shape out of them.

What a lovely place to bury a pet.

I stay there for a few minutes, listening to the wind rustling in the trees above, wondering if 'J' was a cat or a dog. Whichever he or she was, I hope they died of old age.

Then I turn and look back. It's confusing, suddenly, trying to work out which direction I came from. The trees all look the same.

I stare at the ring of bluebells surrounding me. How did I get here? From this way, or that?

I stand up, taking a deep breath. It feels as though I'm in the eye of a hurricane. I'm surrounded by trees on all sides, all identical, all feeling as though they're closing in on me.

For God's sake, Bonnie, get a grip.

I take a deep breath. And then I hear it – a shout, coming very clearly from one direction. Thank God. I blow a kiss at the stones, and head towards the noise.

Eventually, the trees thin out and I can see the edge of the lawn again. I relax, feeling a bit stupid. I follow the line of slightly trampled grass around the edge of the lawn until I'm back at the front of the barn.

Here, there's a classic shingle driveway, the gravel so new it's still dusty. Nicky's car is parked to the left.

I look back and beyond the wildflower meadow where the outbuildings are. There's another barn too, a smaller one that I haven't noticed before, and the row of stone buildings that Selina referred to earlier as the pigsties.

I check my watch – it's just gone 7pm. I have plenty of time to do some more poking about.

As I stride towards the pigsties, I hear something.

I creep closer, hiding behind some tall wildflowers. Will is standing outside the pigsties. As he paces to the left, I spot a young man in front of him, with a mop of dark hair obscuring most of his face. I edge just a little bit further towards them, straining to hear.

'Jesus, Kai,' Will is saying. 'Can't you just do what she asks, just for this one weekend? I mean, really. I don't need this shit. I've got a dinner to cook!'

'Get out of my face,' Kai says, kicking at the shingle. I crouch

104

down, my heart pounding, as Will stomps back to the main barn, slamming the glass door behind him so hard that I'm amazed the whole thing doesn't shatter.

Kai stands there, miserably staring at the ground.

He could be really good-looking. If he washed his hair, anyway. My mate Bella would love him. He's exactly her type with his beautiful, androgynous look.

I march towards him.

'Hello,' I say.

I don't know what makes me do this stuff. I just can't resist stirring the pot sometimes. Plus, you know, families are fascinating.

He glances at me as I come closer. I stop a few paces away, giving him my brightest smile, and pull out my pouch of tobacco.

'Want one?' I say, pulling out a pre-made roll-up and offering it to him.

He nods and takes it from me. I help myself to the other.

'All right,' he says. I hand him my lighter.

He flicks the lighter on and I lean down over it, staring him right in the eyes as I take a deep breath, letting the flames ignite the paper. I tuck the pouch back into the pocket of my dress. His hands are shaking as he lifts the roll-up to his lips.

'You shouldn't be smoking,' he says, in an unexpectedly judgemental way. He flicks his hair out of his eyes as he inhales.

'Cabin fever,' I say, blowing a smoke ring. 'I've been good, mostly. It's only a small one.'

'Yeah, but . . . it's not good for the baby, is it? That shit.'

'Bet your mum smoked when she was pregnant with you,' I counter, holding his eye contact.

'How do you know who my mum is?'

'It's pretty obvious, isn't it?' I say, swallowing. 'You look just like her. Selina.'

'Yeah, well. Look how I turned out.'

I don't know what to say to that. For a few moments we both stand there, smoking. I glance back at the barn, wondering if anyone inside can see us.

'Your dad's about to cook me dinner,' I say, meeting his eyes again.

'He's not my dad,' he says. 'He's just Mum's latest meal ticket.'

'Are you not a fan?'

He sniffs.

'He's as bad as her.'

'Oh,' I say. 'In what way?'

He points his forefinger at the side of his head and rotates it, pulling a face.

'He seems pretty sane to me.'

'Well,' he says, as though choosing his words carefully. 'He's a good cook. And he's loaded.'

I suck hard on my roll-up.

'What happened to your real dad?'

He shrugs.

'Your mum can't have been very old when she had you,' I say, still digging. 'She looks so young now. And you must be, what, twenty-one?'

He shakes his head.

'Nineteen.'

'Wow,' I say, taking a step closer. 'You look older. I'm twenty-two. I thought you were my age.'

'My mum was twenty-three when she had me,' he says. There's a pause, a tiny shifting of his barriers. He looks at my bump. 'Was it a mistake?'

My hand flies to my stomach protectively. I wish I hadn't crossed this line now. *Nothing.* Nothing is more important than my baby.

'What? No, not at all.'

'Apparently having a baby at that age ruined my mum's life.'

'I'm sure that's not true,' I say, dropping the remnants of my roll-up into the gravel. I've had enough of his conversation. It's my fault – never poke a hornets' nest. 'Nice chatting to you anyway.'

'Wait,' he says, holding out my lighter.

I look down at it.

'Keep it,' I reply. 'You're right. I shouldn't be smoking.'

He snorts and I walk away, round the back of the barn to where the kitchen doors open onto the garden.

Suddenly, I find I'm shivering, as though the temperature has dropped.

It's a dangerous game I'm playing. But oh my, is it fun.

GEORGIA

I send Brett a quick message to tell him I miss him.

Out of habit, I re-apply my make-up and throw a shawl around my shoulders. I'm wearing my pale grey maternity jeans with my white broderie cotton blouse over the top, and I smile in the mirror at my reflection.

I've tried so hard to make an effort throughout my pregnancy. I've been completely paranoid at times that Brett would just up and leave me, even though he's sworn he could never do something like that.

'Walk out on the mother of my unborn child? What kind of man do you think I am?' he said fiercely, one night when I sobbed my fears all over him. 'Even if things hadn't worked out with us – which they have – then I would have stayed and supported you throughout, in whatever capacity you needed.'

He wasn't expecting to find out I was pregnant just weeks after our first date, but his reaction was not what I was expecting either.

He was delighted.

'I've always wanted to be a father,' he said, beaming. 'I'm forty-five next year, I was beginning to think it would never happen. This is fate! Meeting you . . . and now this. And the thing is, Georgia, I think I'm falling in love with you . . .'

I had melted then, swept up in his words. It was going to be OK. It wasn't the most conventional of starts to a relationship, but it was going to work out.

I take a deep breath, pick up my phone from the bed, and leave the tent.

It's getting darker now and there are festoon lights strung up all along the back of the barn. It looks like a wedding venue. It would be a great place to hold press events, if it wasn't for the fact that it's in the middle of nowhere.

The kitchen doors are wide open and there's an intoxicating smell emanating from the room. We had to fill out a pretty extensive questionnaire about our food preferences before coming. Despite my nausea, my tastes haven't changed that much, but I know some pregnant women have really strong food aversions. My friend Sara just ate ice cubes and spaghetti carbonara for months.

Pasta is a safe choice, and it's clearly what we're about to eat, as I see Will placing long tentacles of pappardelle into a pan of bubbling water. The other ladies are already there, sitting up against the huge island unit. Selina is pouring Nicky a drink.

'Obviously, we don't want to overcook it,' Will says. 'Nothing worse than overcooked pasta, and because this is freshly made, it cooks in seconds.'

'Good evening, Georgia,' Selina says. 'What can I get you to drink?'

'I'll have a large glass of red.'

109

Her face falls. It strikes me that, while she's lovely, she has no sense of humour whatsoever. She's too intense, too earnest.

'Sorry, only joking. What are the others having?'

'I've made a virgin mojito, but if you don't fancy that, we have sparkling water, some presses from the farm just down the road . . . or herbal tea, of course?'

'Mojito, thanks, sounds lovely.'

With some effort, I clamber onto the chair at the bar. I keep forgetting how much more difficult it is to manoeuvre with my bump.

'We were all just admiring Will's skills,' Bonnie says, winking at me. I look over at Will, but he doesn't respond. He's busy sautéing something in a huge copper pan. His sleeves are rolled up, showing a hint of toned, tanned arm. I suddenly see what Bonnie really meant.

I smile, take a big drink. So, Bonnie likes older men. Interesting. I realise she's never said anything about the father of her baby, and I really want to ask her. I'm so nosey – it's always been in my nature. 'Curious about others' would be the euphemistic way of putting it.

'Your husband's American, right?' Bonnie asks as Will turns away.

It turns out she's just as nosey as me.

I twist my engagement ring round my finger. It's getting a bit tight as my fingers have swollen recently with the water retention – another third-trimester thing apparently.

'Yes, but we're not actually married yet,' I say. 'We haven't been together that long. The baby was . . . well, a surprise.'

It's what I always say.

110

After all, 'accident' would be a lie.

'Oh, that's so romantic! So you got pregnant and then he proposed?'

I nod.

'How long had you been together for?'

I look down.

'Well, um . . .'

But I am saved from answering as, just then, a stocky man enters the kitchen through the barn doors. He's holding a large bunch of wildflowers.

'Sorry to interrupt,' he says, looking over at Selina. 'Just brought you these, as requested. For the table.'

'Oh, amazing, thank you!' she says, her voice sing-song. 'Everyone, this is Badger, our wonderful volunteer – he's responsible for the amazing grounds we have here at The Sanctuary.'

'Lovely to meet you all,' he says and we all smile.

Selina takes the bunch from him and slips it into a huge stoneware vase in the middle of the dining table.

'Please,' she says. 'Take your seats.'

The table has been laid beautifully, with pale linen napkins decorated with sprigs of rosemary. Tiny tea lights twinkle along the centre, and the glassware at each place setting is sparkling in the light.

'Oh wow, this looks beautiful,' I say, pulling out a chair. I pull my phone out of my pocket and take a quick photo of my place setting.

'Thank you,' Selina says. 'I have to say, it's an absolute pleasure to do things like this. I really enjoy it.'

She starts placing bowls of steaming pasta in front of us.

'Let me help you with that,' Badger offers. 'Then I'll get out of your hair.'

'Thank you, Badger. So, here you are, ladies: kale and hazelnut pesto tossed over pappardelle with feta and red onion,' Selina says. 'I hope you all enjoy! And we have the most delicious cheesecake for after – I saw it in the fridge earlier.'

She takes a seat at the end of the table and Badger sets down the last bowl before her. Will is still at the sink, washing up.

'Please, do start,' she says. 'Don't want it getting cold.'

'Are the boys not joining us?' Bonnie asks, looking over at Will. 'That seems a bit unfair, given all their hard work.'

'Ladies only, I'm afraid,' Selina says.

We all stare at Will. He gives a tight smile. Badger has already left.

'I hope you all enjoy it,' Will says, and then he turns and leaves the room.

He seems a bit grumpy. Perhaps they've just had a row.

Poor Selina, she's trying so hard too.

'This is delicious,' Nicky says. 'Must be great, living with a chef!'

'Yes,' Selina says. 'I'm—' But then she stops speaking.

Suddenly her eyes widen and she begins to cough. Her face flushes and bark-like noises come from her mouth as the muscles in her neck strain.

She stares at us with popping eyes, a puzzled yet frantic look on her face.

'She's choking!' Nicky says, standing up quickly. 'She's got something stuck in her throat.'

Nicky rushes round behind Selina and deftly scoops her up under her armpits from behind. She repeatedly jerks Selina's whole body upwards, as though she's a rag doll.

'Oh my God,' Bonnie says, her hands over her mouth. 'She's going purple!'

'Should we call someone?' Poppy asks.

I can't stop staring at the horrific sight of Nicky and Selina, and their entwined, frantic dance, and then, without warning, something flies out of Selina's mouth with such force that it lands right in the middle of the table.

She gasps and splutters, the colour coming back to her face, tears streaming down her cheeks. Nicky rubs her back.

'It's OK, you're OK,' Nicky says. 'Sit down, have a drink, get your breath back.'

She hands her a glass of water. Selina nods and takes a sip.

'How horrible!' I say. 'You poor thing.'

She gives me a weak smile. We all stare at her. She waves a hand in the air as if to reassure us.

'Thank you, Nicky,' Selina says eventually, her voice a croak. 'If you hadn't responded so quickly, I dread to think . . . thank you.'

'Yes, what a hero,' Bonnie says.

'Oh God, it's nothing. I'm a teacher, we're trained for this stuff.'

'Even so, I really appreciate it.'

Nicky nods, sitting back at her own place.

'What was it?' Bonnie asks, staring at the table. 'What did you choke on?'

'I don't know,' Selina says, stroking her throat with her hand. 'It was something hard.'

113

Bonnie leans forward and pokes around the tea lights. We all watch in fascination when eventually she mutters, 'Ah!' and lifts up something shiny.

'It's a tiny silver ring,' she says, holding it up to the light. 'A signet ring, I think. How did that get in there?'

'Let me see it!' Selina says. 'Sorry. Can you show me?'

Bonnie leans over the table and hands it to her.

'Whose is it?' Bonnie asks, and Selina turns the ring over in her fingers.

'I . . . I don't know,' she replies. Her voice is still raspy. 'How strange. I've . . . I've never seen it before. I don't suppose it belongs to any of you, does it?' she asks, holding it up.

We all shake our heads.

'Very odd,' she says, putting it down next to her plate. 'I'll have to ask Will if he has any idea where it might have come from . . .'

She gazes over our heads into the middle distance as if pondering something.

'Perhaps his way of trying to propose,' I joke, but Selina isn't listening.

'Anyway,' she says, her frown magically morphing into that same hostess smile again. 'Please, let's eat. That's quite enough drama for one mealtime.'

And just like that, it appears the subject matter is closed.

POPPY

Poppy feels a curious mixture of exhaustion and exhilaration as they start the journaling session. Seeing Selina choking and gasping for breath, her silky-smooth facade well and truly shredded, gave her a rush of satisfaction.

It's always gratifying to see people getting what they deserve.

Once they've finished dessert, which, after the choking incident, is probably Poppy's favourite thing of the whole day, Selina picks up a pile of soft leather-bound books from the island unit and hands them out one by one.

'These are your journals,' Selina says, the gentle lilt in her voice back. 'Write down anything and everything that occurs to you about today's experience. Write down something you are proud of, and something you would like to work on tomorrow. These journals are completely private, so please don't worry at all about anyone reading them. You'll take them back to your rooms with you tonight. This is between you and your own inner voice. It's a way of emptying your mind of the stresses and successes of the day, so that you can start afresh tomorrow.'

The way she speaks is almost hypnotising. Poppy opens the

cover and stares at the blank page. Leaning down, she inhales the scent of the leather – a meaty, unpleasant fragrance. The paper inside the book has rough edges, deliberately torn, not cut. Rustic.

Poppy glances around at the others. They are already bent low over their books, furiously scribbling. Bonnie, in particular, seems to be writing at incredible speed.

Poppy looks back at her own blank page. And then some words form, and her pencil scratches on the thick paper, as though moved by an unseen hand.

I came here to forgive. But now I realise, I can never forgive you.

She crosses them out, and writes something else instead.

I know what you did. But do you? Do you really understand?

She looks at the words in the notebook, and almost laughs at how ridiculous it all is. Selina is sitting at the end of the table, watching them, with that same beatific smile on her face. Like a frozen yoga queen.

She has no idea.

She is so calm and composed, even her movements seem smoother and more considered than anyone else's.

But Poppy understands now: she's an actress, playing a role. So completely in control.

But she can never escape the vision they all had of her earlier: choking and gasping and clawing for her life.

Two wrongs don't make a right, but would an accident like that have been such a terrible thing? If only Nicky hadn't interfered.

Poppy leans back over her book, holding the cover up on one side, as though she's back at school and worried her mates will try to copy her work. She doesn't write any more words though. She just traces the outlines of stars, hundreds and hundreds of stars, until the page is full of them, and you couldn't read the words underneath them if you tried.

Eventually, Selina rings a small bell on the table. One by one, the writing stops, and they all look up at her.

'Right,' she says, almost whispering. 'Well done. What you've done today is braver than you might think. Please now close your journals. As I said, you'll be taking them with you back to your rooms, so if there's more you want to say, then you can add to them later on tonight. For now though, when we're ready, we'll make our way to the yoga studio for our final session of the day – our courage meditation.'

Yes, Poppy thinks. Courage is what she needs. Courage to see her plan through to the end.

They follow Selina to the yoga cube, carrying herbal infusions in tea bowls. The bowls are handmade, individually decorated, but they are also stupid. It's impossible to hold them without burning your fingers. Poppy wraps hers in the sleeve of her jumper, and treads warily down the gravel path to the studio.

Inside, Selina turns the lights down low. Then she reaches over to her phone, and switches on some music. It reminds Poppy of the music Selina played in their yoga session, but it's even more bland, if that's possible. An endless echoey drone.

Selina must have spotted her expression because she speaks directly to Poppy.

'It's a steel tongue drum,' she says, raising her voice above the tonal chimes. 'Incredible instrument. I have one out the back – I'll dig it out for you all later, and you can try it.'

Poppy is too taken aback by this to reply.

'So,' Selina says. 'Let's all sit down in a position that feels comfortable. Your legs need to feel grounded, connected to the floor, your spine tall and your shoulders down. Now, close your eyes. We do meditation with our eyes closed, to cut out any visual distraction. You need to go completely into your body, your own vessel . . . Let's take a few deep breaths in . . .'

They do as she says and unexpectedly, Poppy finds herself zoning out to the sound of the repetitive music and Selina's soft, beckoning voice. Selina's words remind Poppy of the hypnobirthing playlist she had, how she listened to it in the bath when she was in labour, and suddenly she feels the tears pricking at the backs of her eyes.

'Courage is not the absence of fear. Courage is not the absence of difficulty. It's the ability to acknowledge it, to fully feel it, and to move forward, into and through . . . So notice if there is any fear, any discomfort, how it is showing up in your body . . .'

It feels as though Selina is speaking directly to her. Again, it strikes Poppy that the universe is supporting her in her decision to be here, to be brave, to find a way forward from this pain and towards a new life.

This is just the tip of the iceberg. But it's a start.

'You are in the right place. You have exactly what you need. You are on the right path . . .'

Selina is right. Poppy is on the right path.

After the session finishes, they are all quiet.

Even Bonnie – the one who, despite her boisterous and carefree exterior, is clearly hiding something. There was a moment earlier over dinner, when the others were jokily discussing the things that annoyed them most about their partners, and Bonnie sat silent, turning her napkin over in her lap.

What is it she's hiding? Is it shame? That she's pregnant at such a young age? Or something else?

But Poppy doesn't really care. She doesn't need these distractions.

She needs to stick to her path.

Poppy says goodnight to all of them and returns to her tent. Someone has been in and lit the fire, and turned down the bed.

Will, obviously. He's a very obedient partner.

On the pillow is a small glass bottle with a spray top. It's tied with twine, a sprig of lavender tucked in underneath the knot. She reads the handwritten label on the side.

Organic lavender pillow mist. Spray me onto your pillow for a relaxing night's sleep.

Selina has thought of everything. Poppy is impressed by the sheer amount of work and dedication she has put in, to making every single detail as perfect as it could be.

Everything she is in control of, anyway – the weather, burning scarecrows and choking incidents notwithstanding.

As Poppy spritzes her pillow, she briefly wonders if lavender can be anything other than organic.

She closes off the air vents on the wood burner. The idea of leaving the fire burning all night makes her uneasy, and it's warm enough in here anyway. There are three pom-pom-trimmed cushions arranged neatly on the bed. She takes each one in turn and hurls it into the corner.

She looks over at the welcome pack that Selina left and

119

takes out the card with the Wi-Fi code on it. She enters it into her phone, and waits for WhatsApp to update. There is another message from Ant, of course.

I'm worried. Please tell me you're OK, that's all I want to know.

Her eyebrows rise. Objectively, she will never be OK again. But if he thinks she's come here to kill herself, he's mistaken.

I'm fine, she replies. *I'm just clearing my head. I needed to get away. You don't need to worry about me.*

She almost adds, 'I'm not your problem any more,' but she doesn't want to sound bitter. And it's not really true, is it? They will always be each other's problems in one way or another. They are so inextricably bound together.

The bathroom block – a small building that looks like a log cabin – is just behind the row of tents. Poppy sits on the bed, waiting to hear that the others have finished. She doesn't want to get trapped having to make small talk in a queue for the toilet.

There's also the matter of her bump. It's not huge, but even so, it's annoying and she'd prefer to take it off before navigating the bathroom.

She rolls up her top and unfastens the velcro round the back of the bump. Then she flops it onto the bed. It lies there, like a disgusting slug. She wishes she hadn't had to use it, but she lost so much weight last year there was no way anyone would believe she was seventeen weeks pregnant. Or is it sixteen? She never did work out the dates for her story. Thankfully, no one has asked. No one seems that interested in her.

Not yet, anyway.

Poppy's amazed, given she told Selina what she's been

through, that Selina hasn't taken some time to pull her aside and check she's feeling all right about everything. But then nothing has quite worked out like she planned today. And there's always tomorrow, the one-on-one sessions.

Poppy looks down at her empty, flat stomach. It's covered in red lines from where the fake pregnancy bump has been wrapped tightly around it. In the dull light of the tent, they look like angry red scars.

A visual representation of how she feels inside. Scarred, forever more.

SELINA

Once all the guests are safely in their beds, I stand for a few minutes outside the back of the barn, watching the tents. There's still smoke rising from two of them. I hope they're not cold. I can't believe the weather turned so dramatically earlier.

My throat is still aching and I put my hands to my neck and swallow softly, briefly wondering if some cough sweets would help. Probably not. It's more of a muscle pain.

I'm still in shock after the terror of those few moments, the struggle to get air into my lungs, the blinding, unexpected thought that perhaps this was *it*. How could this be it, the end of my story?

None of us ever know when the end will come.

What a start to the weekend. The only silver lining is that *I* am the one who choked.

I pull the signet ring out of the pocket at the back of my leggings and turn it around in my fingers.

How the hell did it get into my food?

I look down at it. The lettering on the front is almost completely worn away, but if you look carefully, underneath all the scratches you can still see the swirled pattern of her initials.

J.W.

It's silver, not gold. Although that wouldn't have made any difference. Eventually even gold rubs away to nothing.

When I met her she had nothing. No job, nowhere to live, no prospects. I took her in, welcomed her with open arms. She barely had any clothes in the scruffy bag she turned up with. This ring must have been very precious to her.

I go back into the house and close the big barn doors behind me. Will has cleared away after dinner. He's in the pigsty helping Kai now. At least none of the guests have discovered Kai. That's all I can hope for – that he keeps his low profile as promised. I can't afford to have him weeping all over them. He's still so unstable, it would completely ruin the atmosphere.

On my laptop, I check the weather forecast for tomorrow. Intermittent rain, plus unseasonably gusty winds. What are the chances?

I sit at the kitchen table for a few moments, wondering whether or not to pour myself a large glass of wine. It's nearly 11pm, far too late for me to start drinking, but somehow I'm desperately craving it.

Sod it. It's been a challenging day.

I take a glass from the shelf that runs the full width of the kitchen wall and un-cork the bottle Will has left standing on the side. I pour myself a healthy measure and go back to the table.

I promised myself I wouldn't do this. I wanted to come to our one-to-one sessions tomorrow completely neutral, but . . .

Nothing wrong with giving myself a little head start.

I open my emails and find the full name of each of the

guests on their bookings. And then I copy the first – Georgia Delaney – into Google.

I have already seen her Instagram, of course. Her initial email had her Instagram link in her signature, so I knew from the start that she was a journalist and was very active on social media.

She is part of a 'cool' London crowd, friends with lots of influencers. If just one of the really, really popular ones got pregnant and booked onto our retreat then . . . my word, it would change everything. Literally.

As a newspaper columnist, she's a bit of an influencer herself actually. She has more than 4,000 followers on Instagram. We only have 200, despite the *Grand Designs* article.

I click on her latest post – a photo of the inside of her tent, in the same immaculate state as when she first arrived. It all looks amazing: the bed pristinely made, the fire flickering in the corner, the kilim rugs adding the perfect touch of rustic warmth. A warm glow of pride rushes through me at this picture of my own handiwork, passion and care. I did that. I did it all. It was my vision, and I've executed it perfectly.

I scroll down to read the caption.

Home for the weekend!

There are a handful of comments.

Looks lush!

Enjoy!

Well jel!

She's tagged us in the image too, so I quickly share it on our own page adding that we are loving hosting our first retreat.

She could easily have brought up the unexpected rain, the

burning scarecrow, my choking incident, and made some kind of joke at our expense, but thankfully there's nothing negative at all on her feed.

Just goes to show really. Nothing is the full picture.

I click back on Google and scan the rest of the search results about her. Not much personal info, just pages of her articles: her looking smart in the tiny headshot next to her byline. She writes lifestyle features, long ones for the Sunday supplements. She is our most valuable asset this weekend. At all costs, she needs to have a good time. She is the one we need to impress.

And after we gave her a place for free, she owes us.

But what about the others?

Bonnie intrigues me. I copy her name into Google too.

She's got an Instagram account as well, but it's private. I stare at her profile picture. She's wearing a crown of flowers on her head, backlit by a sunset, her curly hair almost completely obscuring her face.

She reminds me of a younger me. A carefree spirit. I swallow another mouthful of wine.

Other than that there's not much about her online – just her Facebook page, also set to private, and an old Tumblr page filled with inspirational quotes and random pictures of beaches in Thailand.

Clearly there's no way she could afford to pay the fee we charged for the weekend. The booking was made by her sister Nicky and the credit card charged belonged to a man with the same surname as Nicky.

I wonder what the father of Bonnie's baby is like. She hasn't mentioned anything about him and I'm curious now.

I Google Nicky next. She's got a LinkedIn profile, saying that she's Head of Year 10 at a secondary school in Bristol. Other than that there's her Facebook page, which is filled with pictures of her with her two sons and husband. They look like a pretty conventional, middle-class family to me. No secrets there.

I wonder how old she is, though. She looks knackered, and has the aura of someone completely depleted in every sense.

Hopefully that's something we can sort out this weekend.

Last of all, I type in Poppy's name. The combination of her name and surname is strangely common and there are lots of results, none of which look like her. I keep clicking, idly, as I sip the rest of my wine.

Nothing. She is invisible. Not a trace of digital footprint.

How strange, for this day and age.

I close the lid of my laptop, frustrated. Will thinks I'm paranoid. But of all the guests on this weekend, somehow I can tell there is more to Poppy than meets the eye.

What is she hiding?

THE MORNING

There is something special about parenting a daughter.

It is a privilege, and a responsibility. Because the world is not kind to women.

The truth is, I had hoped for a boy. But then she was born, and the first time she looked at me my heart tripled in size.

I'll admit I didn't always get it right. I made mistakes. I'm only human, and I didn't have the best upbringing myself.

It's difficult when you have no blueprint to follow. But you know all about that, I suppose.

Is that why you've tried so hard to create a blueprint for others?

I wanted so much for her. I wanted her to live a life of wonder and excitement, to live a life unconstrained by convention or expectation, to live a life where she followed her true passion, where every day she woke up and felt joy at the possibilities that stretched before her. No matter what she did, what she achieved, where she went, who she spent time with . . . I wanted her to listen to her gut – to have faith and respect in herself as an individual – to achieve and experience whatever she hoped for.

I wanted her to understand that she was a one-off, and that her gift to the world was confidence and pride in that fact.

I wanted her to take pride in being a woman. The stronger sex, for sure.

Perhaps I wanted too much.

Perhaps I had too many hopes and dreams.

But either way, it doesn't matter now, does it?

Nothing much matters when you're dead.

NICKY

I wake when the sun comes up. Nothing too unusual about that, of course, but I'd forgotten just how light it is in a tent first thing in the morning. I roll over in bed and check my phone. It's nearly 6am.

I rub my eyes a little and then settle back down. It's amazing not to have to leap out of bed, not to already have some small person climbing on me or demanding I help them on the loo for a wee. Seb has taken to sneaking into our bed at night recently, and I quite often wake to find his elbow jammed into my eye socket.

It was cute the first time he did it; now it's just annoying.

I stretch out my legs so I'm a starfish. It's a very, very comfortable bed; I must remember to ask Selina where she got it from.

I still feel a bit drowsy. Then I remember: I woke in the night. It was pitch-dark and I was sure I could hear something. Something so familiar it had wrestled me from the depths of my dreams.

A baby crying.

Incessantly. The sound I remember so well from the early days of the boys: that rhythmic screech, punctuated by hiccups and desolate gasps of breath.

131

I had sat up in the bed, frowning, straining. It made no sense. There are definitely no babies here. I stepped out of bed and poked my head through the tent door, but the countryside around me was silent.

As I climbed back into bed though, I heard something else. Whispering, coming from Bonnie's tent. So she was still awake. But I couldn't make out what she was saying, and I drifted back to sleep again shortly after.

That's the trouble with these tents – there's absolutely no privacy at all. When I left the bathroom block I heard Georgia having a very loud, loving conversation with her partner over FaceTime. I've got no idea why she didn't use headphones, because everyone must have been able to hear every word he said.

It was all very passionate and intimate and it made me feel a bit sad inside, remembering a time when Jon's and my relationship was like that. When every communication between us ended with the proclamation of our love, and every text message was followed by a long string of kisses.

When I've looked back on old letters and emails he wrote me in the past, I've cringed, feeling embarrassed that we were so . . . juvenile.

But actually, was it juvenile, or was it just innocent and lovely, and something to be treasured?

I flip my pillow over and moan. Despite the deep-seated tiredness that feels as much a part of me as my obsession with raspberry Magnums, I know now that I won't be able to get back to sleep.

It's a horrible combination: a brain that is too awake and a body that's absolutely shattered.

And there's something else bothering me. I need a wee. All that bloody herbal tea. I should know by now that I can't drink anything after 8pm without waking up worrying I'm going to wet myself. Plus, of course, I'm pregnant.

I can't believe I keep forgetting. That's the whole point of this weekend! Perhaps I should bring it up in my one-to-one session with Selina later.

I keep forgetting I'm having a baby because I'm so utterly depressed at the thought that it's plunged me into denial.

Something tells me that that won't go down too well with her. She's a midwife, passionate about all things pregnancy and mothering.

I swing my legs out of bed and push my feet into the slippers that were left for us in our tents. Then I pull the huge fleecy dressing gown on over my pyjamas. It feels chilly out of bed – the fire went out overnight and the air in the tent is crisp and fresh. I like it though. The feeling of the cold on my cheeks.

I leave the tent and pause for a minute, staring at the garden. It's so still and tranquil here. We live in the country too. But as we're in a village, it feels as though all the houses are crammed together in one small area, surrounded by a great expanse of nothing. Like people clinging to a raft in the middle of the sea.

Here, is the opposite. Here, we are *in* the nothing.

I take a deep breath and appreciate for the first time in a

long time how invigorating it is to be the first person awake in the morning.

I wander over to the bathroom block behind the tents. It's basically a log cabin but it does have electric heaters and underfloor heating, and it's surprisingly toasty when I step inside. Along one stretch of wall are individual shower rooms, complete with fresh towels and organic toiletries. On the other side are the two toilets, each with a private basin.

I push open the door to the first toilet cubicle and feel an unexpected resistance.

'No!' a voice calls from inside.

'Oh my God, sorry!' I say. 'I didn't realise there was anyone in here.'

I move along to the next cubicle but the door opens and out comes Poppy. She's swamped by her huge dressing gown and won't look me in the eye.

'It's all yours,' she says, to my feet.

'Are you OK?' I ask, and she looks up at me. Her eyes are red-rimmed.

'What? Yes, I'm . . . I'm fine.'

'Oh God, you poor thing. Morning sickness, I presume? Is there anything I can get you? I saw Selina had left some ginger biscuits in our rooms . . . at least, there were some in mine, so you might have some too. But if not, you're welcome to mine. I'm lucky really, I don't find pregnancy makes me sick, although it does make me want to eat everything in sight, which is almost as bad. No, sorry, of course not. It's nowhere near as bad, I've had friends with horrendous

134

morning sickness and know how debilitating it can be. God, sorry, now I'm just rambling on and on . . .'

I smile at her and she holds my gaze.

'It's not morning sickness,' she says, looking away.

'Oh. Right.'

I don't know what to add. I stand there, feeling stupid.

'That's good then, I guess.'

She looks back at me, her eyes hard.

'Your third baby. You're very lucky.'

I frown at her.

'I know. Listen, are you sure you're all right? Nothing's happened . . . with the baby?'

There's a silence. I feel my heart pounding in my chest. I'm concerned I've overstepped the mark completely.

'Sorry,' I continue. 'It's none of my business. I didn't realise anyone else was up. It's just, after what you've been through, if there's anything worrying you . . .'

'It's fine,' she says, but again I can't read her expression. She seems completely detached, almost as though she's in a trance. 'I don't sleep well. It's difficult. Once you've lost a baby . . . but, well, I won't let that happen again. See you at breakfast.'

And with that, she pushes past me, a little aggressively, and leaves me standing in the bathroom block alone.

BONNIE

I'm just about to leave my tent to join everyone for the morning yoga session when I hear a scream.

I poke my head out of the heavy canvas. The sky above is clear but the air is chilly. The other women are gathered around the yoga studio, staring at something on the ground.

I yank my jumper on and hurry to join them. My eyes are sticky and crusty with sleep.

'What's happened?' I ask. 'What's going on?'

As I come closer, I spot what they're all looking at. Something bloody and congealed, spreadeagled on the doormat outside the studio. I glance up at the other women. Georgia has turned away, the sleeve of her jumper over her mouth. Nicky is staring down at the mess, frowning. Poppy is standing back slightly, her face in that same neutral expression she always pulls. As though her brain has checked out of her head.

Last of all I take a look at Selina. Her face is screwed up like an old flannel, and in the harsh morning light she looks older than ever.

'Oh my God. What the hell is it?' I ask. 'Or was it, should I say?'

Something furry and black, with blood oozing out of what

once must have been its neck. The splash of blood is a particularly dramatic sight, staining the immaculate sandy paving slabs that form a path around the studio.

'Shit. Where's its head?' I say, and suddenly from behind me I hear the sound of retching. Georgia is throwing up into the perfectly manicured flower beds outside the studio.

'Fuck's sake,' someone mutters.

Surely not Selina?

I'm the only one who heard it. Nicky has turned her attention to Georgia, stroking her on the back.

'It's OK,' Nicky says. 'Let's get you back to the kitchen for a glass of water. It makes me feel pretty sick too, to be honest.'

Georgia looks at her and nods. There are tears in her eyes. The two of them trundle towards the house, Nicky still with her arm around Georgia, as though she's an elderly relative who can't walk properly.

'Oh dear. I'm very sorry about this,' Selina says, and I look at her again. She's got her game face back on now. 'Perils of living in the country. What a great shame.'

'What was it?' I say, unable to resist. I take a step closer. It's too big to be a mouse, too small to be a cat or dog. I'm surprised at how hard animals are to identify without their heads. But then I see it, curling out from underneath the body. A tail.

'It's a rat,' Poppy says. 'Without a head.'

Selina's eyes widen.

'What the hell! Do you have rats round here?' I ask. 'Running around? And we're sleeping in tents . . .'

'No!' Selina says, then composes herself. 'I mean, of course there's all sorts of wildlife in the countryside. But none near

137

the house. I expect some animal's just dragged it here and been distracted and left it. I'm very sorry. Let's all go into the kitchen for a cup of tea and I'll get Will to sort it out.'

Will to the rescue again. She really does have him right where she wants him.

In the kitchen, Nicky is sitting next to Georgia, her arm still around her shoulders.

'I'm sorry,' Georgia whispers as we come in.

'Don't be silly,' I say. 'It would have made me puke too, but I'm used to seeing bits of dead animal.'

Georgia looks horrified.

'At college,' I say. 'I'm a catering student.'

'Oh,' she replies. 'I didn't realise that.'

I pour myself a glass of water.

'Yes. I've got another year left. The baby wasn't exactly planned but . . . that's life,' I reply. I grin. 'Well, that woke us all up, didn't it? I have to say this weekend is turning out nothing like I expected and I'm actually quite enjoying it.'

Selina gives me a tight smile.

She doesn't want people like me on her fancy retreat. I'm not her target demographic at all. She wants people like Georgia and other posh ladeez from West London to come and Instagram themselves to death. A scruffy, knocked-up West Country student like me is absolutely not her dream visitor.

'Can I get you anything?' she asks. 'Or if you don't mind waiting here for just a few minutes, I'll get Will to clear up the . . . mess . . . and we can get on with our morning yoga.'

'These things are sent to try us,' I say. 'That's what my mum always says.'

'That's right,' she replies, her lips still pursed. 'But we won't let them.'

She scurries out of the room and the rest of us sit in awkward silence for a few minutes. Poppy is standing by the patio doors, staring out at the yoga studio.

'I wonder what animal killed it,' I ask, and Nicky shoots me a look.

Georgia's head is back down over the glass of water.

'Bonnie,' Nicky says. 'Let's not go on about it.'

'I'm just curious,' I say. 'And why would it just leave it there? And why just take the head? Bit weird. If I was going to have a nice rat supper, the last bit I would leave is the body. The body has all the meat on it.'

'Shut up, Bonnie,' Nicky says. Georgia won't even look at me.

'Yes, Mum,' I say sarcastically. 'I just think . . . well, we've paid a lot for this weekend, haven't we? Perhaps we should ask for a partial refund. For trauma.'

The others just ignore me. So instead I lean over the table to the massive fruit bowl in the middle and pluck out an apple. I rub it on the front of my jumper and take a bite.

'Selina's weird,' I say, munching. 'Don't you think? I can't work her out. It's like she's playing a role. I don't feel like she's very . . . sincere.'

My eyes meet Poppy's. She gives barely anything away, but I can tell by the way she holds my gaze for just a little too long that she feels the same.

'Jesus, Bonnie. What do you expect her to be like?' Nicky snaps. 'She's being professional. She's not about to tell you all her deepest darkest secrets.'

'All right, don't get at me. I just think . . . given that we're guests in her home, it's odd that she's so . . . stiff.'

'*Given that we're guests in her home*, we should probably respect her right to keep some things private.'

I hate it when she talks to me like this. Like I'm just a little kid. Patronising cow.

'I actually met her son briefly yesterday,' I say, ignoring her. 'He doesn't seem to be much of a fan of his mum either.'

'Bonnie . . .'

'And another thing!' I say, taking a second bite of apple. Georgia and Poppy are definitely interested so Nicky can sod off. 'How on earth have they managed to do all this work to the farm, just the two of them?'

Georgia lifts her head slightly.

'They've got that volunteer, remember? I can't remember his name.'

'Oh yes,' I reply. 'How jammy is that?'

Just then, Will comes into the kitchen, Selina trailing behind him. I jokingly clamp my hand over my mouth. Nicky huffs at me.

'Will is going to sort out the, er, mess,' she says. She puts her arm around him, gazing up at him as though he's some kind of hero.

The apple clings to my teeth. Public displays of affection are not my thing.

140

'Good morning, ladies,' he says. 'Perils of farm life, eh? Hope it hasn't put any of you off your breakfast.'

'Good morning,' Nicky says, ever polite. I nod at him, put the apple back in my mouth, but he walks straight past me and into the garden. I watch his back retreat towards the studio. He's carrying a dustpan and brush.

He'll need more than that to get that shit sorted.

'I was thinking,' Selina says, turning to us. 'Let's have breakfast first, and then we can have our yoga session afterwards. How does that sound? I believe Will has made some of his amazing organic granola, but of course we have a huge range of things, and you're welcome to anything you'd like. Let me just get everything organised . . .'

GEORGIA

No matter how hard I try, I can't unsee that dead rat. Or stop thinking about it scurrying into my tent at night, and crawling over my bed . . .

I managed to eat half a bowl of granola, but it felt like wood shavings in my mouth, and tasted of nothing. I know it's pathetic to be this squeamish, but I always have been. Added to that, my stomach doesn't seem to have liked the pasta we had for dinner last night very much.

'Are you OK?' Nicky asks after breakfast, as we sit there nursing our cups of (decaffeinated) tea. Selina is washing up, Bonnie has gone back to her tent and Poppy is over on the sofa, staring into space.

She's so quiet, it's easy to forget she's even here. She was quite friendly at dinner last night but at other times it's as though she's on a different planet.

'Yes,' I reply. 'I'm so sorry. Don't tell Selina, but my stomach's a bit upset today and I just . . . I miss Brett. He's in the States, different time zone . . . I don't know what I was thinking really, coming here. It's the first time he's had to travel since I got pregnant, and I just couldn't bear the idea

142

of being alone in our flat. Which is so stupid. I lived on my own for ten years! I used to *love* being alone.'

'Is this your first baby?'

'Yes,' I say. 'Well, I had . . . I've had miscarriages in the past. A couple. Years ago.'

'I'm so sorry to hear that,' Nicky says.

'Thanks. I was in my twenties. My husband at the time . . . well, we didn't really cope with it very well. We were so young. It's why we broke up. But anyway, it all feels like a very long time ago now.'

'Still, it must be very difficult, even after all this time.'

'Yes,' I say, taking a deep breath. I suddenly want to tell her everything, but of course I can't. I don't even know her. But it would be so nice, just to get it all off my chest . . . 'I suppose it is really. This baby is very much . . . wanted, but it was a surprise, you know, to Brett especially. And I'm a bit scared it'll all go wrong again. I just want to talk to someone, get all these fears out of my head and have someone else tell me I'm not crazy for thinking them.'

'You're not crazy,' Nicky says. 'Not at all. This is my third baby and . . .'

She pauses, pulls in her bottom lip.

'Well, let's say we all have some kind of crazy chat running around on a loop in our heads. It's just part of the joy of being pregnant. That's why I came on this weekend. Well, that and I'm supposed to be spending some time bonding with my little sister. Although heaven knows where she's gone now.'

She looks over my head and through the double doors.

'She seems . . . fun.'

'A liability, more like,' Nicky says, rolling her eyes.

Talking to Nicky has made me feel so much better. I want to reach out and give her a massive hug.

'She seems very young to be having a baby, but I suppose I'm just very old.' I can't help it, my naturally nosey side refuses to be suppressed.

Nicky sighs, running her hands through her hair.

'She's only twenty-two. I know – there's a big age gap between us. Our dad left my mum for hers. But we've always been quite close. Not like normal sisters, but we get on well. As friends really. She can be very funny and entertaining, when she's not being a total pain in the backside.'

'Twenty-two seems so young to me. But of course it's not really, is it? It's probably the perfect age to have a child.'

'I suppose any age is the right age if you're ready for it. Although it'll be a shame if it means she can't finish her course.'

'I'm sure it will all work out somehow,' I say.

'Oh, I have no doubt about that,' Nicky says. 'She always manages to land on her feet.'

There's some underlying tension in her words. Thinking about the way they were snapping at each other earlier makes me wonder how they really feel about each other. I decide to talk to Bonnie later. To take some time to get to know her.

It's good to focus on other people sometimes, to stop going over and over your own problems in your head. To spend that energy trying to help someone else instead.

'What about you?' I ask. 'How do you feel about your pregnancy?'

Nicky's mouth opens.

'Oh well,' she says. 'If I'm honest, it was a huge shock. I thought we were done, you know? We'd even sold all the baby stuff on eBay. I was meant to be going back to work. It was our anniversary, we just got a bit carried away and . . .'

'Gosh,' I say. 'I'm . . . well, that must have been a surprise.' She nods.

'Lots of surprise babies on this weekend, it seems! I'm slowly getting my head around the idea,' she says. 'Life's what happens while you're making plans, eh?'

I laugh. If only she knew how accurate those words were.

POPPY

Poppy looks down at the paving slab. Will has thrown a bucket of bleach and water over the place where the dead rat was lying, leaving a dark wet patch outside the yoga studio.

The earlier sun has disappeared behind a cloud.

Poppy's bump is back on, strapped around her like a back-to-front straitjacket. She has layered two vest tops and a T-shirt over it, so there's absolutely no chance of anyone noticing that it's not real. Underneath the heavy mass of fabric, her skin feels sweaty and uncomfortable.

It doesn't feel anything like it did when she was actually pregnant.

Sometimes she tries to remember it, the heaviness of her stomach, the way she would have to roll onto one side to get out of bed in the morning. Chloe was a big baby. Almost ten pounds. When Poppy pushed her into the world it felt as though her entire body was being turned inside out.

And then she felt that way again, less than a year later, when they told her there was nothing more that could be done.

'Right, in we come,' Selina says, opening the door for them. 'So sorry we weren't able to do this session first thing as planned.'

The others have been chatting non-stop since breakfast: Georgia and Nicky seem to be getting on particularly well. After her cross words with Nicky, Bonnie said she wasn't feeling great and went for a lie-down in her tent but she's back now, cheeks flushed, her long hair a tangled mess hanging in front of her face. Poppy wishes she would tie it back.

They file into the yoga studio. It's chilly inside, and the air smells of stale incense. It reminds Poppy of the village hall where she did her postnatal classes. That same stuffy, musty air that hangs around in communal spaces.

'I'll just warm it up a bit,' Selina says, turning on the air conditioning. 'Won't take a second.'

'It was very cold last night,' Poppy says. 'Wasn't it? I think my phone said it got down to six degrees.'

'Oh, I hope you weren't cold in your rooms?' Selina says. Poppy can't believe she has the audacity to call them rooms. 'I asked Will to light the fires while we were having our last session. It's perfectly safe to leave a good log on them all night.'

'It was fine in bed,' Poppy says shortly. 'I used the blankets.'

Selina nods, but there are two pink flushes on the tops of her cheeks that weren't there a minute ago.

'Now,' she says, turning to Georgia, 'as you're the furthest along out of everyone and feeling the most fragile, why don't you come here near the window?'

She rolls out a yoga mat, as far away from Dead Rat Patch as possible, and Georgia sits down on it.

'Thank you,' she says.

'How is the nausea now?' Selina asks.

'I'm fine,' Georgia says, smiling. 'Sorry to have made such a fuss.'

'You didn't make a fuss at all,' Selina says. 'Right, so, if the rest of you could take a mat and choose a spot, we'll begin.'

Despite herself, Poppy finds that, once again, she enjoys the yoga session.

Selina is good at it – her years of experience, perhaps the one thing which she hasn't lied about, show. Poppy finds herself relaxing so much that at one point her T-shirt rolls right up, almost to the bottom of her sports bra. Thanks to the vest underneath, there's no way anyone can tell that her bump isn't real, but even so, she needs to be more careful.

She pulls her T-shirt down and accepts the eye mask that Selina offers, along with the blanket.

'Now for our final few minutes, let's get into a comfortable position, lying on your side, with the cushion between your legs if needed . . .'

Poppy listens to Selina telling her in a slow, calm voice that every part of her is relaxed. When Selina finally finishes listing each item of her anatomy and tells them to sit up, Poppy finds that she's almost asleep.

'Wow,' Nicky says. Poppy takes off her eye mask to look over at her. 'That was seriously relaxing.'

'Good,' Selina says, smiling.

Poppy notices Selina nervously glance over at Georgia.

Georgia is still lying down on her side, eye mask on, and says nothing. At this angle Georgia's bump looks huge. She looks almost full-term.

'We've got an hour off before lunch,' Selina says. 'So feel

free to carry on journaling, or take a walk across the fields, or come and find me if you'd just like to chat. I'll be in the main barn, so don't be shy. Will'll also be starting to prepare lunch in half an hour, in case you'd like to watch that and chat to him about his recipes. I know he enjoys cooking with an audience.'

'What about your son?' Poppy says. She wants to pin her, like a moth to a board. To watch her wriggle as she tries to work out an escape.

'Sorry?'

'You have a son, don't you?' she asks. 'I'm sure I've seen him hanging around the other barn. What is he doing this weekend? Doesn't he need you? I feel bad, if we're taking you away from him.'

'Oh, don't worry! He's twenty,' Selina says.

'Nineteen,' Bonnie corrects her.

'What?'

'Sorry. Me and my big mouth,' Bonnie says, giggling. 'I bumped into him yesterday and we had a quick chat. I'm sure he told me he was nineteen, but perhaps I misheard.'

'Yes, well,' Selina says. 'He is technically nineteen but he's twenty in three weeks' time.'

'Technically nineteen,' Bonnie says. 'I like that! Don't worry, Selina, I can't remember my own age half the time, and I'm only technically twenty-two.'

'He's an only child, isn't he?' Poppy asks, standing up. She hands back the eye mask, staring Selina straight in the face.

'Yes,' Selina replies shortly. 'He is.' She turns the corners of her lips upwards in a half-smile, but there's something else in her eyes that Poppy hasn't seen before. Is it fear? Or confusion?

Or – surely not – recognition?

'And his father's in prison – that's right, isn't it?'

'What?' Selina says. 'How did you . . .'

Poppy holds her stare. The other women are open-mouthed. She loves this. It's so nice to have some power back. She feels like a cat playing with a mouse, batting it this way and that, listening to it squeak in fear.

'It was very unfortunate,' Selina says, and Poppy is surprised to see tears springing to her eyes. This is Selina's Achilles heel then. Her ex. She is human after all. 'We weren't together when he was arrested. And if you don't mind, it's not something I like to talk about.'

'But how come you didn't have another child? As you obviously like babies so much. A case of one and done?' Poppy says, but she's pushed it too far this time. The other women are all staring at her now, as though she's mooned them.

'A case of . . . timing, I suppose,' Selina says. 'By the time I met Will I was too old to have another baby.'

That's not true.

Selina turns away and starts folding up the blankets.

'And you met Kai's real dad when you lived in the US?' Poppy's armpits are damp with sweat.

Selina looks back.

'Yes. When I lived in the US. His father was American. But, well, that's another lifetime ago. As I said, I'd prefer not to talk—'

'You ran away to California at seventeen, right? Must have

150

been an incredibly formative experience for you . . . Very sad for it to have ended . . . for it to have ended like it did. Must have taken a lot to get over. A trauma, I suppose.'

Poppy has lost it now. This is the most she's spoken since she arrived. The others are all staring at her as though she's possessed.

Somehow she can't shut up. She just can't. There's so much inside her, and she just needs a little release, a tiny release, right now, to stop the whole mess exploding out at the wrong time.

'It was a different time,' Selina says shortly, wrapping a blanket over her arm. 'Our teenage years and early twenties, it's all a time of discovery really, isn't it? Trying to work out who you are and what you want. And Kai's father . . . well, he was a hot-headed man. Got on the wrong side of things.'

'Well, I'm in my twenties and I'm pretty sure fate has decided what I want for me,' Bonnie says, sticking her tiny bump out and laughing. Nicky and Georgia smile. They are pleased she's broken the tension; a welcome relief.

Poppy squeezes her fists together.

'But the father of your baby isn't in the picture either, am I right?' Poppy says to Bonnie, and then she points at Selina. 'So in a way, you two are really very similar. You even look a little alike.'

Nicky frowns. The tension is back.

'Sorry,' Poppy says, but it's too late. Too late to claw anything back. Never mind. It doesn't matter what they think of her anyway. 'I didn't mean to be rude.'

'God, we look nothing like each other!' Bonnie says,

open-mouthed. 'And we're nothing alike either! I mean, no offence, Selina.'

Selina swallows.

Poppy turns and leaves the studio.

It was a welcome release, but it wasn't enough.

SELINA

'That was really out of order!' Bonnie is saying. 'How dare she ask me about the father of my child? She's clearly been secretly judging me since we got here. She needs to mind her own bloody business. Isn't there some sort of etiquette rulebook for these kind of weekends?'

We are sitting in the kitchen. Bonnie is drinking another cup of coffee and talking to Nicky.

Yes, yes, I know it's meant to be a caffeine-free retreat but please, God, don't try to palm me off with decaf, Bonnie said as she helped herself to one of Will's Nespresso pods. *What's good for me is good for the baby. I'm listening to my gut. That's what you told us to do, right? Works for me!*

I let her take what she wanted and drew back to watch, pretending to tidy up.

She's right. Poppy is everyone's worst nightmare. The last thing – sorry, person – anyone would want on a retreat of this kind. I can't imagine what Georgia thought of her strange outburst earlier.

And the longer she's here, the more convinced I am that she has some kind of agenda against me.

Right before the yoga class began, I found an anonymous

note shoved into the pile of mats. A pathetic threat, the kind a child might leave as a practical joke. I thought it was Kai – his way of getting to me – but now I'm sure it must have been Poppy who left it. She clearly knows something. But what?

Oh God. It's all starting to slip away from me. I can't bear it.

How can she have found out about Ron? But more importantly, why would she have wanted to research my background so thoroughly? I feel sick to my stomach.

'How on earth did she even manage to get pregnant in the first place?' Bonnie asks. Her voice is low but I can still hear every word and she knows it.

'Bonnie,' Nicky says. 'For God's sake.'

'She's creepy!'

'Bonnie, stop being such a bitch. You don't know anything about her. Perhaps she's having some . . . personal problems.'

'You think? Not a very relaxing retreat with her in our midst, is it?'

I shrink back. She's right. I need to do something about this situation, before the whole thing implodes.

'I don't like the way she sits there and watches us all,' Bonnie continues. 'The way she listens in on everything. And I don't care if she can hear this. I hope she can hear this, so she realises exactly how uncomfortable she's making us.'

I cough loudly. It's not that I don't agree with what Bonnie is saying, more that I can't bear to hear any more.

Ever since Poppy told me her story, I've had my concerns. It's understandable that she might want to come on a retreat like mine, after all she's been through, but her behaviour since she got here just doesn't add up. There's more to it.

It's not just grief. She's deeply bitter about something. And it feels personal.

She said she lost a child, but perhaps she didn't mean an actual child . . .

No, it's impossible. Poppy is far too young.

My head aches.

I look at the clock above the hob. Not long now until lunch, and then after lunch are the one-to-one sessions. I feel a wave of misery wash over me as I remember how much I was looking forward to them, how excited I was, before everything started going wrong. The scarecrow, the ring, the headless rat, the anonymous note.

I don't need this.

Now I'm terrified of what to expect when I sit down with these women face to face. It's more important than ever that the others enjoy their stay here, but how can I give them the service they deserve when there's so much other stuff on my mind?

I have another retreat planned in a month's time and there are three women booked in at the moment, but if this weekend continues to go from bad to worse and Georgia decides to write a horrible review, then we'll be finished.

The thoughts cycle endlessly. I close my eyes, take a deep breath, try to centre myself. I ask myself if the thoughts I'm thinking are true, and remind myself that I don't have to accept this narrative.

So, Poppy is a strange and difficult guest, but I've had difficult clients before in the past, and I've managed to handle them. I will be able to handle her too. She hasn't said anything concrete about me. And the others think she is as strange as I do. They're not going to judge me, surely, on her behaviour and my past?

Nothing can ever be as hard as last year. I got through that, so I can get through this.

I stand there, mug in hand, my teeth biting down so hard on my lip that it stings. And then I hear a noise behind me and I turn, and into the room strides Will.

Will who always used to care for me, who always saved me from myself, with his stoic sensibility. Will who seemed so sure of himself, who could make decisions in an instant, without looking back.

And now, I don't even have him. I've tried everything to get him to forgive me for what happened last year. Everything. Proving to him that I can pull off this weekend was meant to be the thing that saved us. And now I'm messing that up too.

Bonnie and Nicky turn to look at him as he paces across the room towards me. He's looking down, his cheeks slightly red, his hair combed back neatly. That's good. He's making an effort. I smile, take a few steps towards him.

'Hello,' I say. 'Come to get started on lunch?'

'That's what I'm here for,' he says.

He doesn't kiss me on the cheek or offer any kind of affection. Of course he doesn't. Those days are long gone.

'Well, don't let me get in your way,' I say, but he's walked over to the cupboard and is busy putting on his apron, and doesn't respond.

Bonnie and Nicky have returned to bickering at the table, heads bent low together.

'I'll leave you all to it,' I say, but no one looks up. I feel out of place in my own home, and it's devastating. 'I'll be in the yoga studio if you need me. Looking forward to lunch! I think we're having one of Will's amazing fresh salads. I'm sure it will be utterly delicious.'

Practise what you preach. That's what I need to do now.

THE LUNCH

Will you be honest this weekend?

If you're asked to explain yourself? Your own story?

Or will you lie? Lying by omission is still a lie, you know.

It took some digging – but eventually, I unearthed the videos of you online. Standing beside him, your hero. Ranting and raving about the medical establishment. How birth is not a mechanical process. That medicalising birth is a crime.

The evils of Big Pharma.

Oh, and I know how tragic your own story is.

Unexpectedly complicated birth + human error + uncontrollable bleeding = emergency post-partum hysterectomy. Left infertile at the age of twenty-three.

A tragedy, for sure, but an excuse for all you've done since?

I watched those videos, fascinated. You always became slightly unhinged by the end of the rants. Shouting and swearing and waving your arms around so quickly you almost knock yourself off balance. As though possessed by some other-worldly force.

The fury of the bereaved, perhaps.

I know you've toned things down since then but it's clear your core beliefs remain the same, isn't it?

You've just become a bit more subtle about sharing them.

NICKY

Will is chopping vegetables. He keeps looking over at us from the island unit.

Despite all the drama earlier, a little part of me was pleased that Poppy directly asked Bonnie about the father of her baby, but it hasn't made any difference. She's still not going to tell me anything specific.

'It doesn't matter,' she says, when I ask her again. 'It's a complicated situation. I'm sure you'll meet him one day, but at the moment . . .'

'Do you even know who he is?' I say. 'Answer me honestly. I don't . . . I won't judge you.'

'Of course I do!' she replies. 'Jesus, is that what you really think of me?'

I know she's only my half-sister, but even so, I feel guilty. I should have done more for her, I should have taken more of an interest in her life. I don't even know who her friends are.

But she's so . . . infuriating.

'Is he taken, then?' I ask. 'Or is it . . . what's he called, your flatmate? Jeremy?'

'For God's sake. Nicky, you did not just say that!' she says. 'Don't be so ridiculous. It's not Jeremy.'

It's all for attention, I remind myself. It's how she works. Pulling any trick in the book to ensure that the spotlight is always on her. I sit back on the kitchen bench. I refuse to play this game any more. She's a grown-up. I have enough of my own mess to deal with.

'Forget it. I promised I'd ring Jon before lunch,' I say. 'They'll be home from football now. I'll be back in a bit.'

'Fine. Great idea. You do that,' she hisses. 'Go and mind your own business for once.'

I swing my leg over the bench and make my way to my tent. Bonnie'll probably start flirting with Will as soon as I leave.

The thought brings me up short. Am I . . . *jealous*? Of her youth, her freedom, her charisma? Surely not?

It's chilly again now, the clear sky filled with clouds once more, and I pull my hoodie tightly around myself. As I approach my tent, I notice someone in the distance, by the trees. A figure, crouching down, with dark hair. He's holding something clutched to his chest.

I look around. There's no one else nearby. I don't know if Georgia is in her tent, and I have no idea where Poppy is either.

'Can I help you?' I call, but the figure stands up, his arms still wrapped round whatever it is he's holding, and disappears, running off into the woods.

'Everything all right?'

I turn. Badger is standing behind me, gardener's gloves on, a pair of secateurs in his hands. His eyes crinkle as he smiles at me. His face is tanned, criss-crossed with deep lines. It's one of those faces that you instantly warm to.

'Gosh, you gave me a fright,' I say, putting my hand to my

163

chest. 'Yes, sorry, I just saw someone. Over there by the trees. I didn't recognise him. He looked a bit . . . lost.'

Badger glances over at the woods.

'Probably just Kai,' he says. 'Have you met him? I guess lost is a pretty fair description of him, although really, he's just . . . well, he's had a hard time of it.'

'Oh, right,' I say, flushing. 'Yes, sorry. I knew he lived here too, I just haven't seen him before. I didn't mean to be rude.'

'You weren't,' he says and he holds my gaze. My cheeks burn even more.

'What are you . . . up to?' I say, gesturing at his gloves.

Selina described him as an eco-volunteer, who's helping them with the building and maintenance in exchange for free board.

'Just some pruning. The roses are getting out of control.'

'It's their favourite time of year, I guess,' I say stupidly.

'You a gardener too?'

'Amateur,' I reply. 'We moved to the country a while ago and inherited the most beautiful garden from the previous owners. I can't bear the idea of letting it down. It's caused me no end of stress. Stupid, really!'

He laughs.

'Don't worry about Kai,' he says, smiling. 'He'll be fine, you know. Hope you enjoy the rest of your stay.'

'Thank you,' I say. 'It's beautiful here.'

I leave him to his pruning.

In the tent I take my phone from the side of the bed and tap the app for FaceTime. Jon answers straight away. Seb and Ben are in the background, crowding him off the screen. It looks as though they're walking through a car park, but it's difficult to tell.

'Mummy!'

'Hello!' Jon says, smiling at me. 'As you can see, we're not missing you at all.'

I laugh and blow kisses at them.

'How was football?'

'Wet,' Jon replies. 'We're a bit late – stayed behind and had a catch-up with the Morgans. We're going over theirs later for a pizza and film night.'

I'm surprised. Jon has never voluntarily socialised with the boys' friends' families before.

'Oh wow,' I say. Is that a stab of envy? No, something else. Surprise that Jon has taken over my role so easily? 'That'll be nice.'

'How's the weather there?'

'Let me see your tent, Mummy!' Benj interrupts.

I laugh, and switch the camera around.

'Here, look, it's huge,' I say, panning the inside. 'Look at my ginormous bed! The mattress is so comfy. And there's a fire and an armchair and even a little fridge full of snacks . . .'

'That's *so cool*!' Benj says. 'A fridge in a tent! Awesome!'

I smile at Jon.

'Awesome? That's a new one,' I say.

'I know, God knows where he picked that up.'

'They're so grown up. It's like they've actually grown while I've been away!'

'Nicks,' Jon says. 'You've been away for just over twenty-four hours. I don't think that's even possible.'

'I know,' I reply, but inside I'm wondering how to explain to him that I feel like I'm always missing stuff.

I read somewhere that you only have eighteen summers with your children before they go off to live their own lives, no longer interested in spending much time with you. I found it absolutely terrifying. What a small window of their lives we really share.

Every second that I'm not with them racks me with guilt. It was hard enough dealing with the guilt of neglecting Benjamin when Seb was born. And it's only going to get worse in a few months' time.

How will I ever have enough time or energy to spend with them, when I'm permanently attached to a newborn baby?

'Let me show you the rest of the place – there's an amazing flower meadow.'

I leave the tent and make my way across the huge garden towards the meadow. The sky has darkened even further.

'Oh, that's a shame,' I say into the phone. 'The weather was lovely a moment ago. It keeps clouding over. It absolutely poured it down yesterday while we were out walking. And I've just had a fight with Bonnie, and to be honest . . .'

'What?' The screen turns black. 'Nicks, I can't hear you – your signal's going.'

'Oh! I'm probably too far from the house for the Wi-Fi . . . hang on.'

I turn back but the connection fails, and when I try to call him back he doesn't pick up.

I swallow. It's nearly lunchtime anyway.

I walk back towards the bell tents. But something's not right. Mine looks wonky, misshapen.

I hurry towards it, and as I draw closer I see that the roof of the tent has collapsed in on itself, like a deflated cake.

'What the . . .' I say, pulling open the fabric door and crouching down to see inside.

The tent poles block my way. I back out of the door and stand outside, looking at the other tents. They're still standing.

It's only mine that's collapsed, the canvas walls now heaped on top of all my things. At the back, the lovely vase of wild-flowers has been knocked over and shattered, the water dripping down onto the bed. The middle pole slices through the tent like an iron bar.

I give a little shudder. I was literally in there just a few minutes ago. The poles look heavy.

What might have happened to me if I'd been inside at the time?

BONNIE

'My tent's collapsed!' Nicky says, as she comes into the kitchen. I was wondering where she'd got to – lunch is nearly ready.

'What?' Selina says.

'Oh my God,' Georgia says. 'Are you OK?'

'Yes, I was . . . I wasn't in there when it happened, thank goodness.' I can see she's shocked, and though she's trying to control her voice, she's had a fright. 'But the poles have fallen down in the middle. The whole thing has collapsed on top of all my stuff. I can't get inside.'

'Oh no, how awful,' says Georgia. 'I wonder how on earth . . .'

'The tents are perfectly safe,' Selina says, waving her hands as if to quieten us. 'I'm so sorry, Nicky, I'll get Will to take a look at it straight away. Your tent is on the end, the most exposed. It must have been a particularly strong gust of wind . . .'

She rushes to the hallway door and shouts up the spiral stairs.

'Will! Can you come down? Please!'

As she comes back in the room I notice that her hands are shaking slightly, the colour drained from her face.

'I'm so sorry,' she says. 'Can I get you something for the shock? A nice cup of chamomile, perhaps?'

'Water's fine,' says Nicky. 'Thanks.'

We all stare at Will as he walks into the kitchen and on out through the back doors to examine the tent. There's an awkward silence in the room as we all watch Selina follow him. The two of them have an animated conversation on the lawn outside. She keeps fidgeting with the zip of her hoodie.

Eventually, they both come back in.

'Well, the guy ropes had come loose,' he says, to Nicky. I try to meet his eye but he won't look at me. 'That's why it collapsed. I'll need Badger to help me get it sorted. But your stuff should be fine. If it's not, I'm sure we can compensate you. We have comprehensive liability insurance.'

He sounds so stiff. Nicky frowns.

'Right,' she says. 'I mean . . . I'm not asking for . . . but perhaps we should check the other tents too. I don't . . . I mean, the idea of it falling down when someone is inside is pretty terrifying. It's surely a health-and-safety concern? Those poles are pretty heavy.'

I remember Nicky telling me about the disclaimer that Selina had her sign when she booked our places.

Was that included? *Risk of potential death by tent collapse?*

'I'll check and tighten all the other ropes and stakes,' Will says, looking pained. I feel a bit sorry for him. 'I'm not sure how this happened. I checked those ropes myself . . .'

'Must have been the weather,' Selina says. 'It's very gusty. We weren't expecting the wind. Or the rain. I'm very sorry though, Nicky. But . . . well, hopefully no harm done.'

Nicky twists her lip and takes a sip of her drink.

'But it wasn't raining. I mean, it's a bit cloudy but . . .'

'We can move you into the empty tent, if you'd prefer?' Selina says.

'No, thank you,' Nicky says. 'I'm sure it'll be fine once it's sorted.'

Will leaves and Selina puts a bowl down in front of her, placing a freckly hand on Nicky's shoulder.

'Cucumber, basil and watermelon salad,' she says, with none of the enthusiasm of our previous mealtimes. 'Please do help yourselves to the rosemary and thyme bread.'

'Right, thanks.'

Everyone goes quiet for a bit and then Nicky speaks again. That's so Nick – can't bear to leave things a little uncomfortable, always wants to fill the gaps and make people feel better.

She's such a mum.

'I'm sorry to cause a fuss. It just . . . well, it really gave me a fright.'

'Of course,' Selina says, spearing a piece of cucumber. 'I'm very sorry it happened.'

She looks like she's about to cry.

'The birds were loud this morning, weren't they?' Georgia says, changing the subject. 'A proper dawn chorus. So lovely. You never hear birds in my part of London.'

'Oh, that reminds me!' Nicky says. 'I meant to ask this morning. Has anyone else heard a baby crying?'

I look up at her.

'What?' Georgia says.

'I don't know if I'm going mad or what,' Nicky laughs, 'but I swear last night I heard a baby crying.'

'I didn't hear anything,' Georgia says. 'But I wear earplugs.'

'Are you sure?' Selina asks.

'The sound's so familiar – I guess I'm in tune with it because it wasn't that long ago that I was getting up in the night to feed Seb when he cried.'

Selina nods.

'Strange. Well, no babies round here, I'm afraid. Perhaps it was a dream?'

'I heard it too,' Poppy says, almost interrupting.

Oooh! Was that a flash of anger in Selina's eyes as she turned to Poppy?

'Really?'

'Yes,' Poppy says. 'In the middle of the night. Hungry crying. A baby wanting milk.'

'How peculiar,' Selina replies. 'What about you, Bonnie? Did you hear anything?'

I stare her down. I *really* want to open my mouth and blurt out everything that I know. But I can't.

I shake my head.

'I sleep like the dead.'

'Are you sure it wasn't foxes?' Selina says, turning back to Nicky. 'They can be very noisy at this time of year.'

'No,' says Nicky. 'We have foxes too. This was different. It was definitely a baby . . .'

'Well,' Selina says. 'We have neighbours, the ones who bought the farmhouse . . . perhaps the wind carried the sound. I'm not sure what direction it was blowing in last night . . .'

We all sit there, staring at her. You can barely see the nearest neighbours from here, let alone hear them.

'I can't think what else . . .' Selina says, shrugging.

'Sometimes I wonder if I'm going mad. Hearing things,' Nicky says, laughing. 'But if you say you heard it too, Poppy . . .'

'Definitely,' she replies. 'A baby. Wailing.'

'I mean, my son Kai does like to listen to very strange music at all times of the night . . .'

'It wasn't music,' Poppy says insistently. 'It was a baby crying.'

'Perhaps something on the television then?'

The atmosphere has turned combative again.

I look down at my bowl. This weekend is not turning out how I expected. Not at all. It's awful, but for all the wrong reasons.

'Oh, that might be it,' Nicky says, trying to appease. 'That would make sense.'

'Mystery solved,' Selina says, but no one's buying it.

The awkward silence fills the air again.

'Let's do a selfie!' Georgia says, clapping her hands and holding up her phone. 'Of all of us together. Come on, everyone, gather round.'

'Sure,' I say, 'why not?'

Nicky pulls a face. She hates having her photo taken.

'No, thanks,' Poppy says. 'I'll take it for you though, if you like.'

'Oh, come on, Poppy!' Georgia says. 'Just a quick one, I won't share it anywhere.'

Poppy stares at her as though the decision is too big to make straight away, but then her face softens slightly.

'OK then,' she says.

We stand behind Georgia as she holds her phone up above

our heads. I glance at Nicky but she won't meet my eye. Still sulking about our little spat earlier.

'Squeeze in! Now, say, "Morning sickness"!' Georgia trills.

'Morning sickness!' we all parrot.

'Lovely,' Georgia says, looking at the screen.

I take a glug of my drink and look down at my lunch. I've lost my appetite again.

I have some free time before the one-to-one sessions with Selina, so I decide to take myself off for another walk across the fields and into the woods. Perhaps I'll have a look for Kai too, see if we can have another chat. My phone battery has died again – turns out even though I plugged it in to charge it last night, I forgot to turn the socket on. Very on-brand for me.

I walk round behind the tents.

The sound of a guitar playing stops me in my tracks as I reach the back of the bathroom block. Badger is sitting on an old tree stump, strumming away and singing softly. I hang back so that he doesn't hear me and listen.

> *There is not a star in the sky*
> *That shines*
> *As brightly as you*

There's a lump in my throat, and I put a hand on my stomach. I think about the promises my baby's dad made when we last spoke.

Not long now. I promise. It's all about timing. You know I love you.

I shift on my feet, and Badger looks up.

'Hello,' he says, abruptly stopping. 'Out for a walk before the next shower?'

'Sorry to interrupt. I'm last for my one-on-one session with Selina,' I say, sitting down next to him. 'So thought I'd stretch my legs.'

He nods.

'How long have you been doing this . . . eco-volunteering thing then?'

'Six years,' he says. 'On and off. I get to travel around, see different places. I've been all over the world with it. Borneo most recently. But I've been as far as Tonga, which was pretty epic. Helped a family there setting up their own holiday business – they'd bought an entire private beach.'

'Wow.'

'Yeah, I was with them for nearly nine months in the end. Lovely people. Amazing place, although they're at constant risk of tsunamis, which is pretty stressful. Still, I'll never forget my time over there – barbecuing fresh fish on the beach every night, sleeping under the stars, growing our own veg – really puts life into perspective, you know.'

'Sounds a bit like backpacking for old people.'

'Well, yeah, I guess,' he says, nodding. 'Huh. Old. I guess I do seem old to you.'

'Sorry,' I say, wondering exactly what age he is. It's difficult to tell. His skin is really sun-damaged, but he has more energy than me. I saw him yesterday, hanging from a tree like some kind of crazy acrobat, sawing branches off by hand.

'I'll be fifty next year, as you're wondering. I reckon then maybe, just maybe, you can call me old.'

I laugh.

'I suppose I'd better get back,' I say eventually. 'Although there's a bit of a weird atmosphere going on back there, if I'm honest.'

'Oh,' Badger says. I can tell he doesn't want to be drawn into our drama.

'After Nicky's tent collapsed.'

'Yes, I heard,' he says. 'Someone had let down the guy ropes. That's a nasty trick to play.'

'What did you say?' I say, stunned. 'I thought they had blown off in the wind?'

He laughs.

'I can tell you've not had much to do with tents in your life. Not much chance of that. Hardly been blowing a hurricane today.'

'But . . . why . . . why would someone let down the ropes deliberately?'

'Can't help you with that one, I'm afraid,' he says. 'Someone's idea of a joke?'

'But that's awful, to do that on purpose.'

'Well, perhaps it was an accident,' he says, shrugging. 'Someone started fiddling with them and didn't know what they were doing.'

I frown. It doesn't make any sense. I'll have to tell Nicky, but at the same time, I don't want to scare her.

'Well. That's the end of my break,' he says, getting to his feet. 'Lovely chatting to you . . .'

'Bonnie.'

'Lovely chatting to you, Bonnie. Take care in the woods now. There's all manner of tree roots to trip over.'

He looks down at my Buffalo trainers.

'And they don't look like the best choice of footwear.'

I muster a smile. He leans down and offers me his hand. I take it and he pulls me gently to my feet.

'See you later,' I say, and watch as he picks up his thermos flask and wanders back to the small barn.

When he's safely out of sight, I rush back towards the tents.

'Can I have a quick word?' I say, rounding up all the other women in turn.

Once everyone's sitting inside my tent, I make sure Selina is nowhere in sight, and close the flap.

'I've just been talking to Badger, the volunteer guy. Apparently the ropes on Nicky's tent were let down deliberately. It wasn't an accident after all. It's practically impossible for something like that to happen accidentally . . . I mean, there'd have to be a hurricane or something.'

'But . . .' Georgia begins, looking pale. She strokes her enormous bump. 'Why would anyone do that?'

'I don't know,' I say. 'It's horrible. But I thought I should warn you all.'

I throw a glance at Poppy, but she's got that faraway look in her eyes again.

Understandably, Nicky looks upset.

'I'm so sorry to have to tell you,' I say, hoping she'll believe me. 'I just thought you should know. Because, well, it's a bit freaky, isn't it? None of you have seen or heard anything strange, have you?'

They all shake their heads.

'I mean, I suppose there's Kai?' Nicky says. 'Selina's son? Perhaps he . . .'

'Maybe,' I say.

'Nicky and I swapped tents,' Georgia says quietly. 'Do you think . . . do you think whoever did this meant to target me?'

'No,' says Poppy. It's the first time she's spoken and we all turn to stare at her. 'I'm sure whoever did this . . . I'm sure it was just a random thing. Some horrible joke.'

I look at her again and this time she meets my eyes. I don't know what to make of her.

'I would have thought the farm was quite secure,' Nicky says, and I can tell she's trying to calm herself down. 'It's not easy to get to, is it? You have to go down that really long track to get here. There's no one else for miles around. You have to drive here really, and surely we'd see or hear if someone had pulled up?'

'It must have been Kai then,' I say, nodding, although I'm not convinced.

'I guess?'

'Either way,' I say, my heart beating a little faster again, 'I think we should all just keep an eye out now. Be a bit more vigilant, and if we see anything else that's odd, then make sure we tell each other straight away. Agreed?'

'Agreed.'

GEORGIA

I'm quite nervous as I make my way to the yoga studio for my counselling session with Selina. In my head, I've prepared the speech I think I should make, but I'm still terrified she'll judge me.

I would judge me, if I wasn't me.

I step inside the glass cube. There's a separate section at the back, the 'therapy room' as Selina described it, completely enclosed. I was relieved about that. I couldn't imagine sharing my innermost thoughts in what's basically a goldfish bowl that looks out over the gardens.

I'm a crier, and no one wants to cry with an audience.

It's warmer in here than it was this morning.

Aside from anything else, I'm not really in the mood to bare my soul to Selina after all the strained conversations over lunch, and especially after what Bonnie's just told us. This retreat isn't turning out to be anything like I expected.

But this is what I came here to do, and I have to do it. It's a burden I have to remove from my shoulders. Once I've done it, I will feel better. It's always been that way in the past, so there's no reason to think this won't work.

I make my way towards the door at the back of the studio,

but then realise with a start that I can hear angry voices. Selina and someone else are hissing at each other.

'I'm sick of you and your stupid rules. I've had enough of doing what you tell me all the time!'

Then there's the sound of a slap.

'Pull yourself together.'

My stomach lurches. She must be talking to Kai. I feel a wave of shame for Selina. I can see how desperately hard she's trying to make this weekend a success, and yet she's had non-stop issues ever since we arrived.

And then, of course, there's the strange tension between her and Will. I shudder, thinking back to Lewis, the way he would lash out when he was drunk. Which was often.

I'll never know for sure that the miscarriages were caused by the stress I felt, constantly having to tiptoe around him, but the counsellor I spoke to after we broke up said that it wouldn't surprise her.

Not a professional diagnosis, but enough to make me feel more guilty than I already did. I had brought this on myself, on my babies. I should have left him, and then perhaps they would have lived.

I hurry out of the studio. I can't do it, I can't interrupt them, even though I know I should, really. What if he turns violent? What if he hurts her?

What if it's all my fault, because I'm too pathetic to go in there and stop him?

I race back to my tent, and climb onto the bed. Before I know what's happening, I'm sobbing: great, fat tears.

I *am* pathetic. I've tried so hard – I've worked so hard. On the outside my life is a perfectly curated utopia, but inside I'm just a scared little girl who can't do anything without a man to take care of her. I couldn't even face spending a few nights alone without Brett while he had to work abroad.

I sob noisily into my pillow, not caring about my make-up running, and then I hear a soft voice calling me.

'Georgia,' it says. 'I'm sorry to interrupt, but I'm ready for our session now if you are.'

I sit up and gaze at the entrance to my tent. Selina hasn't come in, at least. I wipe my eyes quickly and glance in the mirror. It'll be obvious I've been crying, even if she hasn't actually heard me.

But that's OK. It's not like I wasn't going to cry in the session anyway.

'Coming,' I say, frantically pawing at my eyes. 'Sorry!'

'Of course, I'll wait for you in the studio. Take your time.'

She clearly doesn't know that I've already been in there, that I heard her altercation. But at least she's OK. He can't have hurt her, or she wouldn't have come and found me so quickly. She wouldn't sound so cheerful.

I wipe my eyes while looking in the full-length mirror, and then use my fingers to pat some foundation over my nose, to cover the redness. Then I take a deep breath and walk back to the yoga studio.

Selina is in there, with a cleaning cloth and some antibac spray, wiping the yoga mats. She puts them down at the side of the studio when she sees me and straightens up.

She seems very composed and not upset at all. Maybe the fight wasn't as bad as it sounded.

'Hello,' she says. 'Come on through.'

We go into the small therapy room at the back. It's set up like a room in a beauty parlour, with a massage table pushed against one side and a small sink at the other. It's dark and cosy inside, the walls painted a soothing cappuccino.

'Oh,' I say, looking around. 'This is lovely. I didn't know you offer beauty treatments too.'

'We don't,' Selina says, 'yet. But that's the plan. Lots of plans! But all in good time.'

She gestures for me to sit on one of the two armchairs placed at the far end of the room.

'Would you like some tea? Or some mint water?'

'Water would be great, thanks.'

She pours a glass and hands it to me. I take a sip and place it on the floor by my chair.

'So,' she says. 'I'm here for you. Happy to listen to anything you'd like to talk about. Happy to have a chat about the weather if you prefer. As I mentioned before, I'm not a counsellor but I am a good listener, and sometimes just having a chat with someone impartial is very helpful. Or I am more than happy to give you tips on the birth – what to expect, how to create a birth plan that works for you. I am a trained midwife and have lots of experience helping women give birth. But ultimately, it's completely up to you.'

I swallow. I'm grateful she hasn't brought up the fact that she just heard me sobbing my heart out.

'I . . . I suppose I would like to get some stuff off my chest.'

Selina nods.

'OK, great. Why don't we start with you telling me what made you come on this retreat?'

I clear my throat.

'My partner, Brett, is away for work,' I say. 'It's the first time he's gone away since we met and I . . . I don't know why, but I didn't want to be left in the flat on my own. I think the issue is, it's all been such a whirlwind. We only met last year, and then I got pregnant, and I suppose it all being so new makes me feel quite insecure. I was genuinely worried when he left that he just might never come back. He's American, and he travels back to the States for work, and his whole family are still over there and of course I've never even met them . . . And he seems committed but what if he goes over there and then . . . well, forgets about me? Or changes his mind?'

I sniff.

'I know I sound pathetic. It's just the distance and the pregnancy, and everything being so quick . . . it feels like our feet haven't touched the ground since we met. And . . . it's not that I wish that I wasn't pregnant, because, God, I've wanted this for so long, but the timing is so terrible and . . .'

'It sounds as though you're not trusting the relationship. Has Brett given you any reason to believe he's not committed to you, or your baby?'

I swallow.

'No, but . . . no, not at all. He's been incredible. He's the most perfect man, but that scares me too, because there's no such thing, is there? Everyone has something to hide. God knows I do—'

'Take a breath,' she says, interrupting me. 'Now I know this

182

might sound silly, but have you tried talking to him about this? Telling him how you feel?'

I shake my head.

'I can't. He thinks I'm so strong; the girl he fell for was so tough. That's what he said he liked about me. That I was confident, that I wasn't scared to walk away from anything less than I deserved. That I wasn't the type to settle. And that I wasn't clingy – he's a busy man. He's very successful.' I pause, aware that I sound like a show-off. 'I mean, he's had a lot of women in his life, I guess. From what he's told me. A lot of needy women, and I don't want to be just another one in a long line . . .'

'But you're pregnant with his baby,' Selina says softly. 'So there's no way he would see you like that. What's he like? Tell me about him. He's successful, that's great. But what else is there to him?'

'He's . . . he's very calm. Self-assured. I think he's the only man I've ever dated that's not insecure. Not in any way. He doesn't seem to have anything to prove. But then in some ways that makes me more nervous, like, he's so complete in himself, that he can just cut people off, if they disappoint him. He's kind of . . . detached, I suppose. It's different from any other relationship I've ever had, where there was always jealousy and insecurity and sniping and just . . . a lot of drama.'

'He sounds absolutely lovely,' Selina says, and I let out a great big half sob, half laugh.

'He is, he really is. But . . .'

The words dry up in my mouth.

'I take it the pregnancy wasn't planned,' Selina says,

bending her head down slightly. She looks up at me, her searching brown eyes scratching at my soul. 'Is that what's worrying you?'

'No, not exactly,' I say. 'It's more complicated than that. It's . . .'

I pause, take a deep breath.

'The thing is . . . I'm . . . I'm not sure the baby is his.'

POPPY

This is it. The moment she has been waiting for. The reason she came.

In the bathroom block, she locks herself into a cubicle and then stands over the toilet pan and retches. Nerves. Nothing much comes out.

She doesn't feel any better. She closes the toilet lid and then splashes water on her face in the sink, looking up at her reflection in the small mirror. She sees the same hollowed-out eyes she saw in the woman who lost her baby that day. They have never left her. Those dark craters of skin underneath eyes that used to sparkle – they are her reminder that her baby is gone, and that she will never be complete again.

Back in her tent, she checks the time on her phone. There's another WhatsApp message from Ant.

Saw Jane in the village today. She asked about you. She was very upset. She's worried about you. We both are. I hope this weekend is bringing you the relief you need. I'm here for you if you want to come home x

Jane.

Poppy pictures the two of them, standing outside Morrisons, having a nice casual chat about her.

How's she feeling? Jane will be saying. And Ant will look down and bite his lip and say, *Not good*, and she'll reach out her hand and pat his arm in sympathy and he'll smile at her and then say, *Fancy a coffee?*

Because he'll want to make her feel better and he won't want to think about Poppy and her inability to cope with – to deal with, to accept – the fact that their daughter is gone.

And that will be it, the two of them, heads together, bonding over Poppy.

And then maybe, in a month or two, they'll start seeing each other more regularly and they'll find they manage to laugh together about stupid things and then one night they'll be at Ant's new flat having dinner and they'll have too much wine and Ant will put his hand on her arm this time and say, *Stay?*

And Jane'll look up, pretending to be bashful but deep down knowing this was what she had wanted all along and then he'll take her to bed and he'll fuck her and he'll do his best to forget about Poppy.

Useless, ridiculous, messed-up Poppy.

She throws the phone across the tent as hard as she can. She wishes she hadn't read his stupid message. How dare he even bring Jane up. She can't think about her. Not now. Jane. Her 'friend'.

The thick-as-shit waste of space that no one is allowed to be angry with because she 'didn't mean it' because she's devastated and apparently her loss is just as bad . . .

Apparently Poppy should try to understand how it feels from Jane's point of view.

186

Apparently people did enough trying to understand how it feels from Poppy's point of view last year, and now it's Jane's turn.

She is so full of rage that she doesn't quite know where to turn. Jane! Seriously. Does he have no idea, still, no idea of what might upset her? Of what she might find difficult?

She thinks of the years she spent with Ant, the love she thought was real, and how it's all ended up. In this absolute mess.

She closes her eyes and tries to pull herself together. If nothing else it's shown her that she made the right decision. That they couldn't go on trying to kid themselves that their relationship could survive this.

She's tempted to take her phone and throw it into the stream at the bottom of Selina's field. To make sure Ant can never, ever contact her again.

But she can't bring herself to completely cut ties with him. He'll always be Chloe's father. They shared the joy of being her parents together – the memory of which is the only thing she has left.

She leaves her tent and practically marches towards the yoga studio. Selina is standing in the doorway. She doesn't look pleased to see Poppy – and no wonder.

Poppy has lost all sense of societal niceties since she lost Chloe – she finds she is unable to care whether or not the way she's behaving makes someone else uncomfortable. It was the same with Bonnie earlier. She just couldn't help herself.

'Poppy,' Selina says, swallowing.

'Hi,' she manages, and then she follows her through to

a small room at the back of the studio. It looks like a room in a spa, and a sudden memory of Jane and Poppy having a prenatal massage together hits her like an ice-cold pitchfork to her insides.

'Please, take a seat,' Selina is saying.

The room shifts. Poppy's eyes close involuntarily.

Suddenly all she can hear is a white noise buzzing in her brain and she squints up at Selina who is handing her a glass of water but then Selina's face starts to blur and distort and a tidal wave of heat rushes through Poppy's body, and she tries to cling to consciousness but it's impossible . . .

. . . her body is fighting her and it wants to go, and she remembers this feeling being exactly the same when they told her there was no more they could do, and before she knows it she's lost again, lost all control, and she's on the floor and everything is black.

SELINA

This can't be happening.

But it is. It really is.

Poppy is now lying on the floor of my treatment room. Unconscious.

I can't believe it.

As she fell, she hit her head on the side of the small, wheeled cabinet that we bought to store beauty treatments in.

I stare at the cabinet for several seconds. Ridiculously, the memory of buying it at IKEA in Exeter comes to mind. The queues, the stress, the way Will barely spoke the whole way home. Painstakingly sitting on the floor, late one night, with a glass of red wine, trying to build the bloody thing. Wondering where I had gone wrong and why he seemed to hate me so much.

It's made of metal. The corners are sharp. Cheap, not finished properly. Wouldn't pass a health-and-safety test.

Just like those tents.

I stand frozen, staring down at Poppy's body. The glass of water she was holding is lying on its side, its contents soaking the floor. I look at her head. Her thick hair is flopped over her face. And underneath there's a smudge of rusty liquid, growing silently larger by the second.

I know what I'm meant to do right now. I'm meant to call for help. I'm meant to phone 999 right now.

Right *now*. That's what I'm supposed to do.

I take a step back from her.

It was an accident. She passed out. She fainted. And then she fell. None of that was my fault. None of it. I haven't done anything wrong. I smiled, I said hello, I handed her the glass of water. I was ready for our session – ready for whatever she was going to throw at me. Because clearly, she had stuff to throw.

And now I can't do any of those things. Now I'm panicking, because one of the guests on my inaugural yoga retreat – the yoga retreat that's been an unmitigated disaster from the start – has gone and fainted and given herself a nasty head injury in my treatment room, in my beautiful pristine treatment room. And now the weekend, which I have worked so hard to make perfect, has gone from bad to worse to absolute fucking disaster.

Before I even know what I'm doing, my foot spasms of its own accord, and I kick her stupid, inconvenient, pain-in-the-arse body in the back.

'No! Poppy!' I shout, the words somehow erupting without permission. 'Wake up! I won't let you do this. Wake up!'

And then I'm sobbing.

I will call an ambulance. Of course I will.

This time, I will.

I will ring them now and I will tell the others and they

will all want to leave and they will all go on about how the weekend has been cursed and then they'll make it into a joke, an anecdote, a little story they tell at dinner parties. And if she actually fucking dies then no one will ever come here again and Will will chuck me out for good and then I'll end up exactly where I started: homeless with a ghost of a son in tow. A ghost of a son who hates me.

It's too much. I have tried so hard. It's not what I deserve. I don't deserve this to be the ending of my story.

I won't do it. I'll take her and I'll go. Somewhere no one can find us.

I look down again at the body on the floor.

I can't believe I just kicked her. What if I've hurt the baby somehow? I could never hurt a baby. What is happening to me? I'm falling apart.

I cover my face with my hands, and then I hear a noise.

A sort of choking sound. I look again. Poppy is moving, her stomach rocking back and forth slightly. Then, a hand goes to the wound on her head.

It's enough to shock me into action.

'Poppy,' I say, leaning down, 'are you OK? Can you hear me?'

She mutters something and her eyes flicker.

'You fell and you've hit your head,' I say. 'Don't move, I'll call an ambulance.'

'No!' she says, surprisingly forcefully. 'I'm . . . fine.'

I crouch down beside her. She hoists herself up onto one arm, and then to a seated position.

'I'm OK,' she says, blinking at me, her hand still touching the side of her head. 'My head hurts.'

191

'You fainted and hit it on the side of the cabinet,' I say. 'Here, let me take a look.'

She moves her hand away and I part the hair gently. It's sticky and matted but underneath there's only a tiny, superficial cut. I breathe a huge sigh of relief.

'You've just cut it on the corner, but don't worry, it's not deep. How are you feeling? Do you still feel dizzy? I think you just passed out . . .'

'I'm fine,' she says. 'I was just a bit light-headed.'

'Pregnancy,' I say. It's all going to be OK, it's all going to be OK. A pregnancy faint is hardly an unusual thing, and certainly not my fault. She might not even want to tell the others. I almost laugh with the joy of it.

But still. I kicked her.

'Let me get this cleaned up for you,' I say, standing. 'I've got some cotton wool here, I'll just dab it gently with water, and then if you want we can go back through to the main house and I'll put some antiseptic on it.'

She doesn't reply, so I busy myself with the cotton wool, dabbing the side of her head until most of the blood has come away.

'It looks fine,' I say brightly. 'You'll be right as rain. How is your head feeling?'

She doesn't exactly smile at me, but for once she's not looking strange. Instead, she looks sad.

'OK,' she says. 'Thank you.'

'Oh, it's nothing,' I reply. 'Pregnancy is a difficult time, physically and mentally. Lots of challenges, lots of room to grow.'

I put the cotton wool in the small pedal bin under the sink. When I turn around again she's sitting up, her knees drawn to her chin. She looks exhausted suddenly, the black rings underneath her eyes more pronounced than ever.

'What would you like to do now?' I say. 'We can carry on with your session, or we can go and get your head looked at properly? You might have a concussion.'

'I feel fine,' she says. 'I just fainted. I didn't knock myself out on the cabinet.'

'I know, but—'

'It's fine,' she says. 'What does it matter anyway, what happens to me?'

I frown at her.

'Do you know how my daughter died?' she says fiercely. The sadness has been washed away by that same anger.

I shake my head.

'She died of measles.'

'Oh. I'm very sorry.'

'More specifically, complications caused by measles – sepsis was what actually killed her in the end. Blood poisoning. Her brain swelled up too. Encephalitis. Her temperature went up to forty degrees. Her whole body changed colour. She didn't even look like my baby, by the end. And she was only in hospital for a week before we were told there was nothing more they could do. That she would never recover.'

'I can't imagine . . .' I say. 'I can't imagine what that must have been like.'

'I'll tell you if you like. It was like a living hell,' she says, staring into my eyes.

I'm reminded of the visceral power of a mother's love, how impossible it is to control, how all-consuming.

'I'm sure,' I say. 'I am so very sorry.'

'The thing is, Selina,' she continues and I start at the sound of my name on her lips. 'She shouldn't have caught measles. Should she? She was eleven and a half months old. She had just a few weeks until she was meant to have the MMR vaccination. We had even booked it in already. Can you imagine? That injection would have saved her life. But she was one month too young, so she hadn't had it yet.'

'I'm sure the vaccination schedule—'

'Oh no, you miss the point.' Her voice is so very angry, it's almost not human. 'There's nothing wrong with the timing. I've done a lot of research. I know the facts. One year old is the perfect age to get the MMR. That wasn't the problem. The problem was that some people, for some reason, think that vaccinations are a bad thing. So they don't let their children have them. And because of them, babies like my daughter are catching measles, and some of them, like my daughter, are dying from it. More and more children are catching it and it's all because some people believe the shit they read on the internet and decide that they won't do what the doctors tell them, won't listen to the tried and tested advice . . . and because of people like that, my daughter is dead.'

'It must be the hardest thing to accept,' I say. 'How very . . . unfair it was that your daughter caught measles.'

'Not really,' she says. 'Why wouldn't she catch measles, when so many people are walking around with it now? Anyone could catch it at any time. No, the hardest thing to accept is that some people still choose not to vaccinate their children. Despite all the evidence. Despite the fact that their actions are literally killing people. Killing children. *That's* the hardest thing to accept.'

I stare at her. I don't know what to say, how to respond. I don't know if I can help her any more. Not now I know she's so full of rage.

'Yes,' I say eventually. 'I'm sure it is.'

'If you have the answer to that, Selina,' Poppy says, standing up, 'a way of teaching me to accept that, then please, I'd love to hear it. I really would.'

'I—'

'No, I didn't think so,' she says. 'Because you and me, we have different opinions on this. Don't we, Selina? But the question remains: what do the others know? Do they know how you feel about vaccinations? Do they know that you used to date the most prolific anti-vax campaigner in America? That when you were young and attractive, you were his poster girl? That he's Kai's father? That he pimped you out to spread his dangerous message to vulnerable parents across the States?'

'I don't . . . That was a long time . . .'

'He was a nice man, your ex. Ron. Not only a passionate anti-vaxxer, he was also jailed for beating someone to death, in a road-rage incident. Sounds like a lovely guy. What do you think the other women on this retreat would say, Selina, if they knew? What do you think they would think, if only someone told them the truth about you?'

'His behaviour has nothing to do with me. Not any more. And all that business . . . that was way after we split up. I don't know what you think you know about me, but whatever it is, you're wrong.'

I close my eyes. It all makes sense now. I know why she's here, and I know what she wants.

'I think you know very well, Selina. I know everything about you. All about your fake qualifications. You're not a midwife, are you? You've never done a day's midwife training in your life. It's just lies. You're a fraud. A charlatan. A quack. All the stuff you thought you'd so carefully kept hidden ... I can't wait to hear what the others make of it all.'

I open my eyes.

Hers are flashing with anger, but I can see she's on the verge of tears too. Just a few seconds from a complete emotional collapse. And then what?

I can't let her do this. I can't let her ruin this weekend, not after all the work we've put in.

I won't.

I will make her see things my way. Even if it's the last thing I do.

THE AFTERNOON

Something I've pondered a lot over the last few months is where to attribute blame.

When someone holds a belief so deeply, no matter how misguided, is it actually wrong of them to try to share this belief with others?

Can you blame them for it?

By spreading your message, are you actually doing the right thing? Should you be admired for it, for your passion for the cause, despite others disagreeing with you?

Perhaps.

But where do you draw the line?

How far are you willing to go, to persuade people your point of view is the right one?

And how many people have to suffer as a consequence?

Let me tell you something. You're about to find out.

NICKY

When I enter the yoga studio, Selina is coming through a door at the back, wheeling out a small cabinet.

'Hi,' I say. 'I hope I'm not too early.'

She looks up at me. Her eyes are bloodshot.

'Right on time,' she says. 'I was just . . . having a tidy-up. Please, come in.'

I follow her back through the door and find myself inside a small room, painted in soothing shades of brown. There's a strange scent in the air, something I can't place immediately. And then I realise: it's bleach. I look down. The floor beneath me is damp.

'I . . . er . . . I spilt some nail varnish,' Selina says, as though reading my mind. 'It made such a mess. I've just been cleaning it up. Sorry about the smell.'

Her nails are bare. I sit in the chair she gestures towards at the back of the room.

'Would you like a drink?'

'No, I'm fine, thank you,' I say. 'I just had a cup of tea. It was lovely – beetroot and hibiscus, I think.'

'Ah yes, that's Will's favourite,' she says. She suddenly seems to unfurl like a rolled-up piece of paper, leaning back in her chair. 'We'll be making our own tomorrow using herbs and flowers from the garden. Nettle tea is really very good for you and not as disgusting as it sounds.'

'Never tried that one.'

She smiles.

'Is everything sorted with your tent?' she asks.

'Yes,' I say, swallowing. 'All fine now, thank you. Will's been great.'

'Once again, I'm very sorry about that.' She gives a forced laugh. 'Got to love the good old Devon weather.'

I nod, thinking about what Bonnie told us. Does she really think it was an accident, or is she actually lying to my face?

I just want to get through this hour now.

'So, Nicky, this is your time. You can use me for anything you'd like – whatever you might find helpful. I'm happy to just have a chat, or we can talk about your thoughts and hopes for the birth, or any anxieties you are having in your pregnancy . . . As you might know, I'm a trained midwife so we can talk about that side of things too, if it would interest you.'

I can imagine Selina being reassuring on this topic – she has a quiet confidence I admire and am sure would be very helpful when you're in labour.

But I've gone through labour twice before and my feelings about it can be boiled down to one simple thought: you can't control it, you just have to trust it will all work out in the end. There is literally no point in having a birth plan. God laughs in the face of birth and life plans alike.

'I . . .' I start, but somehow I don't have the words to continue. 'I don't really know where to start, to be honest.'

201

'Why don't we start by you telling me what made you come on the retreat in the first place?' she asks.

'It was actually my sister's idea,' I say. 'She thought it would be nice, I guess, for us to get away and spend some time together. And she knew I wasn't . . . well, I wasn't exactly happy, when I found out I was pregnant again. I've already got two boys, you know, and I thought that was it for me. That was me done. I didn't . . . I never planned to have three children.'

'Oh,' she says. 'I didn't realise.'

'I know, it sounds terrible. I'm eaten up with guilt about it, but the truth is it's not what I wanted,' I say. 'I was so excited about going back to work. But I've found it difficult to talk to my husband about. He's so busy with his own work, and he seemed so happy when I told him I was expecting again. He had the opposite reaction to me. He doesn't know how I feel. I told Bonnie and she suggested this retreat, said it might give me the chance to think about it – a bit of breathing space, I guess, to come to terms with it, I suppose. But if anything . . .'

'Go on,' Selina says. 'This is a safe space. You'll find no judgement here.'

I take a deep breath.

'If anything it's just confirmed my belief that I don't want to have this baby. But that's awful, isn't it? I mean, women across the world are desperate for babies and can't have them. And look at Poppy—'

'Poppy?' Selina interrupts.

'I mean, she lost her baby, and look how it's affected her. Clearly she's found it very difficult to cope. Understandably.

And here I am, miserable, just thinking why did this happen to me when it was so absolutely not what I wanted?'

A flicker of something passes over Selina's face. It's gone before I can catch it, analyse it, but it looks almost like contempt. I hang my head.

'I'm sorry,' I say. 'I feel terrible, even admitting this to you. It's just . . . it's going to take me a while to get my head around it, that's all. It's a lot to take in. It's somehow harder too, when you know what to expect. When you know the sheer amount of work that looking after a young baby requires. How exhausting it all is. I don't . . . I don't even know if I have the energy for it. I'm sorry, I'm moaning. I know it's a gift. I do, I know how lucky I am. Let's talk about something else. Those yoga stretches you showed us, perhaps, to help loosen your neck and shoulders – do you have any more? My shoulders are always killing me.'

I'm gabbling again, but Selina is still as stone in front of me, watching me with her intense eyes.

'You talk very fast. I think you're too hard on yourself,' she says. 'You clearly have very high standards and you need to let yourself off the hook. The tension in your shoulders is probably coming from this build-up of stress. How is your relationship with your husband?'

'It's . . . well, it's fine. We don't get to spend much time together really, just the two of us, but he's my best friend. He gets very stressed with work. He works very hard . . . I just try to make things easier for him at home, you know.'

'What do you do that's just for you?' Selina says.

'I . . . I sometimes get together with the mums from school.

Not that often though, we're all too tired. I like to read, when I get time . . .'

'Do you prioritise these things? Or are they at the bottom of your to-do list?'

I look down. From nowhere, tears have sprung.

'You don't have to stay with him, you know,' Selina says, leaning forward. 'There is life after divorce.'

'What?' I say, shocked. My heart starts to pound. 'No, I mean, I'm happy generally, he's a lovely man, we've been together since university . . .'

'It's possible to outgrow people,' Selina says, leaning back in her chair. 'There's no reason to believe that what works for us at twenty will work for us at forty, by which time we are completely different people.'

'No,' I say, wiping away the tears. I'm frightened of what she's saying. It's as though there are two sides to me, and she's slowly peeling them apart. 'No, I love him, I do . . . I just . . .'

'It sounds as though the issue here is your husband, not the baby,' Selina says. There's something magnetic about her, the confidence with which she is speaking about my biggest taboo. 'And after all, you wouldn't really countenance having an abortion at such a late stage, would you? Not when you're already a mother . . . not when you know how powerful that bond is.'

I frown. Suddenly, I feel as though I'm being told off.

But at the same time, it's as though she's cut to the heart of me, got straight to the gritty, important stuff that I've been trying to suppress. Her words echo inside a deep chamber within me.

'But what about you?' I say. 'Are you happy with Will?'

'Our situation is very different,' she says, looking down. Her eyes widen, and she pauses.

'And anyway, we're not talking about me,' she says eventually. 'We're talking about you. Now, what are you going to do? Whose happiness are you going to prioritise this time around? Yours or your husband's?'

BONNIE

Nicky has just left the studio after her session, looking pale-faced and vaguely terrified.

'What happened?' I say, walking towards her.

'What?' she replies.

'With Selina? How was it? Are you still upset about the tent thing?'

She presses the palms of her hands together.

'She told me again that it was the weather. Are you sure you got it right? There was no way it could have been the wind?'

'I'm only telling you what Badger told me,' I say defensively. 'But perhaps he was wrong.'

Neither of us believes it.

'Listen,' I say slowly. 'I've been thinking. We could . . . we could always leave. If you like. Go home? I know things haven't exactly turned out how we planned. Not quite the luxury retreat we were hoping for, and the bloody rain doesn't help.'

'What? God, no! Jon spent a fortune, he'd kill me.'

'Don't be stupid. He'd understand.'

'I'm fine,' she says, giving me a half-hearted smile. 'Honest. It's only one more day, and it's been nice to have a break from home. The food is great at least. And like you said, let's all just keep an eye out for each other.'

'OK,' I say. 'If you're sure.'

'Good luck in your session,' Nicky says, glancing back at the studio. 'Selina certainly . . . well, she certainly has a way of making you think outside the box. Ugh, can't believe I just said that! I hate that phrase.'

I smile.

I feel a tingle of excitement as I approach the studio for my session. Since we got here I haven't been alone with Selina, not once. I wonder how she feels about me. Whether or not she even cares if I'm having a good time this weekend.

I've seen the way she's looked at me – dismissed me as some stupid kid who's got knocked up and is headed for a life of failure. Which is a bit hypocritical given how she was almost the same age when she had Kai.

'Hello?' I call out to the empty yoga studio.

I didn't see Selina leave so I go through the door at the back of the studio. But that's empty too. And then I notice it: another door, leading out from the back of the treatment room. She must have gone somewhere.

I look at the clock. I'm on time. She's late. I suppose she'll turn up soon. Perhaps she's gone to the loo.

The room smells weird – like the college toilets after they've been cleaned. A sickly mix of bleach and cheap air freshener. There's a small sink set into a row of cupboards and drawers, with a mirror above, along one wall, and a kind of massage table pushed up alongside the other.

I start opening the cupboards, but they're mostly empty.

Just some screws and instructions for the massage table in one, cleaning stuff in the other.

I pull open the top drawer and it's full of the kind of junk you'd expect to find in a newly refurbished house. But there's something at the back that's sticking as I try to pull the drawer open wider. A piece of paper. I push my fingers through and yank it out.

It's screwed up, as though someone has shoved it in the drawer in a hurry.

Inside, starkly printed in capital letters, are the following words:

YOU WILL NEVER UNDERSTAND THE DAMAGE YOU'VE DONE. THAT IS WHY I'M HERE.

'Are you OK?'

I turn, red-faced, to see Selina standing behind me. I stuff the note into the pocket of my dungarees.

'Yes,' I say, holding her stare. 'I thought I'd come in and have a nose while I waited for you. It's nice in here. What were you planning on making it? A beauty parlour?'

'I have a friend who does acupuncture and craniosacral therapy,' she says. If she saw what I was reading then she isn't letting on. 'We'd like to offer it to guests on the retreat, but we couldn't make the schedules work this weekend.'

'Ah, shame. I'm a huge fan of acupuncture,' I lie.

'Really?'

'Really,' I say, in a sing-song voice. 'Anyway, shall we get started? Bet you're worn out listening to us all whining on about our pregnancy woes!'

She bites her top lip.

So much contempt, Selina, but why? Do you know the truth about me?

'Please, have a seat.'

We sit in the small tub chairs opposite one another. I imagine the others here, dabbing away their tears as Selina royally fucks with their minds.

'So, Bonnie,' Selina says, smiling that same fake smile. Behind it though, I can see she's knackered, and stressed about something. I think about the note I just found, how it might have affected her. Who might have sent it. How many enemies does she have? 'Congratulations on your pregnancy. Is there anything in particular you're worried about, or would like to discuss?'

'No, I don't think so,' I reply. Now I know what she's really like, I can beat her at her own game. I'm two steps ahead of her. 'I mean, the bigger stuff sure, like how am I going to cope bringing up a baby when I don't even have a job and I live in a house share with a bunch of students who are mostly four years younger than me, but other than that . . . I dunno. As for the birth . . . well, I've got a pretty high pain threshold.'

'Labour is a different kind of a pain,' she says. 'I always encourage women to see it as a positive pain, a pain that tells you things are happening. It's a pain that has purpose.'

'I suppose you don't believe in drugs and all that shit. Epidurals, or whatever they're called.'

She pauses. I can see how carefully she's choosing her words.

'I believe that women don't need these things, but at the same time, if *they* believe that they need them, then it's hard to convince them otherwise. Some women are . . . let's not say weaker, but less able to cope. But generally speaking, the way we have medicalised childbirth . . . no, it's not something I am a fan of. Women did perfectly well for centuries giving birth alone underneath trees . . .'

'Underneath trees?'

'I'm being glib. I just mean, other mammals manage to give birth perfectly healthily and safely by listening to their instincts. I think it's a shame we've been taught to ignore our own.'

'Yeah,' I say, pausing. 'I suppose deep down I am really nervous about the pregnancy . . . the birth. I hate hospitals. I mean, I know no one much likes them, but I really hate them.'

'I'm the same.' She smiles. 'They're not the nicest places for pregnant ladies, or the nicest places to be born, either. Much better for everyone if babies are born at home in a calm, loving environment.'

She sits back in her chair.

'It's great that you're so open to this,' she says, and I wonder briefly whether I've managed it – I've actually managed to fool her. I get a little thrill at the thought.

If only she knew the truth.

She's still talking, oblivious.

'Most women your age are not so brave. We've been conditioned to believe that giving birth is some kind of medical emergency, rather than the most natural thing in the world. I've got lots of information on this I can share with you – lots of books in the barn I can lend you. So, tell me, how does the baby's father fit in? Is he supportive and fully in the picture?'

I beam.

'Oh yes,' I lie. 'He's amazing. We haven't been able to be together as much as we would like but that's going to change soon. We have plans, you see. He's always wanted to be a father. And I just know he's going to be brilliant at it.'

GEORGIA

After my therapy session, I decide to go for a long walk.

Selina didn't seem particularly shocked by the revelation that the baby I'm carrying might not actually be my partner's. She was surprisingly kind, but also, unexpectedly, well, *supportive* of the idea that I just carry on pretending and not worry about ever telling Brett the truth.

'The truth is you don't know,' she said. 'Right? You don't know whether this baby is Brett's, or whether it's the other man's? So is there any benefit to confessing right now, when you're heavily pregnant and really need to prioritise your own mental health and the baby? All of this can be resolved, eventually, later down the line.'

I had stared at her in surprise. It wasn't at all what I had expected her to say. I thought she'd be, well, more morally upright than that.

I couldn't decide whether it made me like her more or less. Was she just telling me what she thought I wanted to hear?

She was so opinionated too. So sure of herself and the advice she was giving.

'But . . . surely, surely he has a right to know?'

'Do you have any idea how many children are currently

being raised by men who aren't biologically related to them? Do you think, really, deep down, that it actually matters?'

I stared at her. I couldn't say, well, yes, actually I did think it mattered, a bit at least, because I knew that Will wasn't her son's father, and I didn't want to upset her.

'I don't know,' I said. 'I just feel like I'm not being honest with Brett. And I love him so much – honestly, I can't believe that he's come into my life. This perfect man. Exactly what I was asking for, what I hoped to find. And now I've somehow managed to mess everything up . . .'

'No man is perfect,' Selina said. 'You just haven't had to deal with his bad bits yet.'

I frowned at her. The session was making me feel worse, not better.

'Sorry,' she said, noticing my face. 'I just don't want you to put him on a pedestal, to see yourself as somehow lesser. It's the feminist in me! Us women put ourselves down so much, we constantly look up to men as though they're the answer to all our hopes and prayers, as though without one we can't be seen as successful or powerful. And it's all bullshit. They are the lucky ones. They are the ones that get to be with us – women, the most powerful, resilient, caring beings on the planet. Do you think if the situation was reversed, that your partner would be tearing himself into pieces with guilt over this?'

It was the most animated and angry she'd been since we arrived.

'I . . . I don't know,' I said. 'I think he's pretty moral, but—'

'Like I said,' she interrupted. 'You don't even need to deal

213

with this yet. You have to prioritise what's important, and what's important is taking care of your own health, your own stress levels, to ensure both you and the baby are healthy. Once he or she is here, then there'll be plenty of time to deal with this stuff. You also might find that you just know, instinctively, whether or not he's the father . . .' She paused, pursing her lips. 'The other man . . . is he someone you knew well? An ex-partner? Would he want to be involved? Is he still in your life?'

'No!' I said. I didn't want to admit the whole sorry story to her. It was too embarrassing. 'No, he wouldn't want to be involved. It wasn't like that.'

She paused for a few seconds, watching me.

'Georgia,' she said, piercing me with her laser-like eyes. 'I think you are going to be the most wonderful mother to this baby, and I think your partner is going to be the most wonderful father too. Listen to me. You need to let yourself off the hook here. The fact that you are worrying so much about it proves just what an amazing woman you are. But tell your brain that you're done hearing this self-abuse. Enough now. Babies are a privilege, a gift, a joy. I believe they are always bestowed for a reason. You said you'd always wanted to be a mother, that you'd dreamt of this all your life. It's here now. Don't waste this precious time being eaten up with guilt about something that you can't control. You can't go back and change it. You can deal with this at the appropriate time, when you need to. But not now. You've left it this long without telling him – a few more months in order to ensure your baby is delivered into a supportive, safe environment won't do any harm. And as I said, when the baby is born you might find you know either way – that you can tell whether or not the baby is Brett's. A mother's instinct is very strong.'

It was all very well her saying that – and the conviction in her voice was certainly reassuring at the time – but deep down I knew it didn't change anything.

It felt like she was letting me off the hook, but whatever she said, she couldn't make me let myself off it.

And strangely, her words have helped me to decide what I need to do. The opposite of what she advised, in fact.

Brett is due back from New York next Wednesday. It seems clear to me now that I have to sit him down and tell him the truth.

How it all came about.

It was my friend Lucy's idea. She had an older friend who'd done it – said how straightforward it was. She found a clinic, chose the donor, and paid to have a fertility check. Then, at the perfect moment, had the sperm injected directly into her uterus. It wasn't as scary as IVF. It wasn't as expensive either. And it worked. She ended up with twin boys.

It felt like the clock was ticking. I kept looking at my life, nearly thirty-nine, and wondering how it had got to a point so far removed from what I had pictured.

By now I thought I'd be living in the suburbs, with two kids, a husband who travelled into the city every day, and perhaps a Labrador. I would have given up my newspaper column to go freelance, and my children would be my priority.

My life would look a bit like Nicky's, I guess.

But somehow it hadn't happened. I had pushed so hard for

it, that I'd pushed it away. Instead, I was nearly thirty-nine, living in a one-bedroom flat in London with a huge mortgage, a high-pressure job and an addiction to spin classes. I drank too much, I slept too little, I ate too little.

I was not who I was meant to be.

I stood staring at myself in the mirror and suddenly imagined my life in ten years' time, continuing exactly the same. Only I'd be more bitter, and it would be too late.

I made an appointment with the clinic the next morning. It was all quite straightforward, and I wasn't the only single woman in the waiting room.

I got chatting to one of them – Bethan – and she told me that she was forty and she'd just broken up with her husband because she realised that she wasn't prepared to give up her dream of being a mother after all. He had never wanted kids. She seemed sad but sanguine. We ended up swapping numbers, texting constantly throughout the whole process.

But then shortly after, I met Brett.

I would never normally sleep with someone on a first date. He said the same but now I know him better I'm not entirely sure that was true. He was a gentleman though. No pressure. It was all driven by me. My euphoria, the feeling that finally the pressure was off.

The irony.

I pause, realising I'm slightly out of breath, and decide to sit down on a tree stump at the edge of the woodland. My stomach is still a bit sore.

Taking back control of my life – my fertility – in that way had left me feeling carefree. And perhaps that's what Brett saw – perhaps that's what first attracted him to me. I had just had a meeting with a PR in a bar of a hotel and was finishing up some work on my laptop before going home when he came over.

He asked me if I could recommend anywhere decent to eat nearby. He was new to London he said, and keen to get a more authentic experience than the places the hotel recommended.

'I'm not a tourist,' he explained, probably noticing my confusion at his interruption. 'I've just taken up a new position at the UK arm of my firm.'

He was charming and lovely and we chatted – I was in such a good mood. We stayed in the hotel bar for ages, and then in the end went for dinner. He came back to mine.

It was only two days after my insemination. Perhaps it was disgusting to be sleeping with someone so soon afterwards, but I didn't think I had anything to lose. I didn't even expect to see Brett again.

Perhaps deep down, I thought I was just upping my chances. I don't know. I was drunk. We should have used protection, but we didn't.

Then just weeks later, there it was. The positive pregnancy test I'd hoped for – making all my dreams come true. And also, in the background, surprisingly still there and still very much 'into' me: Brett. My new boyfriend.

I thought when I told him I was pregnant that he would run for the hills. We literally barely knew each other. But he didn't. He didn't put any pressure on me either. He was perfect.

I know I should have told him then. But I was too scared. And soon afterwards, too ill. My morning sickness was crippling, leaving me no headspace to deal with the conversation I should have been having.

And now . . . now it's too late.

Except it's not. I can do this. He will understand. He has always understood. He's never let me down before.

I stand again and continue walking towards the woods. Not long now until our next yoga session. It has been good to get away this weekend – it's been weird, for sure, but good too.

I take my phone out of my pocket and gaze up at the trees above me. It's so quiet in the woods, so peaceful, yet there's still something sinister about being somewhere so isolated and maze-like. No matter which way you turn, it all looks the same.

I'm about to take a photo of the branches above me, the dark sky peeking through, when I spot something else further ahead. Something bright pink.

I walk towards it, confused. Then I realise what it is.

A scarf. I pick it up. It's old, dirty, interwoven with gold thread. Like something you'd buy on a market stall on holiday.

I pick it up and turn it over in my hands and then I spot something. A stain. Dark brown, crisping the fabric at one edge. I run my thumb over it. Surely not . . . blood?

I frown, almost dropping the scarf in disgust.

I look around again, wondering how it got left out here.

It's not something I recognise as belonging to any of the others, but I decide to take it to our next yoga session, just in case.

SELINA

Of course, after what happened earlier, Poppy doesn't come to afternoon yoga. The others make a big fuss of her absence, as though they're all close friends suddenly.

I can't bear it. I am exhausted. And there's still this evening and all of tomorrow to get through. What was I thinking? Trying to run a retreat after everything that's happened here?

'Right, ladies, you have an hour before dinner – please do take some time to rest – or go for another walk, whatever you'd like to do . . .'

They start gathering their things together.

'Oh!' Georgia says. 'I forgot to say. I found this in the woods . . . not sure if it belongs to any of you guys?'

She takes something out of the pocket of her hoodie. Something bright pink. I recognise it instantly, the bile swimming to my throat.

I lean against the wall, trying to compose myself. How the hell . . . how could she possibly . . .

'It's a scarf, I think? Is it any of yours?'

The others stare at it, shaking their heads.

'It's . . . it's mine!' I squeak. 'Thank you, Georgia. I've been looking for it everywhere.'

I take it from her.

'I'm not sure how it got into the woods. How very ... peculiar.'

The fabric feels like burning coal in my hand. I close my eyes briefly, thinking of the last time I saw it. I was so sure ... I was so sure it had been buried with her ...

'Is that ... blood?' Bonnie says, pulling a face. 'It's really stained.'

'I ... I haven't seen it for months,' I say. 'I must have dropped it outside, and it's been through the wars since. Never mind. It's not precious.'

'Glad you got it back,' Georgia says. 'It's really pretty.'

I nod, my eyes fixed. I can't trust myself to speak.

'I hope Poppy's OK,' I hear Nicky saying to no one in particular. 'Strange how she didn't turn up to the session.'

'Perhaps she's having a nap?' Georgia says.

'Maybe,' Nicky says.

I put the scarf down at the side of the room where I don't have to look at it and carry on piling the blankets and spritzing the eye masks with antibacterial spray. If I'm quick, I've just got enough time to check on Kai.

Poppy can wait.

'See you at dinner, ladies,' I call, trying to sound as cheerful as possible.

When they finally leave, I sit in the silence, thinking about the scarf. I have never believed in ghosts, but this weekend I have felt continuously haunted by her presence. How the hell did this scarf get out there in the woods? Unless ... some animal . . . no, surely not. He promised me he would take care of it properly.

Please God, surely not.

I take a deep breath. There's no way out of it. At some point, I'll have to check the site hasn't been disturbed. Or ask Will to. But first, I make my way to the pigsties.

I don't bother to knock. After all, it's not his property, is it?

Instead, I push open the heavy wooden door and peer inside.

Kai is sitting on his bed, headphones on, staring at something on his phone. Despite the newly painted white walls, it's really dark, and my eyes struggle to adjust to the change in light. He hasn't bothered to raise the blinds. The place is a tip, and smells musty.

So far, so normal. But it's not good enough, is it? It's not good enough for her.

He can't cope.

I rush towards the cot.

There she is. River. My perfect little angel. She's awake, staring up at the beamed ceiling and making shapes with her hands.

'Hello, sweetheart,' I say, scooping her up. 'How are you?'

Out of the corner of my eye, I see Kai has finally noticed me. He yanks off his headphones. I look over at him.

'She's too hot,' I say crossly. 'She doesn't need this many layers on. For God's sake, Kai. It's May. Letting babies overheat can be incredibly dangerous.'

He stares at me.

'Right. Sorry,' he says, and then he turns back to his phone.

I want to reach over and strangle him. But I can't. Because

I'm holding River, and she's gazing up at me with her huge blue eyes. She squirms in my arms, hiccupping.

It's only been twenty-four hours, but I have missed her so much. She is the only joy in my life right now.

'She needs winding,' I say, laying her over my shoulder. I rub her back, jiggling her up and down several times. Eventually, a bubble of air escapes from her tiny mouth.

'That's better, darling, isn't it? That's better, my little poppet. Did you have a bubble in your tummy? Did you? Poor Riv-Rivs. Poor baby.'

I wish I could take her back to the house with me right now, look after her myself, but of course I can't. Too many questions. No one can ever know she's here, especially when Kai is still such a mess, and I can't trust him not to blurt out the whole sorry story.

But it's so exhausting, trying to keep the guests away from this part of the farm.

'It's only for a few days, my angel,' I say to her. 'Then you'll be back with us. I know, I know. I miss you too, my darling.'

'She's fine,' I hear Kai say. 'We've been fine.'

'Has she had her baby rice?' I ask. There's no point in trying to engage with him in any other way. 'You were meant to go into the kitchen while we were doing yoga.'

'No, I completely forgot to feed her,' he says. 'That's why she's just needed a burp. 'Cause her stomach is empty.'

The sarcasm brings me up short.

Nasty as it is, it's a good sign. A sign that he's finally coming to terms with everything. I'd far rather this than the shell-shocked zombie that we've endured for months.

'How much did she eat?' I ask. 'And how much milk did you give her after? She's very gassy.'

'She had a whole bottle like normal, and she ate most of the bowl.'

He finally stands up and walks towards us. I'm always surprised at just how tall he is.

'I'm not a complete idiot,' he says, taking her from me. He kisses the top of her head. 'Despite what you think.'

'Darling, I don't think you're an idiot. Of course I don't. I just know you're very fragile at the moment. And understandably, after everything you've been through.'

A tiny piece of my heart breaks as I look at River. It's been so hard pretending she doesn't exist this weekend.

'Take that cardigan off before you put her back in her cot,' I say. 'She doesn't need it. And don't let her nap for more than forty-five minutes this afternoon, or she'll be awake in the night again. Two of the guests heard her crying last night. We can't have that happen again.'

He nods. I leave the pigsty before looking back. Just watching him holding her makes my heart hurt, but what choice do I have?

NICKY

I sit on the bed in my tent, still processing my conversation with Selina earlier. Thinking about what she said, about how she told me I didn't have to stay with Jon. As though she actually thought I'd be better off if I didn't.

It was the most transgressive, shocking thing anyone has said to me in the last decade. And now, turning it over in my mind, it still makes me feel uncomfortable, itchy in my own skin.

How can she just say that, so blithely? It's insane. I've built a life around Jon. Around our kids. It's my entire world.

The thought of just leaving that behind makes no sense to me whatsoever.

But even so . . . there's part of me, perhaps 10 per cent, that finds the idea of starting over intoxicating. Alluring. Exciting.

Perhaps she's right and he's the reason I don't want this baby? Perhaps it's not the baby that I don't want, but him?

What other life might I have had if we had broken up when we left university? Rather than doggedly continuing with our relationship – me moving to Bristol to be close to him and his work, even though all my family and friends were still in Exeter.

Is this what a midlife crisis looks like?

I sigh. It's all very well thinking this. But it's a fantasy, and I know it. The truth is that the grass is always greener, but it still needs mowing.

Our life may not be exciting, but it's safe and secure and that counts for a lot.

I send Jon a text telling him that I love and miss him and the boys, but he doesn't reply. I expect they're out in the garden, burning off the last bit of energy before heading to the Morgans'.

There's a shout from outside.

I poke my head out of my tent. Georgia is walking towards me, one arm wrapped underneath her bump.

'She's not in her tent!' she shouts.

Bonnie comes out of hers.

'What?'

'Poppy, she's not in there,' Georgia says. She's panting slightly.

'That's weird,' I say. 'But don't worry, I'm sure she's fine. She's probably just gone for a walk.'

'Another walk?' Georgia says. She glances towards the woods. The sky is gunmetal grey above us, the evening drawing in. I think of my tent collapsing again, and shiver. I'm dreading trying to sleep in there tonight. Perhaps Bonnie was right. Perhaps we should go home. 'When did you last see her? I'm worried . . .'

I rack my brains, trying to remember.

'I think I saw her just before her counselling session,' I say. 'But only briefly. I heard her leave her tent, and then she walked towards the yoga studio.'

'You haven't seen her since?' Georgia says, eyes widening. 'That was hours ago.'

'I saw her go into the studio too,' Bonnie says. 'But I didn't see her come out.'

'What?'

'Nothing,' she says. 'But who knows what goes on in Selina's secret room . . .'

'It's not funny, Bonnie,' I say. 'Something might have happened to her! Think about what happened to my tent. There's something going on, and I don't like it. We need to tell Selina.'

Georgia nods and we walk towards the barn together. Bonnie hangs back.

As we approach the kitchen doors, Badger appears from round the side of the building. He's pulling off a pair of gardening gloves, his face lined with dirt.

'Evening,' he says. 'Looks like we're in for some thunder tonight.'

'Have you seen Poppy?' Georgia asks.

'Poppy?' he says.

'Yes, we can't find her,' I reply. 'She's got short brown hair, kind of cropped in a bob. She's pregnant, obviously. Quite a thin face.'

'Oh,' he says. 'Yes, I remember. I saw her this morning, just before lunch, I think. But not since then, no, sorry.'

I glance at Georgia.

'She's not in her tent. We're a bit worried about her; no one's seen her all afternoon. We need to tell Selina.'

Inside the kitchen Selina is sitting at the dining table, tying

226

napkins with twine and placing cornflowers underneath the bows. She looks up.

'Poppy's not in her tent,' Georgia says, 'and no one has seen her for hours. Might she have got lost in the woods?'

Selina stares at me. She doesn't say anything.

'Is it worth calling the police?' I say. 'Especially after the thing with my tent. Perhaps there's a prowler around?'

'How did she get here?' Georgia asks. 'Does she have a car?'

'No,' Selina says. 'She came on the train, then got a cab, I think. But I'm sure she's fine. Let's take a look around the grounds together. She could have just gone for a quick walk. No need to panic.'

I'm frustrated that Selina isn't taking this seriously.

We all trudge outside, following her as she walks round the front of the barn and across a field full of flowers. There are more outbuildings here – I didn't notice them when I first arrived.

'Should we check inside?' I say.

'No, they're the pigsties,' Selina says. 'They're just full of junk now – she won't be in there.'

I think we should be checking all the same, but don't feel I can disagree with her. It's not my home, after all. And I guess I wouldn't like strangers poking around inside my outbuildings, if I had any.

'What about this place?' I say, pausing outside another, smaller barn.

'That's where I sleep,' Badger says. 'Don't judge, it's a work in progress. I'll have a quick check – I was just in there myself though, so I doubt it.'

We wait outside for a few moments while he disappears into the barn.

'Nothing,' he says. 'Sorry.'

'Let's keep looking,' Georgia says. 'I know it's daft but I'm really worried. You can tell she was a bit out of sorts earlier, and it looks as though it's going to pour again any minute.'

'How did she seem in her therapy session, Selina?' I ask, wondering if Selina, in her unconventional style, said anything shocking to Poppy that might have set her off. Especially after the way Poppy was needling her this morning.

'She was . . . she had been feeling a bit faint,' Selina says, staring down at the gravel driveway. 'But she was fine.'

'Did you know she lost a baby?' I say. 'Last year. I don't know any of the details but perhaps she's found this weekend has brought up some stuff she hasn't been able to deal with. Maybe she feels guilty about the new baby, replacing the old . . .'

'That doesn't explain her just upping and leaving though, does it?' Georgia says. 'We were getting on quite well at lunch. She wanted to be in the photo . . . I thought she was beginning to settle in a bit. I know she was a bit . . . prickly to begin with, but some people are just like that around strangers. They take time to warm up.'

We continue our search round the barn and gardens, but she's nowhere to be seen.

'If she doesn't turn up we'll have to call the police,' I say, staring across at the woods.

'Of course,' Selina says. 'But let's just hold fire for a little bit longer . . . She could easily be just across the Nine Acres in our

228

neighbour's field. There's a map in your welcome pack, it's the guided walk I was going to take you on yesterday.'

'Is there someone we should call?' Georgia says. 'Her husband?'

Selina shakes her head.

'I don't have any of those details, I'm afraid. Please, try not to worry. I'm sure she'll turn up.'

How can she be so sure? I look over at Badger.

'I'll check the woods,' he says. 'Don't panic. We'll find her, I'm sure. She can't have gone far without a car anyway.'

'Thanks, Badge,' Selina says.

The rumble of an engine makes us all turn back towards the barn.

'It'll just be Will,' Selina says. 'He had to go into town this afternoon to get some bits for supper.'

'Oh,' I reply, but Georgia is already hurrying back towards the driveway.

We follow her.

Will slams the door of his Land Rover shut and stares at us. He's carrying a bag of shopping.

'What's happened?' he says.

'Poppy's gone missing,' Georgia says.

'No, she's—' Will says.

'Badger's gone to look for her in the woods,' I say. A rumble of thunder goes off in the distance, and like an egg cracking open, rain begins to fall.

Out of nowhere, Bonnie appears.

'Any luck?' she says. 'I just did a search of her tent. And I found this.'

BONNIE

I hold out Poppy's journal.

It's the same as all the rest of ours, but somehow looks more aged. More used. Small drops of rain splash on the cover, darkening the leather.

'I found it under her duvet,' I say. 'I probably shouldn't have looked inside but . . . well. Open it.'

'We shouldn't . . .' Selina begins but it's too late. Nicky turns the cover.

Inside, the first page is almost black with scribbles – layered on top of each other so that it now looks like someone just scratched out the whole page in black ink.

'Turn over,' I say.

Selina inhales sharply.

The next page is empty except for one short phrase, written in the middle in capital letters. I think of the note in my dungarees. But that had been printed on a computer. This is written by hand, in precise, neat lettering.

ONE LIE IS ENOUGH TO QUESTION ALL TRUTHS.

'What does that mean?' Nicky says.

'What does it say?' Georgia asks. 'Let me see.'

Nicky hands her the journal. She frowns as she reads it.

'That poor woman,' she says, as she hands it over to Selina. 'I think we need to call the police. Perhaps she's having some kind of mental breakdown?'

'I think she still feels incredibly guilty about losing her baby,' Selina says slowly. 'And now she's pregnant again. I expect it's just a lot for her to cope with.'

'Even so,' says Nicky, frowning at Selina. 'I don't like it. This isn't normal. What's underneath all those scribbles? And what is she talking about? What lie? I agree with Georgia. I'm not comfortable about this at all, especially after what happened with my tent. We need to tell the police—'

'Sorry,' Will says, cutting in. I glance at him, notice the flush of red on his neck. He won't meet my eye. 'But who are we talking about? Poppy?'

'Yes,' Nicky says. 'She's disappeared.'

'Oh, but no,' he replies. 'She's fine, I just gave her a lift into town . . .'

'What?'

'Yes, she said she had a friend that lived in Okehampton and she wanted to get out and see her for the afternoon. She said her back was hurting and she didn't fancy yoga. She knew I was off to buy some bits for supper and she asked if I could drop her off there. She said she was going to get a cab back later.'

My heart is pounding. Something about what he's saying doesn't ring true. But at the same time, why would he lie?

'How did she seem though?' Nicky asks. Despite how much she winds me up, I admire how fierce she sounds. She'd have made a good police officer.

231

'I don't know really,' Will says. 'Quiet. She didn't really want to chat. We listened to Radio Four. She was wearing her coat, cross about the weather. When she first got in she complained the seat was dirty, and so I gave her a plastic bag to sit on.'

The details feel authentic, but even so. I just know he's hiding something.

'I don't understand why she wouldn't have let us know she was going,' Nicky says.

'You should have told me you were giving her a lift,' Selina says sharply to Will. 'Would have saved us all a lot of worry.'

'I assumed she would have told you herself,' Will says.

There's what people call an 'awkward silence' only it's more than just awkward, it's excruciating. I want to reach out and squeeze his hand, to tell him I'm on his side. But he doesn't look at me.

'Well, at least she's safe,' Georgia says. 'Should we text her anyway?'

'I will. But let's all go inside before we get completely soaked,' Selina says, clutching Poppy's soggy journal to her chest. 'I'll make us all some nice tea.'

Selina is obsessed with fucking tea.

We follow her into the kitchen. It's a cosy haven in comparison to the wet and wild outside. I can't believe how much a place can change with the weather – one minute it's like paradise, the next like something out of a horror film.

I look over at Will. He's already behind the island unit, getting prepped for dinner.

We sit on the sofas in the corner, sipping Selina's homemade nettle tea.

'Good for your kidneys,' she said, as she handed us all a cup.

'What about Badger?' Georgia says suddenly, almost spilling hers. 'We forgot! He's out in the woods on his own in the rain.'

I watch Selina. She almost rolls her eyes. There's no hiding it. She's ice cold, that one. Clearly finds other women infuriating, despite all her feminist chat.

'Badger will be fine,' Selina says. 'He's not scared of a little bit of rain. But I'll try his mobile. He might not have it on him. He's not the type to be glued to it.'

'He's great,' I say. 'He's had such an amazing life. I got chatting to him yesterday.'

Selina looks at me. I take it as an invitation to continue, because I know it definitely isn't.

'He's travelled all over the world volunteering for people. Seen all kinds of sights. What a way to live.'

'Wow,' Georgia says. 'I've always been . . . such a city girl. I think it's a reaction to growing up in the country where life seemed to be, well, a bit dull really. Although now I think dull sounds lovely. I think this is also known as ageing.'

She laughs at her own joke.

'I don't think there's anything dull about living in remote Fiji,' I say, but in a friendly voice.

Georgia's all right. She seems quite fragile underneath her charismatic, Instaworthy persona.

'How long is Badger staying with you for?' Nicky asks Selina.

Selina puts her phone down.

'I've texted Poppy and I've left Badger a message to say that she's safe,' Selina says. 'And I'm not sure really. He seems quite happy with us. His aunt lives nearby, and she's getting quite elderly, so I think he's keen to stick around a bit. He visits her every week. And he's got so many projects on the go – the next one is finishing up the small barn.' She pauses, swallowing. 'So, you know, we're certainly not in any hurry for him to leave.'

'What's he doing to the small barn?' Nicky says.

I am staring at Will. His head snaps up. He's frowning. Something they don't agree on, clearly.

'Oh,' Selina says. 'We . . . well, we thought we'd quite like to turn it into self-contained accommodation. With its own kitchen, etcetera. You know, so that people can come and just stay on the grounds. Then if they'd like to join a yoga class or whatever, they'd be quite welcome.'

'That sounds nice,' Nicky says blandly. I scratch at my shoulder. The polo neck I'm wearing under my dungarees feels itchy against my skin.

'Will Badger be joining us for dinner?' I say. 'I'd love to hear more of his stories.'

'No.' Selina smiles. 'He prefers to keep himself to himself.'

'Shame. Feels a bit servants and masters.'

'Not at all,' Selina says. 'He's one of the family. But he's very private really.'

'And what about your son?' I ask. I can't resist pushing her buttons. All the time, I'm glancing over at Will, to try and work out how he feels about my questions. His face remains neutral, but little twitches around his shoulders, and the way he's aggressively chopping vegetables, tell me he's feeling the pressure.

'What about him?' Selina says, and for a second her mask

slips. More of that coldness and irritation escapes. I have no idea why this woman thought she'd be the right person to run a hospitality business.

She seems to mostly hate people, except when they're lying on yoga mats, unspeaking and listening to her every word.

She seems to hate people, except for when she's in control of them. Literally controlling them – their minds and their limbs.

'Will he be joining us for dinner?' I say. 'When I spoke to him yesterday he seemed a bit . . . well, I hope you don't mind me saying so, Selina, but a bit lost?'

Nicky shoots me a look. So I've crossed a fucking line. Who cares?

'He's had a difficult year,' Selina says. 'But he'll find his path. We all do. Everyone has their mountain to climb, then they can see the way ahead clearly. The view from the top is always worth it.'

'That's beautiful,' Georgia says, and I want to kick her for being so idiotic. She'll probably Instagram it later.

Who am I kidding? She definitely will.

Selina smiles at her. Teacher's pet.

'Now,' she says, turning back to us, glass teapot in hand. 'Who's for some more tea?'

SATURDAY EVENING

GEORGIA

After dinner, Selina asks us to go and get our journals, for our next session. I think about what was written in Poppy's as I walk towards my tent. Selina had left it on a bookshelf in the kitchen, and the creeping sense that Poppy will never return to open it again overcomes me.

One lie is enough to question all truths.

What on earth could she have meant?

It's horrible. I hope she's OK. She clearly needs more help than Selina can offer on this retreat.

I pick up my own journal, stroking the cover. It's soft and warm beneath my fingertips, but I can pick up the faint scent of leather even holding it away from my face. I wonder if my sense of smell will ever return to normal. It's hard to imagine how normal will feel.

The baby rolls over in my stomach, giving me a satisfying kick to the bladder. He seems to have sunk lower into my pelvis over the past few days. I wish Brett was here so I could put his hand on my stomach and watch his face light up as he feels the baby wriggling around inside me.

Back in the kitchen, I accept Selina's offer of an oat-milk hot chocolate and settle myself at the table. Selina has dimmed the main lights and lit another row of tiny tea lights that twinkle in among the foliage on the table. Despite everything that's gone wrong over the past couple of days, I feel a welcome sense of calm descend as I open my journal and start to write.

Brett loves me. I know this. He's proved it to me in a hundred ways ever since we met. If I want to continue with our relationship in the spirit of openness and sincerity, which I DO, then I understand that I need to explain to him about the fertility treatment, about the fact that, very possibly, he might not be the biological father of our baby. And I have to trust that the love we have built between us is enough for him to try to understand why I haven't shared this before.

And if he doesn't understand this and cannot accept it, then I know deep down in my soul that things would not have worked out in the long run. I might have 'got away' with not telling him for a while – maybe years – but eventually, the truth would have come out, because that's what always happens, and the pain that the truth would cause if it came out at a later date would inevitably be far greater than if I told him now.

There is also, of course, the possibility that he is the biological father, and that I have nothing to worry about. But either way, I love and respect him and I want to do the right thing. Because doing the right thing is important to me, and this is a child's life we're talking about, and it matters, and the long-term damage is too great to contemplate.

I pause, reading over what I've written. It sounds a bit pompous, but as I read I realise that my eyes are wet with tears, and I wipe them away as subtly as I can with the sleeve of my jumper.

I look up at the clock. It's nearly 10pm.

'Is Poppy still not back?' I say to the quiet dining room.

Selina is sitting in the far corner, on the sofa, writing in her own book. 'Did she reply to your message?'

'No. I'll call her,' Selina says. 'Perhaps she's decided to stay overnight with her friend.'

Selina leaves the room and I look up at Nicky. Bonnie is still writing in her journal.

'I really hope she's OK,' I say to Nicky. 'I know she was a bit strange but I'd hate to think of her getting into some kind of trouble.'

'I'm sure she's fine,' Nicky says, smiling. She has dark rings under her eyes that I haven't noticed before. I want to tell her to go to bed, but it's not my place.

'Hmm.'

'We don't really know her,' Nicky continues. 'We shouldn't speculate too much – or get too worried. At the end of the day, if Will says he dropped her in town then we have to assume she's OK.'

Will. I think about him, his strange, evasive manner, the way he looks as though he wishes he wasn't here. Charming on the outside, but somehow inauthentic.

'Yes, but . . . do we trust Will?' The words are out before I have time to consider them.

'Oh. He seems very nice to me,' Nicky says. Bonnie looks up. 'I mean, he's not hugely talkative, sure, but . . .'

'It's always the quiet ones,' I say, thinking of Lewis. 'Still waters—'

'What are you talking about?' Bonnie interrupts. 'All he's done is cook for us and look after us since we've been here.'

I bite my lip and look down. I'm definitely not in the mood

to get into a fight with Bonnie. She has a 'don't give a shit' attitude that I simultaneously admire and dislike.

Selina comes back into the kitchen and we all look up like guilty children.

'She didn't answer her phone,' she says. 'But I left her a message. I'm sure she's just decided to stay on at her friend's house. Will says he'll go over there in the morning and check she's OK if we don't hear anything – he remembers where he dropped her off.'

It sounds like a lie. Perhaps I'm just tired. I definitely get more paranoid when I'm tired.

Selina hands us all a hot-water bottle – 'It's chillier tonight' – and it feels like a way of politely asking us to leave. So we do. Nicky says I can go in the bathroom block first, so I use the toilet and wash my face and brush my teeth in the dim light of the log cabin.

Just one day left here, and despite everything, I feel as though I have the answers I need. As though I got what I came for.

I take a photo of my bump from above and upload it to Instagram.

My back is aching slightly from the yoga earlier. I'm missing my pregnancy pillow.

I step out of the bathroom block and take a deep breath. The sky is clear tonight, the earlier rainclouds gone. The air smells sharp, clean, countrified. Dangerous.

I glance over at the woods as I make my way back towards my tent. The sound of voices stops me short. It's coming from just beyond the small barn, and without really understanding why, I tiptoe towards it.

'Is it true?' a female voice is saying. I close my eyes to concentrate. It's definitely Bonnie. I'm sure it's Bonnie.

'What?' the other voice replies. A man, but who?

'That you took Poppy to Okehampton? Tell me the truth, Will.'

'Why would I lie?' he replies.

'To cover for Selina – God, I don't know. I found this weird note in the yoga studio . . . and then there's that stuff written in Poppy's journal. What's going on, Will? Seriously? I don't understand . . .'

'Darling, please. Keep your voice down,' Will whispers. 'She already suspects . . .'

Darling.

'Why wouldn't she have said goodbye? Why would she simply disappear like that?'

'I don't know,' he says. 'I was just doing her a favour. But she was fine, I promise you. She was absolutely fine.'

'There's something not right about all this. I don't like it. I know you're hiding something.'

I take a few steps closer and then I see the outline of the woman talking – the purple dungarees confirming my suspicion that it's Bonnie. But it doesn't make any sense. The way she's talking to him – as though they're close, as though they know each other well . . .

He called her *darling.*

And then it dawns on me. The way Bonnie reacted when Poppy challenged her about the father of her baby. But no, surely not?

Then I remember: Bonnie is a catering student. And Selina mentioned that Will was teaching at a local college. Surely . . .

It's like puzzle pieces clicking into place.

I can't believe it.

'I have to go back inside,' Will is saying. My heart is beating so loudly in my ears I can barely make out what they're saying. 'You don't know what you're dealing with. We can't risk it. She'll wonder where I am.'

He leans down and wraps his arms around her tightly, and they kiss.

A hungry, passionate kiss. The kiss of illicit lovers.

'Will,' Bonnie says, when they break apart. 'Just tell me the truth. I'm scared . . . I don't know . . . Selina . . . she's not what I expected, and now this . . .'

'Just stay away from her,' Will says, his voice unexpectedly fierce. 'My love. Please. You should never have come here. Just keep your head down and don't draw attention to yourself. Trust me. It's for the best. Everything will be better next week. I told you, I'm going to sort it.'

'But . . . Poppy . . .' Bonnie says.

'For God's sake! Will you listen to me? Poppy's fine! Stay out of it.'

Bonnie's hands fly to her face.

'Oh God, darling, please don't cry. I'm sorry I snapped. But I have to go. I have to go.'

He places a hand on her stomach, looking down at it.

There's a rustling from behind the trees and I hurry back to my tent, scared they might have seen me. Inside, I pull my dressing gown tighter round my shoulders. I'm cold to the bone.

What the hell is going on?

SELINA

'Goodnight from me and the bump.'

I'm immensely relieved to read Georgia's Instagram post from this evening. She's taken the picture in the bathroom block, and hasn't mentioned anything about what a massive mess this weekend has become.

No, that's negative thinking. It's not a mess. All of the guests – apart from Poppy – are happy, having a good time. I've given them all good advice.

All except Poppy. Well, at least she's gone now.

I have no idea where the scarf came from, but it must have got lost in the woods afterwards, and I just remembered wrongly.

I sit down on the toilet in my own bathroom and feel my insides practically unwind with relief. The only thing I need to focus on now is making sure Georgia has a good weekend. That I counsel her properly through this whole dilemma she has about telling her new boyfriend he might not be the father of her baby.

Which is the most ridiculous idea I've ever heard. What kind of idiot would tell a man that information so close to their due date? There's literally no need for him to know at all.

But all that matters is that she comes away from this weekend feeling positive, empowered . . .

She wouldn't write about Poppy in her review anyway, it'd be a breach of confidentiality. It's *me* she should be impressed with.

I just need this tiny little snowball to take off and start running, and then we'll be home and dry. The newspaper will publish the review, then more people will come to the next retreat . . . and everything will be OK.

Will will forgive me. I'll have proven to him that I'm not as hopeless as he thinks I am.

River will have the upbringing she deserves.

River.

I hate that she'll be sleeping with Kai for another night. But there was no way we could risk any of the guests seeing her. It'll be easier to explain it all away when she's older. But no one would believe that a baby that young would be left by their mother. They'd start asking questions, and I'd never be able to rely on Kai not to collapse under the pressure.

I brush my teeth and scrub my face with a home-made salt scrub then regard my reflection in the mirror. Will and I haven't slept together since . . . well, since River was born. But he's still here. That means something.

In the bedroom, I find him leaning down, rummaging through the chest of drawers on his side of the bed.

I think of the scarf. I haven't told him about it.

'What are you looking for?' I say, trying to keep my tone light, to be friendly.

'Nothing,' he says, straightening up.

246

'Why are you being so weird?' I say.

'I'm not. What are you talking about?'

'You are! You've been funny with me all weekend. It's not helpful. I need us . . . I need us to both be on the same side. It's so important that Georgia has a good time . . . I can't do this alone.'

He stares at me.

'Don't be so melodramatic,' he says, sighing. 'You're not alone. I'm here, aren't I?'

I'm so frustrated I want to scream.

'You're here, but you're not here! Not really! Something's going on. I know it. I know you!'

'Jesus Christ, Selina,' he says, rubbing his hands through his hair. 'You really are something else. I have literally bent over backwards for you, all weekend. Followed your commands like a dog. Do you think any of those women have any respect for me at all? Or do you think they all see me as a hen-pecked drip?! Do you know how it feels, to have them look me up and down like some kind of servant?'

'Oh my God, is that what this is about? Because I didn't agree to let you run your stupid cookery school first?'

'Stupid,' he says. 'Thanks very much.'

'You know what I mean.'

'No, that's just great, Selina. Tell me how you really feel.'

'No! You tell *me* how you really feel. I know you're lying about something. Hiding something. I just know it. Is it Poppy . . . did you . . .'

'What?'

I wasn't going to bring it up but I can't resist now. I yank out the scarf from where I hid it under the bed earlier.

247

'Georgia found this in the woods earlier,' I say, holding it out to him.

He shrugs.

'Do you know what it is? It's hers! She was wearing it at the time! I used it to soak up some of the blood after, look!'

I turn the scarf over and show him the stain.

'I've never seen that before in my life.'

'What?' I say. 'What are you talking about? Of course you have! It's her scarf!'

'It's disgusting, that's what it is.'

'You promised you'd sort it. But now one of our guests has found this! Evidence. Have you any idea . . .'

'What the hell are you talking about? You're delusional,' he says. 'Seriously. Completely cuckoo. And you're meant to be helping these women. Jesus.'

'Don't you dare! Don't you speak to me like that!'

Months' worth of pent-up stress is starting to unleash. I am so angry, I can barely see. I spin on the spot looking for something – anything – to throw at him. The only thing to hand is the huge lump of Himalayan pink salt on the chest of drawers by the bed.

I grab it, its rough uneven texture like a thousand pins and needles against my skin, and I throw it as hard as I can at Will.

He ducks but he's tired and he's too slow and too late. The rock hits him on the side of the head, and he falls to the floor.

NICKY

The wind is literally howling outside my tent. It's so insubstantial a shelter and I feel so vulnerable, especially after what happened earlier.

We discussed it again before bed and Bonnie suggested that perhaps someone had tripped over the guy ropes and pulled them loose, then tried to put them back and done it wrong. It didn't sound that convincing.

Either way, someone *must* have been fiddling with the ropes on my tent for it to collapse like that. There was no way it could have been the wind.

And it's even windier tonight. There's nothing but patchwork flimsy fabric protecting me from the elements. And what happens if the tent collapses again, with me inside?

Unsurprisingly, I'm finding it impossible to sleep. I've tried – I've tossed and turned, I've listened to a meditation podcast, tried to read a book on the app on my phone, then spent hours scrolling through photos of the kids, which only woke me up more.

Part of me wants to get in the car right now and drive home to my babies.

Bonnie doesn't seem to have been enjoying herself much

either. She's been so difficult the whole time – angry, tense, mocking. But also, seemingly excited and distracted.

Earlier this morning, Poppy whispered something to me at the end of breakfast.

You can't trust her.

It was quite peculiar and at the time I thought she was talking about Selina, but now I'm not sure. Did she actually mean my sister Bonnie?

What the hell is going on?

And why was Selina so twitchy about us going into the pigsty earlier, to look for Poppy? I've been lied to so many times by the kids at school, I can tell when someone is hiding something.

I climb out of bed and pull my waterproof trousers over my pyjamas. The wood burner is almost out, so I put another log on, and open the grille slightly. It's comforting somehow to watch the flames, to be reminded that whatever else happens, some things remain the same. And there is nothing quite as lovely as a proper fire.

I pull on my fleece-lined coat and add my wellies to the attractive ensemble. It's just gone midnight and there's no light coming from any of the other tents. The other two must be asleep already.

Perhaps I'll just go into the kitchen, and grab a knife to hide under my pillow.

There's a light on upstairs in the main barn, but the kitchen doors are firmly closed. Two dark rectangles of glass shining in the moonlight. I try the handle but it doesn't budge.

Of course, they will have locked up for the night. It strikes

250

me as ironic that Selina has made sure she and Will are pro-
tected from harm, even though we, her cherished guests,
aren't.

Overhead, I hear an owl hooting somewhere nearby, and
when I look up, the sky is filled with tiny stars. Despite my
fears, it's absolutely beautiful to be out here, alone, the great
expanse of clear sky above me, to feel like the only person
alive.

The wind slaps my hair across my face as I make my way
round the main barn towards the vast gravel driveway, where
my car is parked, sitting waiting for me like a faithful dog.

I think again about the way Selina reacted when I suggested
we search the pigsties. It was so nuanced, such an individual
reaction. A mixture of anger, fear and something else that I
couldn't put my finger on.

I could understand her frustration at Poppy's disappearing
act, at her irritation at the thought of people poking around
her private spaces. She's incredibly house-proud – her attention to detail is one of the things that's made this weekend
special. But why the fear?

I pause for a second, realising how ridiculous it is that I'm
standing out here on a cold, dark night, trying to . . . what?

Investigate a disappearance that someone has already said
is not a disappearance?

But Will seemed like he was hiding something earlier
too.

Why didn't he tell us straight away that he had taken
Poppy to Okehampton? Why didn't he tell us before he took
her?

Why did he look so nervous; why did he keep looking across at Selina, as though 'checking in' with her?

Why did Poppy tell me not to trust someone? And who did she mean?

I make my way across the field to the pigsties. As the light from the main barn gets further and further away, it gets incrementally darker, the moonlight insufficient to see more than a few paces ahead. I have my mobile phone in my pocket, and I pull it out, but I'm too nervous to switch on the torch function just yet. Selina or Will are clearly still awake and I don't want them to look out the window and see me lit up like a Christmas tree.

My heart is thumping in my chest as I approach the pigsties. There's a dim light coming from inside. I creep round to the front. And that's when I see him.

A young man.

Sitting there, alone, on the step in front of the door.

Smoking, and flicking a lighter on and off with his thumb.

It must be Kai, Selina's son.

I know, in my heart of hearts, that now is the time to go back to my tent, and hide under my blankets.

Above me, the owl hoots again.

I take another step forward. What am I expecting to find if I confront him? Poppy, tied up inside the pigsty? Bound and gagged, her face streaked with tears?

I have definitely watched too many crime dramas lately. There's literally no reason why Selina – or Will, or Kai – would do that to her.

But what about the weird note in her journal, the burning

scarecrow, the beheaded rat? Did someone actually let my tent down deliberately? Was it a mistake, was it meant to be Georgia's tent?

I glance back at the main barn. The light in the top bedroom has gone off.

I take a deep breath and step forward.

Kai looks up at me from his seat on the step and I feel irrationally terrified. To have been caught out, to be guilty, to have done something childish and wrong.

To be a *snoop*.

'I . . .' I start. 'I'm sorry, I thought I heard something . . .'

It's only then I notice that surrounding him, like a halo, are empty bottles of beer.

I feel stupid, embarrassed. He's a teenager, and clearly I've stumbled on the place he comes to get pissed and wallow in his teenage angst.

It doesn't entirely explain why Selina was so twitchy about us looking in here earlier – but perhaps she was just worried we would find him out for the count. Or smoking a spliff.

'Are you OK?' I say, teacher mode kicking in. 'It's very cold tonight.'

Kai gives a kind of strange laugh.

'Why don't we go inside? It's pretty miserable to be sitting out here all alone in the dark. I can make you a cup of tea or something?'

'Will you read me a bedtime story too?' Kai says, looking up, and although his words were clearly intended to mock, his eyes are wide with a kind of denied longing.

'I've got two boys under eight,' I say, sitting down next to him on the step. 'I'm very much enjoying the break from reading bedtime stories this weekend.'

He sniffs again.

'I'm fed up of everyone treating me like a child. I'm nineteen years old. I'm a . . . I'm a grown man.'

'Of course.'

'Well, she needs to treat me like one,' he says, and although he hasn't said it, I can tell he's talking about Selina.

'Yes, but sometimes it's really hard, being the mum of boys,' I say. 'It shouldn't matter, but the truth is, we don't know what it's like to be a boy. All I know about my own is that they've got more energy than I could ever dream of.'

He scratches at the ground in front of him with the base of the bottle of beer he's holding.

'Don't remember much about when I was a kid,' he says eventually.

'Where did you grow up?' I ask tentatively.

'All over the place,' he says. 'She liked to move around. To move on.'

'You don't get on well with your mum at the moment,' I say, more as an observation than anything else.

He does his snort-laugh again.

'Look, I don't know her, but I know she's probably just doing her best. Like most mothers.'

I think about how scared I was that I'd find Poppy here, injured or worse. And although I feel some sense of relief that this is clearly not a horrible crime scene, the hostility Kai feels towards his mum doesn't exactly reassure me that all is well.

Perhaps he let down my tent? Perhaps he wants to sabotage this weekend for her?

'Her best,' he says. 'Yeah. That's what she always says too.'

'I'm sure she loves you very much.'

I have the sense that I am out of my depth now, and no idea how I'll extricate myself from this situation. Serves me right for poking about where I don't belong.

'That's the thing. I'm not sure she does love me. I ruined her life, and she's never going to let me forget it.'

He suddenly starts to sob. Great, heaving sobs that take me by surprise. He leans forward on his arms and from nowhere it feels as though his whole body is convulsing.

Alarmed, I put my arm around him.

I try to imagine I'm comforting Seb after a nightmare, and sit there on the cold hard earth and shush and stroke him, as though he's the child he just insisted he wasn't.

SUNDAY MORNING

Do you think about her death?

I do. Often.

Not just in my nightmares either. But also when I'm walking around, you know, living my life. It'll catch me off guard, an invisible wounding by an unseen force.

The thoughts of her last moments on this earth are the most excruciating of all.

I imagine the pain on her face, the way it would have twisted and distorted with the realisation of what was happening.

I imagine her mouth, wide open and screaming, before her breath disappeared forever.

That's difficult enough.

But worse still, I imagine you. What you were thinking. What you were saying. How you were trying to convince yourself – and them – that the course of action you took was the right one. That it was in any way defensible.

That's what torments me.

You.

Just you.

The cause of her death.

BONNIE

'Good morning, good morning, good morning!'

The sound is coming from outside. I pull my duvet over my head.

'Five minutes until morning meditation starts! Hope to see you all there!'

Selina pokes her head through the entrance to my tent. What the actual . . .

'Morning!' she says. I peer at her through blurry eyes. Her face looks almost frantic.

'What time is it?'

'Nearly eight! Freshen up and then meet us in the studio for meditation – I promise you'll feel better for it.'

'Urggh,' is the only reply I can manage.

How can she be so cheerful? I'm beginning to seriously question her sanity. After what Will's told me about her in the past – sketchy stuff mostly, but even so, the whole vibe was weird – and now her behaviour this weekend. It's like she's on drugs.

And what about Poppy? Doesn't anyone think it's a bit peculiar that she just upped and left yesterday without saying goodbye to anyone, and hasn't come back? Are we just going to all pretend she doesn't even exist?

I'm not sure what to do, but I'm awake now anyway, so I grumpily get up and get dressed.

The last day. God, I can't wait to go home tomorrow. I've hardly had any time alone with Will. No plans have been made, nothing's been sorted.

I was an idiot really, coming here. I thought it would force his hand. Make him realise things can't continue like this.

I know how sensitive he is, how kind and concerned he is to do the right thing by Selina and Kai. But it hasn't changed anything.

In fact, it's pushed him further away.

I check my phone. He hasn't replied to the text I sent him earlier. I always send him the same message, every day, wishing him a good morning. He usually replies within minutes.

As I walk to the bathroom block I see Nicky coming out.

'Hi,' I say. The morning sun is making me squint. 'How did you sleep?'

She looks dreadful. Really knackered, like she did when I went to visit her after Seb was born.

'Not great,' she says. 'I heard some noises in the night.'

'Foxes?'

'I don't know,' she says. She won't look me in the eye. 'Maybe. To be honest, I . . .'

She sounds weirdly sad.

'I'm really looking forward to going home.'

'Oh God, me too!'

261

'I feel bad, I know it was your idea to come here and that you meant well . . .'

'It's not exactly gone how I planned,' I say, looking back at the barn. The kitchen doors are thrown open as usual, but there's no sign of Will inside. I look over at the studio. Selina, replete in yoga pants and gym top, is busy lining up the mats on the floor.

'I'm sorry I suggested it,' I say, looking directly at Nicky. She frowns at me, but reaches out a hand and rests it on my arm.

'You were trying to be nice,' she says. 'Don't be daft. It was really kind of you.'

'Yes, but . . .'

'You weren't to know Selina was a total nutjob,' she whispers, and I laugh. I love it when Nicky's inappropriate. It's so rare, but it reminds me she's human.

'And I'm sorry about yesterday,' I say, looking down. 'In the kitchen.'

'What?'

'When you asked me about the baby's father. I'm just scared you'll judge me. I'm scared I've been a fool . . .'

'Oh, Bonnie,' she says. 'I won't judge you. I promise.'

'It's just . . .' I say. 'I'm scared I might . . . the dad . . . he might not be able to handle it. I'm frightened I might have to do it on my own, after all.'

'Oh, sprat,' Nicky says, squeezing my hand. 'You'll never be alone. You know that. We all love you.'

I nod.

'I just . . . I know you all think I'm a failure, that getting pregnant was the worst thing I could have done. But I thought it was going to work out. I really did.'

262

'And now you don't?'

I shake my head.

'I don't know. Maybe. I still hope so. It's . . . complicated.'

'Well, you know you can always talk to me about it. If you want to.'

I smile.

'Thanks. Do you think . . .' I say tentatively. 'Do you think we should take another look in Poppy's tent? See if we missed anything?'

'I don't know,' she says. 'It's an invasion of her privacy, isn't it?'

'I know but . . .'

'Let's ask Selina whether she's heard from her first. See you in the studio,' she says.

In the bathroom block I think about why I invited Nicky.

It wasn't just to get Jon to pay for our places, was it? Am I really that shallow and awful a person?

No, it was worse than that. It was because I wanted some back-up, for when the shit hit the fan.

I was too cowardly to face this situation alone. I wanted to feel like I had someone on my team next to me. Someone who would *have* to love me, despite everything I'd done.

I'm going to make more effort with Nicky. To focus on her for the rest of our time here. And make the most of the yoga, seeing as, actually, I do quite enjoy it.

I lift my top and stroke my minuscule bump. I'm fourteen weeks today – the app on my phone told me. I haven't really thought much about the baby lately. I've been too busy thinking about the dad.

As I brush my teeth I remember the way that Will promised me – the way he swore – that he had taken Poppy to Okehampton yesterday. I can't believe he would lie to my face, just like that.

But I'm scared now. I'm scared I don't know him at all. The way he warned me off – told me that I should never have come here.

Stay away from her! You don't know what you're dealing with!

I've never heard him speak like that before. He's always been so kind, so loving. To me, at least.

What if Will is actually a psychopath? What if he's not the person I thought he was?

From nowhere, the waves of nausea come, and before I have time to think straight, I find myself leaning over the toilet, retching. As I do, I think about the way Selina proudly told us that the toilets were completely eco-friendly. Sawdust toilets, where the waste is shovelled out and composted over time. The thought of this makes me retch even more.

I start to cry. I just want to go home, but at the same time, my 'home' is a shared house with a bunch of students. We constantly run out of loo roll and have had to enforce a cleaning rota because the bathroom gets so filthy.

That's not the home I want.

I want the home that Nicky has. That Georgia has – I've seen pics of it all over Instagram. It might be small but it's certainly perfectly formed. All soothing shades of grey with splashes of tasteful patterns on the blinds and cushions. Her kitchen worktop is marble – but not actual marble, as she told her followers in a kind of smug but helpful way.

It's actually composite stone, but doesn't it look like the real thing?! Half the price, twice as strong! I LOVE IT!

Her baby is going to grow up surrounded by lovely things and is going to go to lovely baby clubs and have lovely friends and wear clothes from posh boutiques on the King's Road.

And then there's Nicky – Nicky's baby is going to grow up in chaos, wearing hand-me-downs but surrounded by that safe, stable love that I used to think was boring but that I now, suddenly, completely understand.

And me? My baby is going to have a father who doesn't keep his promises. And a mother who's still in college and has no idea how the hell she's going to provide for them. I'll be relying on handouts from local charities, and then after a few months I'll probably give up and move back into the three-bed semi I grew up in with my mum and dad.

And Mum will hover over me all the time telling me I'm doing everything wrong, and the baby will probably prefer her to me, and everyone will agree that I had the baby too young, and what a fool I was.

Is this my punishment for being the 'bit on the side'?

No. He promised we were different.

I'm not going to let Selina stand in the way.

I leave the bathroom block and scan the field around the tents. No sign of anyone else. I look at the barn, but the back of the building is in shadow and it's impossible to tell whether there might be anyone at the window, watching us.

I square my shoulders. So what if they see me?

Without hesitating, I let myself into Poppy's tent. Everything's in the same place as it was yesterday, when I found her journal in the bed. I crouch down beside the bed and rummage through her bag, but there's nothing interesting in there. Just clothes. No washbag that I can find. The bedside tables are bare – just the lavender pillow spray and small vase of wildflowers that were there when we arrived. The towels Selina provided are folded over the armchair in the corner of the room. Poppy hasn't made use of the hanging rack.

I sit on the rush floor, frustrated. And then I spot it. Something squishy wedged under the bed. I twist my neck to get a better look, before moving onto all fours.

It looks like a cushion. I pull it out. It's wrapped in a baby blanket, and as I unfold the fabric and reveal what's inside, I recoil in disgust.

Something slimy, made of flesh-coloured silicone.

A silicone baby bump.

GEORGIA

I'm first to arrive for the meditation session. Selina is wiping down the mats. I feel a pang of guilt as I watch her, thinking of what I heard and saw last night. She clearly has no idea that Bonnie and Will are having an affair. I turned it over in my mind repeatedly when I was back in bed, trying to work out exactly how involved the two are. Does this mean Will is the father of Bonnie's baby? It would make sense, in one way, but the sheer brazenness of Bonnie to come on this retreat if so . . . And to sit there, smiling at Selina as though she has nothing to hide.

I can't quite believe it. I want to be wrong. I want to have misinterpreted it all.

It's not my place to tell Selina what I saw; I should probably confront Bonnie instead. But part of me also thinks I should just mind my own business.

'Morning,' I say, as brightly as possible. Selina turns around and beams at me.

'Good morning,' she says. 'How did you sleep?'

The pang of guilt turns into a tidal wave. She's so kind. She's tried so hard this weekend, against all the issues – the unpredictable weather, Poppy's behaviour, her partner being, well, distant and, even more awfully, the kind of man that has got another woman pregnant.

'I slept really well, thank you,' I say. 'How about you?'

She smiles.

'Oh, I always sleep like a baby,' she says.

I stand like an awkward statue for a few moments. Inside my mouth, the question is trying to escape. *How's Will?*

But I don't let it.

Selina hands me a glass of mint water.

'Thanks,' I say, taking a sip.

'The others will be here soon,' she says, smiling again. Her skin seems even slacker today. As though she's lost weight overnight.

'Any word from Poppy?' I say, because it stops me asking the other question.

'No,' Selina says, putting a blanket down beside each yoga mat. 'Maybe it just wasn't for her, this weekend.'

'It's so strange,' I say.

'Yes,' she says, pausing briefly, 'but what can you do?'

I open my mouth – I'm about to say, 'Well, you could probably try and look up her next of kin and get in touch with them' – but I decide it's not my place to put any more pressure on her.

'Please,' she says, gesturing to the mat nearest my feet. 'Have a seat, child's pose or cross-legged, whatever's more comfortable for you. I'm sure the others won't be long. We had some reluctant risers this morning . . .'

I smile and then sit down on the mat, folding my legs under me. As I do so, I feel a stab of pain in my left side.

'Ow,' I say, my hand automatically rubbing the area.

Selina paces over.

'Are you OK?'

'Yes, yes, I think so. Just a twinge. I've been getting them . . .'

'Braxton Hicks?' she offers.

'Is it not too early?'

'Georgia, I've been a mid— I've worked with pregnant women for more than fifteen years, I can tell you're further along than you said. Not only that, you admitted it when you told me you had fertility treatment last year. I'm not great at maths, but I can do it at a push! Why did you feel you had to lie about it?'

'I was worried you wouldn't want me to come. That you might worry about me going into labour or something.'

'Georgia, I would absolutely love you to go into labour. I mean, probably not right now, we want Baby to cook a bit more first, but helping mothers give birth is my greatest passion in life. It would be an honour to have a baby born here at The Sanctuary. And what a wonderful story for our first ever weekend!'

I smile.

'Well, I'll bear that in mind,' I say. 'But I think Brett would be very disappointed to miss the birth. He's been going on about it for ages.'

'He'd get over it!' Selina says, waving a hand. She seems louder this morning, more frantic and less considered in her speech and mannerisms. Perhaps she's finally beginning to relax with us. 'Now, promise you'll tell me if you get any other pains. How far along exactly are you?'

'Just gone eight months.'

'Right. Well, it's good to keep moving – you don't want to become a complete vegetable. But at the same time, you must give your body lots of time to rest too. This is when the heavy lifting starts – the baby starts to get big and fat and strong so that she can survive in the outside world.'

'Oh, it's a boy,' I say.

She pauses, looking at me.

'Really?' she says. 'Interesting. I could have sworn you were having a girl.'

'Nope, we've had three 3D scans, plus the blood test that tells you the sex. We're going to call him Calvin.'

'How lovely,' Selina says.

Nicky comes into the studio.

'Morning. Sorry I'm a bit late; I know it's breaking the rules but I had to get one of these.'

I turn and smile at her. She's carrying a cup of coffee. I haven't drunk caffeine at all since I fell pregnant – I've been too nervous. It felt like an unnecessary risk.

I'm envious of her carefree attitude to her pregnancy. I guess that's the reward you get for having already had two children. Life's proven to you that it's possible, that you have nothing to fear.

Of all the women here, it's Nicky I envy the most. Despite the fact that you can tell she's a bit run-down – 'depleted' as Selina described it – she has a warmth to her that can surely only come from being surrounded by loved ones.

'Didn't sleep?' I say, smiling at her as she sits on the mat next to me.

'Oh no, I . . . I thought I heard something. Owls perhaps. I got up to investigate but . . .' She pauses. She doesn't look at Selina. 'I get a really overactive imagination when I'm pregnant. Last time I started having the strangest dreams.'

'All totally normal,' Selina says. 'You can blame your lovely friends the hormones for that.'

'Bane of women's lives,' Nicky says, stretching her arms above her head.

'There's lots you can take to help balance them,' Selina says. 'Once Baby's here, of course. Evening primrose is great – I've got some handouts on this I can give you later.'

'Thanks,' Nicky says, but I can tell there's something bothering her. I suppose she's probably worried about Poppy too. 'That'd be great.'

'And Bonnie! Last but by no means least,' Selina says.

Bonnie is standing in the doorway, her hair piled on top of her head in a bird's nest of a bun. She's not wearing any shoes or socks, and her feet are wet from the morning dew on the grass.

My jaw tenses. How can she be so shameless? I'm going to have to confront her.

'Full house, excellent. Let's get started. We'll just do a quick fifteen-minute meditation and then we'll reward ourselves with breakfast.'

SELINA

I've been up since 5am getting everything ready. I had no choice, of course, because as usual, I'm alone in this now.

It's my fault, I guess, but I am alone.

'No Will?' Bonnie asks, as we settle round the table after our morning meditation session. She takes a huge helping of his special granola. There's not much of it left, and it costs a fortune to make with all the various raw ingredients and expensive dried fruit in it. Georgia looks miffed, helps herself to a small spoonful and tops it up with berries and yoghurt.

'He's had to go and help a friend today,' I say, staring her straight in the eye. 'So it's just us girls.'

'Oh, that's a shame,' Bonnie says.

'And Kai?' Nicky asks.

'Oh, Kai's probably still asleep.' I smile, hoping my tone will tell them not to ask any more.

Nicky doesn't reply. She's been acting strangely all morning. Perhaps she heard something? No, she can't have done.

When the rock hit Will and he fell, he didn't make a noise. No shouting, no screaming. Maybe a dull thump, but nothing more than that.

I close my eyes to block out the visions that swim to my mind.

'More tea, Georgia?' I say, offering her the pot, which she takes. 'I can't believe it's our last day together today. So, just to say, I hope you all feel you've moved forward with your aims, and that you're ready to face the challenge of motherhood. Having got to know you a little, I can honestly say that I have no doubts you are all more than capable of being the most wonderful mothers. You just need to trust yourselves a little more. But we'll talk about that more today. So, we have yoga at ten thirty am, and then lunch. After that, you have a free afternoon – no unannounced trips to Okehampton though, please! If you'd like, Badger has volunteered to take anyone who's interested on a little tour of the vegetable and kitchen garden. He's very passionate about his plants. Then we'll come together for our exciting tea-brewing session – using flowers and herbs you'll pick yourself – and after that we have dinner, followed by our amazing fireside session! I can't wait for that; it's a truly magical experience. And then, one by one, we'll spend the time literally burning your fears. I hope that all sounds good. Any questions?'

'Will Poppy be coming back?' Nicky says.

I take a deep breath. Fucking Poppy.

'I'm afraid I simply don't know,' I reply. 'I've left her another message.'

'It's a bit worrying. Should someone go and check she's at her friend's or something?'

'I'll send Will over there later, if we haven't heard anything. Don't worry. I'm sure she's absolutely fine.'

'Technically speaking, she shouldn't come back. She wasn't even pregnant,' Bonnie says.

'What?' Nicky turns her head.

I stare at Bonnie. I can't tell if she's making this up or not. It wouldn't surprise me.

'She was pretending,' Bonnie says. 'I found a fake silicone baby bump in her tent.'

'Are you sure?' Nicky says, frowning. 'Why . . . why would she do that?'

'God knows,' Bonnie says. 'But she's definitely got some kind of agenda.'

'Wow,' Georgia says quietly. 'How bizarre.'

'I . . .' I say, interrupting. Despite the fact that my life is collapsing around my ears, the most important thing of all is that Georgia still has a good weekend. I feel like I'm clasping at the edge of a lifeboat, my fingers slipping as the sea tries to drag me under. 'I did speak to Poppy in our one-to-one and I'm afraid that you're right, Bonnie.'

The lies come so easily, I impress myself. They all look at me wide-eyed.

'As you might know, she lost her baby last year, and she's been having a very difficult time – understandably – ever since. She confessed everything to me when we spoke, and I'm sure that's why she left the retreat. She probably feels very ashamed. I've reached out to her, and she knows she's very welcome to come back whenever she wants to but . . . what I really want to say to you all is – please don't worry about her. I know we all care – and it's great that you do – but she's my prob— issue. And I want you to have the best weekend – it's so important to me that you put your own needs first today. It's not for you to worry about. Now, if you'll excuse me, I'll leave you to it. I have to go and feed the chickens.'

I hurry out of the kitchen doors and go back round to the front of the barn, letting myself in. Then, with trepidation, I climb the spiral stairs and push open the door to our bedroom.

Will is lying in the dark on his side.

He grunts at me as I come in.

'How are you feeling?' I say, as I try to muster up some sympathy for him. 'There's a kitchen full of people downstairs wondering how you are.'

'My head is killing me,' he says.

I march over to the window and pull back the curtains, letting the bright sunlight flood the room.

'Ugh,' he says, rolling over, his hands over his face. 'It's too bright.'

'Let me see your head,' I say, kneeling down next to him. 'Don't be such a baby. It's only a scratch.'

Last night he lay on the floor for several minutes after the rock hit him, and even though I was terrified, deep down I somehow knew that it was all for show. That he was fine, he just couldn't bear to face me. He just wanted me to go away.

I've felt like that a lot recently. Like he wishes he had never met me. Despite everything I've done for him – the purpose I've given him. This place. This business. This amazing business, that would be viable if only he would meet me halfway.

He wasn't even knocked unconscious.

I pull off the wadding I taped over the wound last night. Underneath is a sticky mess, his thick curly hair entangled in

275

the layers of shredded skin. An orangey viscous liquid seeps out.

Two head injuries in two days. What are the chances.

'You'll probably need stitches,' I say. 'Fuck.'

'It's fine,' he says. 'I just have a headache. Leave it.'

He pulls the wadding away from me and tries to stick it back down on the wound, but the surgical tape has lost its stickiness.

'You can't stay in bed all day,' I say, going to the chest of drawers. The first-aid kit lies sprawled open on top. I cut some more surgical tape and push the original dressing back over it. He winces as I press down hard on the sides of his head to make sure it stays put.

'My head is killing me,' he says. 'Just let me sleep it off for a bit.'

'What am I going to tell people? They're already asking where you are. We're meant to be a team. Remember that? Remember what you promised me?! You and me, against the world?'

'What are they saying?'

'Bonnie seemed quite upset you weren't there this morning,' I reply. 'Perhaps she has a little crush?'

'Don't be stupid.'

I stare at him. I'm being paranoid. He'd never do that to me. I know he wouldn't. Things have been difficult between us over the past year but we are unbreakable. I know that.

I blame that fucking scarf. It's thrown me.

'I'm sorry,' I say, with difficulty. 'It's just been an immensely stressful weekend. And all these things keep going wrong . . .

sometimes it feels as though I'm cursed. All these reminders of her . . . it's like her ghost . . . She's here, haunting us! She won't leave me alone.'

'Jesus, Selina. Don't be silly. You just need to relax. Take some of your own medicine from time to time.'

'It's not just that . . . You and me . . .'

'What about us?'

'We're OK, aren't we? It's just . . . it feels as though things have been off between us for a while now and . . .'

He doesn't say anything.

'My head's really hurting,' he says. 'I think I should get some rest. Let's have this discussion another time.'

I swallow away my anger. He's right. We don't have time for this now. But even so. I want to cry. Why won't he tell me he loves me? Why won't he do it?

It's all I've ever wanted. To be loved.

I close my eyes. An image floats to my mind, of myself when I was much younger. I wish I could reach through the mists of time and wrap my arms around twenty-three-year-old Selina, who's still so hurt and broken, and reassure her that, if nothing else, I love her and I always will.

NICKY

There's about half an hour to go before our yoga session.

'What do you make of the Poppy thing?' Bonnie says.

'I think it's really sad. If it's true . . . then, well, it's heart-breaking. I accidentally walked in on her in the bathroom block when we first arrived and she bit my head off. Now I know why. She must have been worried I'd see the fake bump.'

'I don't know,' Bonnie says, frowning. 'There's something about it that doesn't make sense. Why would she be so hostile? And what did she have against Selina? It was all so peculiar.'

'Because she's grieving,' I say. 'I expect she's incredibly jealous of us all.'

Another pang of guilt hits me as I remember telling Poppy that my pregnancy was unplanned. The poor woman, how heartless and selfish I must have seemed.

'There's still something fishy about it all, if you ask me. What if she's done something awful?' Bonnie says.

'Like what?'

'I don't know . . . harmed herself in some way?'

'I'm sure she's fine,' I say, more to reassure Bonnie than anything else. 'Will says he dropped her off in town and she was fine.'

'Hmm. Where are you off to?' she says, as I gather my stuff together and stand up from the kitchen table.

I know it's not my problem, but I can't get the image of Kai crying on that step out of my mind. I can't trust Selina enough to ask her if he's OK, and so I want to go in search of Will.

'Er . . . I wanted to ask Will something. About last night's recipe. It was delicious. Thought I'd take a wander and try to find him.'

'Selina said he'd gone into town, remember?' Bonnie says, eyeing me suspiciously. She's eating a bowl of fruit salad now, on her second cup of coffee.

'Oh yes, silly me. I'll just have a little walk then.'

Bonnie frowns but lets me go without any more fuss. I smile at Georgia who's, as usual, doing something on her phone, and slip out of the room.

I'm confused about what Selina said about Will, because his Land Rover is still parked outside the front of the house, and it doesn't seem to have moved since he arrived back yesterday afternoon. Perhaps they have another car.

I wish I had Poppy's number and could check she was all right, or at least apologise, but I guess Selina is right about one thing – she's an adult, and this isn't a prison. We're not friends, after all; we barely know each other. If she wants to leave, there's not much we can do to stop her.

It's overcast again now and I hug my hoodie tighter round myself as I walk towards the wildflower meadow, which is alive with bees. Just beyond this area is the kitchen garden. I gaze over at it. In the middle of it all is a beautiful greenhouse. Inside, I can see someone moving about.

Perhaps it's Kai.

When I left him last night, he had stopped crying, but he wasn't really talking, and I couldn't get any more out of him. I still have no idea what exactly was so upsetting for him.

I'd looked back over my shoulder one last time as I walked away. He'd probably fallen into a drunken coma and woken up with a headache and barely any memory of our conversation, or his emotional meltdown.

But even so. Being a teenager is tough, and thinking about the way Kai was last night got me thinking about all the kids at school that I used to have to look after.

I could always recognise the vulnerable ones – the ones that put on a little too much bravado in front of their classmates, but deep down cared what marks they got. The ones whose parents forgot to turn up for parents' evening, or turned up and spent the whole time staring at me blank-faced, expectant, wondering what it was I wanted from them.

But Selina. Surely she's not like that? She's a midwife. Surely she cares about her son?

I'm nearly at the greenhouse entrance now and I realise that, of course, the vision inside the condensation-lined windows isn't Kai. It's Badger.

Still, he probably knows quite a bit about the situation.

I tap on the window and he looks up. He frowns momentarily but then gestures for me to come in.

'Sorry!' I say, closing the door behind me. It's incredibly humid in the greenhouse, and I can almost feel my hair curling in the heat. 'Don't want to disturb you.'

He's staking tomato plants. I know because we did it last

weekend – the boys tried to help, but it all got a bit stressful and in the end Jon finished the job alone while I gave them their tea.

'That's an impressive crop,' I say, nodding towards the vines bursting with green tomatoes.

'Easy-peasy,' Badger says. 'It's the celery we're having trouble with. All leaves and no stalks. They don't like variations in temperature, you see. They end up bolting too early.'

'I've never tried celery,' I say. 'But there's nothing quite like growing your own food, is there?'

'Most satisfying thing in the world,' Badger says. He leans over and picks up a thermos from the shelf behind me, then takes a swig.

'Cold,' he says, pulling a face. 'Selina makes it for me every morning but I forget to drink it. Get so damn engrossed in here.'

'Don't you get a break?'

'A break? What from? I love it. The work keeps me sane. You've got to find work in life that keeps you healthy, otherwise, well . . . What do you do?'

'Oh,' I say, slightly embarrassed. 'I'm . . . I'm a teacher.'

'Most important job in the world. I'd doff my cap to you if I had one, but I can never get them over my curls.'

I laugh. His hair is chin-length and impressively untamed.

'I haven't worked for a few years now though. Not since my second son was born. And now . . .'

I look down at my small, but visible, bump.

'That's OK,' Badger says, 'you're still raising the next generation. Wish my mum had been a teacher. Would have made my life very different.'

281

'I suppose,' I reply. 'Being a mum's not quite the same though. I miss it. I was a secondary school teacher, specialising in pastoral support.'

He frowns.

'Oh, kids who had extra challenges. I worked in some of the most deprived schools around Bristol. It was great. Exhausting, stressful, but so rewarding . . .'

I tail off. I'm not meant to be talking about that.

'That's why I wanted to talk to you actually,' I say, feeling my cheeks flush. 'It's just . . . I don't suppose it's appropriate for me to ask Selina, but I saw Kai last night and . . .'

'What's he said?' Badger says, setting down his thermos.

'Nothing,' I say. 'That was just it. He was . . . well, I thought I heard a noise, so I went to investigate and I found him in the pigsty – you know, round the front. He said he sleeps in there, but that can't be right, can it? Why doesn't he sleep in the barn with Selina and Will? We got chatting and he'd had quite a lot to drink. But then he started to cry, and he said all this stuff about his mum, and I just . . . I don't know. He seemed very fragile.'

I think about Poppy, her warning that Selina couldn't be trusted. But then, she was the one who was lying all along.

'I guess I'm worried about him. Can't help it, occupational hazard . . .'

'He's had a hard time lately,' Badger says, turning back to his tomatoes. 'I shouldn't tell you this but . . . a few months back, he tried to kill himself.'

'Oh God,' I say. 'I'm so sorry. I should never have pried.'

Badger looks at me.

'It's all right. He's getting the help he needs. You really don't need to worry about Kai,' he says. 'He's got lots of people looking out for him. He'll be OK.'

I smile and nod.

'I'll leave you to it,' I say, turning to go out of the greenhouse. 'I did want to say though, what an amazing job you've done – with the grounds and everything. It's just glorious. Selina and Will are very lucky to have you.'

'The flowers of all the tomorrows are in the seeds of today,' he says, looking past my shoulder. His eyes flick back to meet mine. 'Just remember that.'

I'm not sure how to respond, so I just smile, and leave him to it.

BONNIE

Clearly, Will hasn't gone into town, because his Land Rover is parked out the front. I try his mobile, despite the obvious risks – Selina could walk in at any moment – but he doesn't answer.

That's not that weird – he's quite often 'unavailable' when I try to call him – but the fact that Selina lied about where he was certainly is.

Perhaps he's with Poppy. Perhaps . . . No, surely he can't be seeing Poppy too? That can't be it.

But why would she have come on this retreat otherwise? Why would she pretend to be pregnant?

My heart thumps. Pregnancy hormones are making me paranoid. Of course he's not seeing Poppy.

I finish my third breakfast of the day – I'm finally getting the hang of this eating-for-two thing. Nicky has left and it's just Georgia and me in here. I carry my bowl over to the sink and look across at her.

Our eyes meet. She doesn't smile.

'Are you OK?' I say, confused.

'I know,' she says. 'I know about you and Will.'

'What?' I say, choking on a laugh.

'You know what I'm talking about, Bonnie.'

'He's my tutor at college,' I concede. 'I didn't want to make a big fuss . . .'

'Not that,' she says. 'I know that he's the father of your baby.'

I take a step backwards, as though that might put some distance between her words and the truth.

'Listen,' she says, her tone kinder. 'It's none of my business. But Selina's been good to me. I feel a bit . . . well, uncomfortable about the whole situation. I wanted you to know that I know. I hate being lied to.'

'I haven't lied.'

'No, I know,' she says. 'But . . . well, like I say, it's none of my business. But if I found out . . . then you ought to be aware that it's going to be easy for Selina to do the same.'

'How did you find out?' I ask. There doesn't seem to be much point in denying it. And part of me almost feels excited. This was what I wanted, after all, wasn't it? This was the whole reason I came on this weekend.

'I saw you talking outside,' she says. 'Last night. More than talking actually . . .'

I look down. My cheeks burn.

'I know it might sound stupid to you, but we're in love.'

Georgia screws her nose up and looks away.

'We are,' I say, and suddenly my eyes are damp with tears. 'It's been so difficult . . .'

'I don't really want to get involved,' Georgia says. 'Sorry. It's just . . . no good ever came from being the middleman.'

'He wants to leave her,' I say, ignoring what she's said. 'He does; it's just very difficult with Kai . . .'

285

'I'm sure he wasn't expecting you to get pregnant,' she says shortly.

'No,' I reply. 'It wasn't exactly planned.'

He didn't plan it anyway.

'Like I say,' Georgia says, raising her arms. 'None of my business.'

'I didn't know he had a partner,' I say. I reach out and grab her arm. 'He wasn't wearing a wedding ring. I had no idea. I'd been out drinking with some of my course mates and he was there in the corner of the pub, with a pint of bitter and looking fed up. I'd invited him over to our table and he'd refused to tell us what was making him look so miserable, but he cheered up as we got talking and drinking more. And then afterwards, the others thinned out until there was only me and him left.'

'You don't need to tell me any of this,' Georgia says, her eyes widening. 'I actually don't want to know.'

'Please,' I say. 'I'd really like to. Please.'

It's suddenly so important for me to get this off my chest. To unburden myself.

She takes a deep breath.

'All right,' she says. 'Can we sit down though? My back is killing me.'

'It was just before Christmas. We were both very drunk when he walked me home,' I say. 'But I honestly thought he was single. We hadn't talked about his home life, or anything like that. We'd just been talking about college, taking the piss out of one of the other teachers, all that kind of stupid banter. Then he came in for another drink and one thing led to another . . . I thought it might have been a one-off but he took my number and called the next day, and he was kind and seemed concerned about how I was, and how I was feeling about everything that happened.'

She raises an eyebrow.

'I know. I thought the same. Was he just covering his back though? Did he think he might get reported to the college? We were both consenting adults, it wasn't like he was my teacher at school or anything. But then it started to get weird. It didn't take much to work out he had a long-term partner that he lived with. That I'd been that idiot, that fool. And then a few months after we got together, I found out I was pregnant.'

'I'm sorry that happened to you,' she says. 'But you must be able to see now that you were deceived? That he's not a nice person, and he can't be trusted?'

'I know I'm the oldest cliché in the book, but I love him. And I think he loves me too. I really do . . . But there's something holding him back.

'He's scared of upsetting Selina, of leaving Kai. I thought if I came here, it would, well, force his hand, I suppose . . . I thought the second he saw me he'd confess all – or at least, later that night, he'd call me in and we'd tell Selina together, hand in hand, and hope for the best. But that first night when he first saw me, he ignored me completely, and it hurt. Then later, when everyone was in bed, he came to find me in my tent and told me I shouldn't have come. That hurt too. A lot. But then I saw how Kai was, and then peculiar Poppy got thrown into the mix, and I could see that I was wrong. It wasn't the right time to be telling anyone anything, and I'd just have to be patient. So that's what I'm doing. Being patient. I don't exactly have much choice though, to be fair.'

Georgia takes another deep breath.

'Oh, honey,' she says. 'What a mess.'

'I'll be all right,' I say defiantly. 'If he doesn't want to leave. I know I can cope. I've got Nicky's support. And I'm glad I came. It's been so good to see things up close, for how they really are. After all these months of being "told" the way things were. I mean, clearly, it won't be easy for him to untangle himself from her life. Not given this place, and Kai. But that doesn't mean it won't happen.'

'I think you have to be prepared for the fact it might not though,' Georgia says.

'But I'm carrying his baby! He might be fond of Kai, but Kai isn't his biological child. He said he and Selina couldn't have children, that something terrible went wrong when she was giving birth to Kai. He told me it broke his heart when she told him because he's always wanted to be a dad. A real dad. So surely, once the baby is born, everything will change? I'm sure of it anyway. I just need to be patient.'

I'm convincing myself more than her.

'What about Selina?' Georgia says. 'Don't you think . . . it was a bit cruel coming here? She will find out eventually, surely, and then it'll be like you've rubbed her face in it.'

I shrug.

Have I thought about Selina at all, in this situation? Yes, of course I have. Over the past few months, I have endlessly obsessed over her: her thoughts and feelings, the ethics of what I've been doing.

'If he loves you, why didn't he just leave?' Georgia says, her questioning gaze so intense I have to look down.

'I told you,' I say feebly. 'Because of Kai. And . . . and . . .'

I tail off. The truth is that I don't know the answer to that question. It's the question that has taunted and haunted me every night since I found out I was pregnant.

The question that fills me with shame, that makes me feel as though I am letting myself down. That I'm deluded. That I'm a stupid fool.

Why won't he just leave her?

I don't know.

All I know is that something terrible happened to them last year, and that he can't – or won't – tell me about it.

GEORGIA

It's none of my business.

None.

But still.

Selina. Poor Selina.

I decide to take a quick walk around the grounds before yoga, to see if it helps my backache. It's not raining, but it's chilly and dull. It's such a shame we only had that beautiful bright sunshine on Friday.

I'm glad to be going home tomorrow. Even though I was desperate to escape, I now can't wait to get back to my own surroundings. I suddenly feel a strong desire to start nesting. I stroke my bump. Not long now.

I follow the gravel path round the edge of the garden and up to the brick wall that divides this part from the wildflower meadow. Here, you can't be seen from the barn. I pause for a minute, leaning against the bricks, taking deep lungfuls of air. And then I hear something surprising.

The sound of someone crying.

But it's not a woman. It's a man.

I peer round the corner of the wall. There, sitting on the ground, is Will, his knees drawn up to his head, his arms wrapped round himself. He is crying. On one side of his head is a huge white gauze, stuck down with surgical tape.

The sight of him is so shocking that I almost stumble backwards. He hasn't noticed me. I stand for a few seconds, staring, wondering whether I should just sneak off and pretend I never saw anything. But then he gives a great heaving sob and looks up.

'I'm so sorry!' I say, as though I've been caught stealing. 'I . . .'

He stares at me. His face is red and blotchy.

'Shit,' he says. He draws his hand across his eyes in an aggressive swipe.

'I'm sorry,' I say. 'I wasn't . . . I just wanted to go for a walk. Are you OK?'

He stares at me, eyes wide. And then he shakes his head.

'I can't do it any more,' he says. 'I just . . . can't. I can't play this role any more.'

I take a deep breath and walk a few steps towards him. Then, with difficulty, I lower myself onto the ground and sit beside him.

'Are you talking about Bonnie?' I say. 'Because . . . I know. I know what's going on. She told me.'

'God, it's all such a mess,' he says. 'I love her, you know. I really do.'

'That's what she said about you,' I say. 'But where does Selina fit into all of this?'

He shakes his head again.

'I can't talk about it,' he says. 'Things are . . . more complicated than they seem. There's stuff about her you don't know.

Oh God, I should never have agreed to this . . . to this insanity of a weekend!'

He thumps the ground beside him with his fist.

'What . . . what have you done to your head?' I say.

'Not me,' he says. 'Her.'

'Selina did this? Why?'

'Who knows why Selina does the things Selina does,' he says, staring down at the ground.

'Have you had it looked at?'

'It's fine,' he says, shifting away from me. 'It was an accident really. She was cross and she just . . . threw something and I got in the way. I don't care about that. I'm more worried about . . . about . . . everything else.'

'What?' I ask.

It's the journalist in me. I'm like a moth to a flame, unable to resist the allure of a scandal.

'You're very pregnant,' he says, looking at me. 'You have to promise me that you won't . . . The thing is . . . Selina. She's a qualified yoga teacher. That's real. But the midwife stuff . . . it's . . .'

'What?'

He gives a great sigh.

'It's not true. I'm not sure she's ever even *studied* mid-wifery. I do know she doesn't have any official qualifications. She thought it would encourage people to trust her, you know, when they did her yoga classes. She specialised in prenatal women, but there's so much competition in that space, so she started marketing herself as a former midwife, said she qualified in the States, but I had my suspicions.

292

I started to look into it recently and I think . . . I think it might all be lies.'

I blink.

'Oh God,' he says. 'I should never have told you . . . I could be wrong. There's so much stuff I don't even know. She's hiding things. A couple of years ago, she began working with this woman, giving her advice throughout her pregnancy – some kind of pregnancy counsellor, I guess – and then . . . I don't know what happened, but something went wrong . . . perhaps because of the advice she gave. I don't know for sure, but anyway, they fell out and now . . . I'm just so worried that she'll tell someone the wrong thing and their baby will be at risk.'

I'm stunned by what he's saying.

'If you knew all this . . . then why on earth did you let her organise the retreat?' I say. 'We trusted her!'

'I didn't know!' he says. 'I promise. I had my suspicions that she might have been exaggerating her achievements so I contacted the place where she said she qualified in the US. I heard back from them this morning – they have no record of her.'

He points to his head again.

'She's so unpredictable . . . you just don't know what she's like.'

'Will,' I say. 'You can't keep this to yourself . . . you need to tell someone.'

'I know but . . . I don't have any evidence. I don't know what went on. I was going to start making notes, you know. To see if there was something I could do. But when I was looking through her stuff last night, she found me, and she went ballistic, and . . .'

'Why haven't you just left her?'

'I'm trapped,' he says. 'This is my farm. *My* family's farm. I can't leave, and I can't make her leave either. She wouldn't go even if I asked her to. And what about Kai? He tried to kill himself earlier this year. He has . . . issues. I can't leave him at the moment. Not with everything he's still dealing with. He needs some stability in his life. And I don't have enough evidence to . . . what? Call the police? And then there's Bonnie. That was never meant to happen. I should have left then . . . I've made such a mess of everything . . .'

'God, Will,' I say, staring out at the flowers.

'Exactly. It's a nightmare.'

'Your head wound . . .' I say. 'That's assault. You know that.'

'It was an accident. And anyway, I'm a cheat! I deserve it.'

'Does she . . . does she know about you and Bonnie?'

He shakes his head.

'No. God, no.'

'Perhaps you should tell her,' I say. 'Perhaps she'd leave if she knew.'

'She wouldn't,' he says darkly. 'She'd more likely murder us both.'

I stare at him.

'Shit!' he says, slapping himself on the forehead with his palm. 'I shouldn't have told you all this. Oh God, what have I done? Please . . . promise me you won't tell anyone.'

'Will . . .'

'You have to promise. Please. I'll leave her. I will. Let's just finish off this blasted weekend, and then when everyone's left, I'll sort it. I'll make sure she never runs a retreat like this again.'

'I can't . . .'

'Please. There's only lunch and this afternoon to get through. She can't do any more harm. There's just the tea-infusing, and I'm leading that.'

A stabbing pain strikes the underside of my bump, as if to remind me I have more important things to think about than Selina and Will's mess.

'I don't know,' I say. 'I'll think about it.'

He nods, his eyes filling with tears again.

'I'm sorry to drag you into all this. But thank you for listening,' he says, gripping my hand. 'It's really helped. It's been . . . good to get it off my chest.'

SELINA

I am nearly at the end of my tether. After our final yoga session, during which both Georgia and Bonnie stared at me throughout, I escape to the toilet, trying to do some meditation, but I'm so overwhelmed and exhausted I find myself wanting to collapse into sobs.

I resist. I am in control of my thoughts. I am in control of myself.

I leave the toilet, the tight knot of stress still firmly lodged in my chest. It feels a little like I can't breathe. I've had panic attacks in the past, of course. After Kai's birth, they came thick and fast. Times when I felt like I was dying. Like the world was folding in on me, crushing me to nothing.

It got so bad that once I even went back to the hospital, convinced I was having a heart attack. The hospital where it all happened. The hospital that stole my life and future away from me at the age of twenty-three.

The consultant told me my symptoms were just 'panic'.

Just 'panic'. They made me breathe into a paper bag.

It helped, for a few minutes, but then the overwhelm returned. I never went back to that hospital after that.

I need Will. I can't do this weekend alone. Not when her shadow continues to follow me everywhere I go.

But as I walk into the kitchen, he is there. Miracle of miracles.

He looks terrible – purple rings under his eyes, his skin dry and flaky. But there's no time for that now. I swallow. All that matters is that we finish this retreat.

'You're up,' I say, as brightly as I can manage. 'How are you feeling?'

'All right,' he says, pushing past me. 'I'll get on with lunch.'

'What about . . .' I begin, looking at the side of his head. He's taken off the dressing and stuck a large plaster down over the area instead.

'I'll say I whacked it on a beam,' he says. 'If you're worried.'

'Of course I'm worried!' I practically shriek. 'I want to make sure you're OK. It looked nasty.'

'It was nasty,' he says, his eyes staring straight through me.

'I'm sorry, but . . . look. We have to move on. Doesn't it bother you at all that if this weekend isn't a success, it makes it ten times harder to hold one again, to build up any kind of reputation? Do you realise how people can make or break businesses online with just one shitty review? Don't you care?'

'You know what, Selina,' he says. 'I'm not sure I do. Not any more.'

'Well, I do!' I shout. 'I care! I'm determined to keep this family together. You loved me once.' I start to cry. 'You did.'

'Like I said, I'm going to start the lunch,' he says. 'You can sit here and feel sorry for yourself for the rest of the day, for all I care.'

I feel utterly hollowed out. Despite everything, I thought he adored me. That's what people said when they met him – *Oh, Selina, you can see how much he adores you*. He used to look at me with a combination of lust and intimidation that I absolutely loved. He told me I was the most fascinating woman he had ever met. He didn't even mind that I had a teenage son in tow.

Mind you, I was younger then, and that was Before. I should never have told him the truth. About my infertility. Everything changed after that.

The front door slams and I look over, wiping my eyes hurriedly. Kai has come in. His face is shiny with sweat.

'Where's River?' I snap.

'Badger's watching her. I'm just gonna have a shower. If that's all right with you.'

He sounds angry.

'Kai . . .' I begin. The situation with him is just another festering wound in my life. 'Are you OK?'

I don't know how to make it better. How to make him better.

'I'm fine,' he says, pushing past me. Does he even notice that I'm upset? Can he even tell that I've been crying? How much of our fight did he hear?

'Listen,' I say, pulling his arm to stop him. He flinches. 'Let's spend some time together tomorrow. Just you, me and River. When everyone's left. I know it's hard for you, having all these people here. We can go into town. I'll get you some new clothes . . . What do you think?'

He rolls his eyes at me, then stomps up the staircase.

He's still a teenager. Teenagers hate their parents. I was the same, with my mum and dad. Only . . .

Only I ran away and never went back. And not just away. Away, away.

I babysat for all the local kids from the age of fifteen. My mum suggested me when her friend Pat was moaning that she never got to spend any time with her husband because they had four kids. I didn't expect to be paid – I was just pleased to be able to get out of our toxic home for the evening. But then when Pat got back from her night out she was clearly pissed, and she pressed a tenner into my palm and asked me to come back the same time next week.

And that was the start of a lifelong love affair with children. It didn't matter what age they were – I loved them all.

I'd been a very lonely only child. I found the interaction of Pat's four children fascinating. The fighting, the sharing, the power-play. And the baby . . . the baby, little Bella, was an adorable thing. Bright brown eyes like chocolate buttons, ears that were a bit too big for her head, but somehow she was insanely cute. And happy. The happiest baby I'd ever seen. Always smiling, always gurgling. I used to creep into her room once she was asleep and just stare at her little face, watching her chest rise and fall, wondering how anything could ever be that peaceful. Wondering if I ever had been. Because I certainly couldn't remember it.

I handwrote flyers and pushed them through all the letter-boxes in our local area. Soon, I was babysitting four nights a week.

I loved it. It got me away from my dad's drunken rages, my mum's cowering. And best of all, it earned me money.

I saved it all up. Hid it in a biscuit tin my gran gave me. I thought one day I'd use it to get a taxi to London, or anywhere more exciting than the dull village we lived in outside Exeter.

But then my mum got sick. And my dad couldn't cope. And my plans got put on hold.

It all came to a head when I was seventeen. I was trying to study for my BTEC, but I was exhausted, looking after both Mum and Dad. And all the time I felt this overwhelming feeling of anger. Thinking about Pat's kids, their childhood and how different it had been from my own. Thinking how unfair it was, that no one had ever spoilt me, or put my needs first. That I had such selfish parents. A drunk for a father, and a wimp for a mother.

My tutor told me I was probably going to fail. I didn't see the point anyway. I didn't know what I wanted to do, but I knew whatever it was, I would never be able to do it while I was living with my parents, in the most miserable town in England.

I had been saving the babysitting money for years by then. I never touched a penny of it. It was all still stuffed in that tin under the bed. I took it out that evening and carefully counted it, laying the notes down in neat little piles.

I couldn't quite believe how much I'd managed to save. It felt like millions. The next day, I went straight to the travel agent and booked myself a flight to Los Angeles.

City of Stars.

As running away from home goes, it was quite a dramatic move.

It would be twenty years before I came back.

And when I finally did, I had a son with me, and the emotional scars from a life-changing injury that wasn't my fault.

SUNDAY LUNCH

How do you think it's going then, this weekend?

Not quite how you'd planned.

The guests are revolting. Ha ha.

One gone without a trace.

Another sniffing around your relationship.

A third just desperate to get home.

And the fourth . . . well, she has secrets of her own.

Have you worked them out yet though?

Perhaps there's a lesson here. Before inviting strangers into your home for a weekend of relaxation and joy, perhaps ensure it isn't a toxic hotbed of secrets and lies.

Just a thought.

POPPY

Poppy wonders if they're all worrying about her, about what's happened to her. Or whether they don't care.

What will Selina have told them?

Has Will told them that he dropped her in town? Or will Selina have made up some lie about her wanting to go home? Probably.

She's reminded of her GCSE History, a quote about the aftermath of the First World War. It had always stayed with her: 'Squeeze the German lemon until the pips squeak.'

A phrase that went round and round her head when she booked this weekend.

Her plan is to squeeze Selina until her pips squeak.

But when she was finally face to face with Selina, she fainted.

Typical.

It's a bit frustrating not knowing what's going on at the farm now, but whatever they are saying, Selina will be feeling the pressure. And that makes Poppy happy.

She checks her watch. 12pm. Still hours to go until she can return.

Poppy thanks Mabel for her hospitality – she really is

very sweet and kind, considering her age and the fact that Poppy just landed on her with no notice – and she leaves the small terraced house, turning left then right until she's on Okehampton High Street.

There's not much to write home about here, but she goes into the first welcoming coffee shop, orders a cappuccino and sits in the corner by the window, wishing she had a book. She only has her phone.

Selina left her a strange, stilted message late yesterday evening.

Just checking that everything is all right. Also that you are feeling OK after your faint. Please do let me know if you'll be returning to the retreat. We would, of course, love to have you back.

Selina was clearly acting. Poppy imagines the others, huddled around Selina, listening to her leave the message. The short shrug she would have given as she put down her phone. *What can you do?* she would have said to the gathered crowd. *Perhaps this weekend just wasn't for her. I do try so hard to please.*

And they would have all looked on, sorry for her, reassuring her what a wonderful time they were all having.

But perhaps by now, someone has searched her room and found the bump. She didn't hide it very well. That will have got them asking questions.

Selina is the only one who has phoned her. She hasn't heard from Ant again. He's given up. Moved on with Jane, perhaps.

The thought curdles the milk in her stomach.

Selina will have to pay for what she's done. To her family. To her. Poppy is unrecognisable from the woman she once was, and it's all Selina's fault.

And yet she continues, peddling her crap, influencing vulnerable minds, without ever looking back, or wondering what kind of damage she might be causing.

Poppy has a long day ahead. Killing time in this miserable town.

But she'll be back at The Sanctuary for 5pm. For the grand denouement.

The magical fireside session. What fun they will have.

NICKY

I am first to arrive at the kitchen for lunch. There's no one else in here except for Will.

He looks up as I come in, offering me a wide smile.

'Good morn— Nope, looks like it's past twelve. Good afternoon then, Nicky,' he says, slapping his hands together.

Despite his friendly welcome he looks tired.

'Do help yourself to some water.'

'Sorry, looks like I'm too keen,' I say, pouring some of the mint water from the jug on the island unit. I feel awkward, like I've interrupted him.

'No such thing!' he says heartily. He turns his back to me and continues chopping salad leaves.

He has a large plaster stuck to the side of his head. I'm sure it wasn't there yesterday.

I'm relieved when Bonnie joins me after a few minutes. She stares at Will, but he's so focused on his cooking he doesn't even acknowledge her. It's odd, given how friendly he was to me just now.

'What's he done to his head?' Bonnie whispers to me as soon as he turns the giant industrial extractor fan on, the noise loud enough to drown out our conversation.

'I don't know,' I reply. 'I didn't want to ask.'

Bonnie frowns, staring at him.

'That's a big plaster. I hope he's OK,' she says.

'I'm not sure about him. Or Selina,' I whisper. 'Do you think their relationship might be violent? Kai is so unhappy . . . Badger told me that he tried to kill himself a while ago. Perhaps Will has been beating Selina up?'

'No,' Bonnie says firmly. 'No, I'm sure it's nothing like that. He's not violent. I can . . . I can just tell. He's not that kind of man.'

'Well, there's something going on,' I say. 'I'll be honest with you – I don't trust any of them.'

'Don't be so melodramatic,' Bonnie says, pushing me. 'It's probably always like this when you stay in someone's house. It's not the same as staying in a hotel. And it's not their fault if Kai has gone off the rails. I bet it's really stressful trying to run a business with him around.'

I'm surprised to see Bonnie sticking up for them, considering how biting she's been all weekend.

'Suicide attempts in young men are on the increase, you know. He's suffering – I don't know what from exactly. But he's clearly dealing with something more than the norm.'

'Well, if you're so worried about him, why don't you go and have a chat with him after lunch? See if you can find out what's really going on.'

'I might,' I say. 'It would make me feel better.'

Bonnie stands up and walks over to Will. He stiffens slightly as she approaches.

'Aren't you going to talk us through what you're doing?' she says. 'We'd love to hear.'

I look up at them both. She's standing too close to him. He takes a step back, but instead of irritation or confusion on his face there's something else. I can't quite tell what it is.

Fascination? Attraction? Pleasure?

Surely . . .

He is smiling at Bonnie. But more than that, his eyes are alight with something pure and undeniable.

Affection. Genuine affection.

It feels as though the clouds are parting and there ahead, in the sky, clear as day, is the answer to the biggest question I've been asking.

No, it can't be true. He can't be . . .

I am speechless, my throat suddenly dry. Is this what she's been hiding all this time?

Surely . . .

I stare at them both. Will turns back to his cooking, and then the corners of Bonnie's mouth turn upwards, just slightly, but enough for me to recognise the smile that she shares with our father.

'Are you . . . is he . . .' I begin, but my voice is so quiet they don't hear me. And then Selina comes in the room.

'Hello,' she says. 'How are you both doing?'

She looks tired. I glance back at my sister, who's moved away from Will. She's staring at the floor.

'We're good,' I say. I've got it all wrong. I can't believe how wrong! Suddenly I feel incredibly sorry for Selina, and also, incredibly worried about what a mess my sister is in. 'Hungry.

This morning's yoga session was great . . . worked up quite an appetite.'

'I'm sure lunch will be delicious. No Georgia?'

'No, we, er, haven't seen her yet,' I say, gabbling. My hands are shaking. 'I think she wanted to go back to her tent for a bit to see if she could get hold of her fiancé when he woke up . . .'

'I'll just check in and make sure she's OK,' Selina says. 'That smells amazing, Will.'

He doesn't acknowledge her comment and she slips past him and out through the double doors.

Bonnie sits back at the table. We both continue to stare at Will's back, as he leans over the hob.

'Please tell me . . .' I whisper. 'Please tell me Will is not . . . please tell me what I'm thinking is wrong.'

'He's a tutor at my college,' she says, staring at me wide-eyed.

'And . . . ?'

'Let's talk about it later,' Bonnie says, laying a hand over mine. 'It's OK. You don't need to worry about me. I promise.'

I shake my head at her in utter disbelief. I wish Jon was here to hear all this. What has she done? He must be twenty years older than her at least. And he's with Selina! They have a business together, a home; he has a stepson.

Is that why Kai is so upset? Does he know what's going on? Perhaps he knows but Selina doesn't? Perhaps he's eaten up with trying to keep the secret?

How could Bonnie have done this? How could she have suggested we come on this weekend?

Why would she want to come here? To force him to leave?

He's clearly never going to do that. I feel sick. I should have seen it coming. I should have been a better sister.

'After lunch,' I hiss at her. 'You and me are going to sit down and discuss this properly. In private.'

'Of course,' she says, smiling. 'But honestly, it's not . . . what it looks like. I promise.'

I can't do anything but shake my head.

Georgia and Selina come back in and we all sit down at the large table together. Georgia seems quieter than usual and this time there are no fresh flowers, and our napkins haven't been folded or tied with string.

We still have our tea-infusing session this afternoon and our fireside ceremony to come. I wonder how I will be able to bear to sit through them, knowing everything that I do.

And what about Selina's advice to me? The way she tried to encourage me to leave Jon. And yet, and yet . . . her own situation is clearly more dysfunctional than I could ever have suspected.

I think about Jon and I think about tomorrow when I'll be back at home with my boys, and I realise how utterly grateful I am for the simplicity of my life, for the fact that my boys love me, and for the first time the solution to my problem seems clear.

It's not that I don't want this baby. It's that I don't want to give up everything to have it.

I am going to talk to Jon, as I should have done all along. I'm going to tell him that I want to go back to work as soon as I can after the baby is born. Perhaps we can do shared parental leave – his company started offering it a couple of years ago. There's no reason to think he wouldn't be pre-pared to try it.

Perhaps I have been naive all this time, thinking that Jon loved his role of provider, and loved me in my role as stay-at-home mum.

Perhaps he would love the opportunity to have a break from work, to take care of one of his children full-time. He's often said how jealous he gets about my time with the kids. He adores being a dad, and he's coped brilliantly this weekend without me. It seems so obvious now that I feel ashamed. Why have I never even asked him if he might want to switch roles with me for a while?

I've always just assumed. Played my role of burning-martyr mum to perfection. I haven't been fair.

And we'll manage financially, somehow. It will be worth the sacrifices.

We're a team. A family. A unit. The most precious, valuable thing in the world.

With Jon's support, the baby growing in my tummy will be fine, and so will I.

BONNIE

In a way, it's a good thing that Nicky knows. After all, it was my goal for this weekend for the truth to come out and for Will to leave.

But I'm still pretty terrified.

We sit down to eat our lunch. Nicky won't even look at me, and the others must have noticed how quiet she's become. At one point in the meal Georgia and I lock eyes for a second and she looks away, frowning.

They all hate me.

I feel too sick with excitement to eat and so I push the food around my plate. After we finish, Selina clears away the plates and announces that the time has come to head outside to pick herbs for our tea infusions.

'We're planning on launching our own range of organic infusions eventually, using plants grown here on the farm,' Selina says. Her eyes are bloodshot. 'We'd love to start selling them – at farmers' markets to start with, but then who knows. It's a lovely, joyful thing to do.'

It's never going to happen, I think, but I smile at her and nod.

I'd love to do something like that too – develop my own line

313

of food or drink – but there's just so much competition these days. She's so clueless. Ever since that man went on *Dragons' Den* with his reggae sauce, every man and his dog is coming out with a condiment or jam or protein bar.

'Will Badger be joining us?' I ask Selina as we walk down the side of the lawn towards the meadow.

'Yes,' she says. 'He's going to talk you through all the various plants we have growing here on the farm. But Will is going to share his specific thoughts on infusing.'

She smiles her fake smile and glances over at Will. He's lagging back. I want so much to take his hand and squeeze it. To tell him that I love him, that it's going to be OK.

I feel myself shrinking a little inside as I realise I don't know how he'd feel if I did that.

I shake the thoughts away. He made me a promise. I have no reason to think he's changed his mind.

There are bees dancing across the bobbing petals on the meadow. The whole thing is alive with movement.

'Now,' Will begins and we all pause. Georgia doesn't stop staring at him. Nicky looks distraught. I swallow. 'When it comes to making a herbal infusion, it's important to remember that technically these are not teas, unless they have green or black tea in, which many don't. The key thing to think about is blending. So, ideally we'll have a nice, level mix of flavours with different notes that come through at different times when you're drinking the infusion. It's a bit like wine. I always suggest starting with a flower note – so that can be something like chamomile –' he leans down and plucks the head of a flower and holds it up to the light – 'or violets.

Dandelions can work too, as can rose petals. Then, we'll add a stronger flavour, to ground everything. Nettles, perhaps – which we have back in the kitchen. After that, you can add a more fruity flavour – lemon being the obvious choice, but there's also rosehip or hibiscus. Then, last but not least, I like to add a cooling herb such as mint or borage. But, really, the possibilities are endless. So I suggest you get picking – pick the colours, scents and shapes you are most attracted to, and we'll take them back to the kitchen and start sniffing and blending.'

He hands us each a wooden trug and a pair of secateurs.

'Oh, and just to say, we have lots of roots available back in the kitchen too – ginger, burdock, liquorice, chicory . . . You'll find plenty of options if you'd like to add a bit more of a kick to your infusion.'

I watch Georgia as she waddles through the wildflower meadow, snipping at the long, narrow stems. She's barely said a word since lunch.

'Hang on,' Nicky says, stopping short by a bright red flower. 'Isn't this a poppy? If I put this in my tea, am I going to get high?'

She laughs.

'Different type of poppy,' Will says. 'The red poppy contains no narcotics, I'm afraid. You need the opium one for that, and we don't grow them here as we like to stay on the right side of the law. The red poppy is traditionally used as a sedative though, so you might want to give that a miss . . . And as you're all pregnant, we also want to be careful with raspberry leaf, as this can be linked to premature labour. But we don't have any of that here anyway.'

We wander and snip and pick and soon our trugs are filled with heaps of colourful flowers. I look back at the meadow and am amazed to see it barely looks as though we've made a dent in it. Which is good because I was feeling bad about leaving it looking sparse.

'Wonderful,' Selina says, looking around at all our trugs. She has one herself.

She notices me looking.

'I've gone for a lot of chamomile, it's a classic. My favourite. And if it's good enough for Peter Rabbit . . .'

I've picked a whole load of different things.

'How did you do, Nicks?' I say to Nicky.

'Yes, great. Really enjoyed it,' she says, looking down at her trug, her voice clipped. She's still furious with me. But it's OK. She'll get over it, when she realises what Will and I have is special.

I love him so much.

'Right,' Will says. 'Let's head back and then we can look at what we've got and start blending.'

The kitchen table is laid out for us all, with laminated cards listing exactly what each herb or flower is, and what they're used for. There's also another A4 sheet that Selina asks us to pass around, listing all the herbs that are not recommended in pregnancy.

'Although the likelihood of any of these causing you harm is minuscule, I'd rather not take the risk,' she says. 'So if you have picked any of these, please throw them in the bin behind you. And if you're not sure, then just check with me or Will.'

We wash our leaves and flowers then set to work blending

and mixing, with Will overseeing everyone's combinations and offering advice as he goes.

It's just like when we're at college and I remember again why I love him – the depth of his understanding and the passion with which he talks about this stuff is so attractive.

When he comes to me I can't help but brush my arm against his, to lean in closely as he talks. He keeps a straight face as he advises me that too much liquorice would be unpleasant, but all the while there's a look in his eyes – a look of longing. I want to tell him that I don't care, that I understand how difficult it will be to break up his situation, to leave it all behind, but that it will all work out for the best. I lay my hand over my bump and he rests his eyes on it, and then when I look back up and our eyes meet again, he stares at me.

I love you, I mouth at him.

He blinks twice.

'Good stuff,' he says, moving past me.

It's OK. He's just frightened. It's going to be a big change for him.

Badger has joined us and is commenting on everyone's concoctions, telling Nicky that horseradish tea is his favourite. Everyone stares at him.

'Puts hairs on your chest,' he says, laughing. 'But too much can give you a dicky tummy, so you know, you have to be careful—'

'Let me know when you're ready and we'll start infusing,' Will interrupts.

The atmosphere is excruciating. Selina is talking too loudly, too animatedly. She's trying too hard. We each have a glass

317

teapot in front of us, plus a cup and saucer, and we gently spoon our carefully mixed concoctions into the diffuser, pouring boiling water on top.

'Of course,' Will says, 'each different tea requires a different amount of time to brew, but let's start with four minutes, and then we can do a taste test to see . . .'

I'm quite pleased with how mine has turned out. Nicky says hers is too bland. Georgia's just used mint and a tiny bit of ginger root, which strikes me as rather unadventurous.

'Yes, it's delicious,' Georgia says, without meeting my eye. 'You can really taste how fresh it is.'

'How's yours, Selina?' I ask.

The table and floor are a complete mess, covered with petals and stalks and other remnants from our potion-making.

'A bit bitter,' she says. 'I think I got muddled up with something . . . one of the roots. But it's a learning process. A really interesting session, I'm sure you'll all agree.'

'Yes, that was really relaxing,' Nicky says, sipping from her glass cup.

'I know it's probably hard to imagine doing something similar when you're all back at home,' Will says. 'But actually you can make your own infusions using ingredients from your kitchen cupboard, or local health food shop. You don't have to actually pick things fresh.'

'Much better if you do though, right?' I say.

He smiles at me.

'Well, obviously I would say so, but then I'm biased . . .'

We hold each other's gaze a little bit too long. I feel my

neck warming, and he slowly blinks at me, and I know, in that second, that it's going to be OK. That it's all going to work out.

I can feel Nicky's eyes boring into the side of my head in anger.

'Right,' Selina says, interrupting my teenage daydream. 'Who fancies a maple syrup flapjack?'

GEORGIA

I'm not sure if it's the herbal tea, my worry for Poppy, my low-level fury about Will and Selina's situation, or the fact that I've been on my feet for too long while we were collecting the plants, but my back is aching even more than normal.

'I'm just . . . I'm just going to go for a lie-down, if that's OK,' I say, pushing my chair back. A wave of pain ripples across my lower back. 'Ooof.'

'Are you OK?' Selina says.

I smile at her.

'Yes, yes, just more Braxton Hicks, I think.'

'If you're sure,' she says. She looks around at the mess on the table. 'You didn't accidentally drink any raspberry leaf, did you?'

I smile. Will's face is thunder.

'She can't have done,' he says. 'I was very careful, there's nothing harmful in here.'

'I'm honestly fine,' I say. 'I've had these pains for a few days now. They come and go. I'll just go and rest.'

I support the underside of my bump with my forearm. I wish Brett was here. It's so horrible to think of him being so far away, across the Atlantic.

'If you're sure. I'll come and check on you in twenty minutes or so,' Selina calls. 'If that's OK.'

I nod at her and hobble out of the kitchen, towards my tent. Then I collapse on the bed, rolling onto my side, and I wait for the waves of pain to pass.

SELINA

The last thing I need is for Georgia to go into labour. I don't think I could cope with that. Not along with everything else.

Although it would be quite the story . . . would definitely put us on the map. If I could pull it off . . .

Of course I could.

A tingle of anticipation comes over me.

There is nothing that makes you feel more alive than witnessing the miracle of birth.

'We've got an hour or so before our fireside ceremony,' I say to everyone. 'So please feel free to spend this time as you'd like. Whether that's walking in the grounds, chatting to Badger about the plants, or writing in your journal. Or having a nap, of course!'

I look over at Badger. He's helping Will clear away the remnants of plants that litter the table and floor, but he looks up and smiles.

'I think I'll go and see if I can FaceTime the boys,' Nicky says. 'Do you want to come with me, Bonnie? I'm sure they'd love to chat to you too.'

'What? Oh, sure,' Bonnie says. She's been much quieter in the past hour or so. None of her usual wisecracks. But still, it'll be good to have some downtime. Especially if I'm going to be needed later, to help Georgia . . .

I smile gratefully at Nicky. She can clearly see that I'm worn out, that I wouldn't mind a bit of headspace before this evening.

'Are you going to finish this?' Will says, handing me my teacup, which is still half full.

'Oh,' I say. 'Right, yes.'

I swallow the bitter liquid in one gulp. It's not any better now it's lukewarm. I've never managed to get the hang of this infusing lark. It's definitely Will's thing.

Plus, if I'm honest, I prefer wine.

'I'll leave you boys to clear up, if that's OK?' I say to Will and Badger when the others have left. 'I've got a bit of a headache coming on.'

'No worries,' Badger says cheerily. Of course, Will doesn't respond. I can't even bear to look at him.

I turn to leave the kitchen and go through to the hall. Standing by the front door is Kai.

He's strapping my huge rucksack on his back. Just seeing it brings a lump to my throat, remembering all the places I fled to, how at many points it held all my worldly possessions, because I owned nothing, literally nothing but the clothes on my back.

Next to him, just behind the front door, is River, asleep in her car seat.

I grab his arm and yank him into our living room. The blinds are down and it's dark inside.

'What the hell are you doing?' I hiss. 'I told you! I told you not to bring Riv in the house while the guests are here! Anyone could have seen her! What are you playing at?'

'I'm waiting for my taxi.'

'Your taxi? What are you talking about? Where are you . . . what's in the bag?'

He looks down at me. He's nearly a foot taller than me. I can see the open pores on his nose as he leans in close.

'We're leaving. I thought you'd be pleased. You'll never see us again. You won't have to worry about us cluttering up your life any longer. Your perfect life with—'

'What are you talking about?'

'I can't live with you two any more,' he says. 'Not now I know about him. You are aware he's been sleeping with the one with curly hair, don't you? That it's his baby in her stomach?'

I swallow. No! Surely not . . . not Bonnie. He wouldn't . . . he couldn't . . .

'What? Don't be ridiculous.'

'Even Will has had enough of you. I thought she was weird when I first saw her. So I followed her, and guess what? She's been having secret chats with him about their baby. And I thought – do you know what that means? That means I'm going to end up stuck with you for the rest of my life. With you hovering over River, trying to claim her as your own! Won't that be fun? After what you did . . . and now he's gonna swan off into the sunset and have his new baby, his real baby, and leave us and it's all because of YOU. Because of what YOU DID. And you know what? I'm not doing it, I'm not doing this any longer. I'm done. I'm a grown-up. We've been fine, over the past few days. Me and River. We don't need you . . . You tried to persuade me I couldn't take care of her but I can! I'm nineteen. She's my daughter. Not yours. Mine! I'm going to start again. Somewhere far, far away. And I'm going to live the life I—'

I slap him round the face. It's becoming a habit. I don't care that the door is open, that anyone walking through the hall will be able to see me. I just need him to shut up.

Not Will. Not Will and Bonnie. No. It's not true. My ears begin to ring. I shake my head from side to side. I refuse to believe it. He's just saying it to hurt me.

'Kai, you're being ridiculous,' I say. 'Where will you go? How will you provide for River? How could you possibly meet her needs? You're behaving like a child.'

He puts his hand to his cheek, eyes flashing. For a second I think he might hit me back this time, and I realise suddenly how much stronger he is than me. He's not just taller, he's a man now. Not a child. I take a step back. I'm shaking, my stomach turning over.

'I can meet her needs a hell of a lot better than you can! I can spend my time doing something worthwhile, rather than having to be your emotional punchbag, spending my life listening to you moan on about what a hard time you're having, how much harder your life is because I'm in it, how nothing ever goes your way, how you were mutilated by a doctor who was trying to save your life! Well, what about me? What about my happiness? What about my family? You stole it!'

I slap him again.

'How dare you speak to me like that! Everything I've ever done has been for you!'

He takes two steps back from me. I hear the crunch of gravel as a taxi swings into the driveway outside. A familiar mewling sound follows from the hallway. River is waking up. In seconds she'll be bawling her eyes out.

'River . . .' I say, eyes wide in fear. 'You can't take her.'

'River's mine!' he says. This is the most he's spoken to me in weeks, and he suddenly sounds so much older. 'Despite you referring to yourself as Mummy! I heard you, so don't bother trying to deny it.'

'You can't take her. I won't let you.'

'There's only one way to make you suffer,' Kai continues. 'Only one way that you deserve. And that's to lose a child. And as a bonus, a grandchild too.'

'Listen to me,' I say, taking a step towards him. 'You're my son. It wasn't my fault; you know I did everything I could to save Josie . . .'

'That's not true,' he says. 'You were happy she died. I've seen the way you've been over the last few months and it's obvious. It was what you wanted all along. You couldn't stand for me to be happy, to be growing up and moving on, to not need you . . . to love someone else . . . You wanted River for yourself!'

'No, no, no . . .' Tears are flooding my cheeks.

'You wanted Josie to die. You killed her.'

'I didn't,' I say, doubling over. My whole body starts to convulse as I sob the words out. 'It's not true. I tried my best. I've attended hundreds of births. There was nothing I could do—'

'You're a LIAR!' he screams in my face. 'You wanted her dead. You wanted her out of the way so you could take River—'

'No, no, no, Kai, please . . .' I collapse to the floor, wrapping my arms around his ankles. My face starts to tingle, my stomach is swirling with nausea. 'It's not true. I didn't want any of this, I didn't, I wanted you, me and Will . . . just to be happy . . . I just wanted us to have a better life . . .'

'Well, you failed. Because he's going to leave you anyway. To be with his bit on the side. And I don't blame him at all. You're going to end up alone, Selina. Exactly as you deserve.'

He kicks me hard in the chest. I gasp, the wind knocked out of me by the pain and force. I lie there on the carpet, watching through tear-filled eyes as he stomps out of the room. I try to stand up, but my legs are jelly, and so I crawl through the doorway into the hall and reach desperately for the car seat, with my baby girl in it, but I can't get close and as I lie there, helpless as a newborn myself, Kai scoops up the seat, River screaming her head off now as he slams the front door behind him.

'No!' I shout, before I begin to cough. An agonising, hacking cough that racks my whole body and burns my oesophagus. 'No! Not River!'

My eyes blur with tears and I can't see properly through the glass barn door and instead I just lie there and listen to the sound of a car door opening then shutting, and the engine purring as it pulls away.

My baby girl has gone. And I know for sure that I will never see her again.

NICKY

Bonnie is sitting on my bed. Her neat chin is lifted in defiance as she tells me all about her relationship with Will.

'He's not happy with her,' she says, turning her hands over in her lap. 'You can tell from the way he is around her. He's miserable.'

'Maybe he's miserable because you're here,' I say, as gently as possible. His behaviour makes perfect sense to me now. 'He probably feels incredibly uncomfortable about the situation. Having both of the women in his life in the same room together, knowing that he's being two-faced to Selina. I'm sure you think he loves you but . . .'

'He does love me.'

'Well, I know you don't like Selina, and I have to say I'm not sure what I think of her either,' I pause, thinking of the strange, boundary-crossing advice she gave me about Jon, 'but even so, it's not very fair or kind to her, is it? If she finds out . . .'

'When she finds out. That's why I came,' Bonnie says. 'I knew I had to force his hand. I knew otherwise he'd never leave.'

'But what do you really know about him?' I say, exasperated. 'Clearly, his relationship with Selina is pretty shaky, given what's been going on . . .' I tail off, a thought occurring. 'How could you ever trust him? What about all the creepy things that have happened? The dead rat, the burning scarecrow, the tent collapse? Please don't tell me . . . that wasn't you?'

'No,' she says. 'Don't be stupid, I'd never do anything like that. I don't know who was responsible for all that stuff.'

I breathe a sigh of relief.

'Well, even so, they're clearly having marital problems . . .'

'For fuck's sake, they're not married!' Bonnie shouts. 'Kai's not even his son. He's been unhappy with her for ages. Sometimes, when he's had a few drinks, he starts to open up a bit. About their life together. He's only stayed with her because of Kai, because he was worried about leaving him. But Kai's got to stand on his own two feet. That's why I came here. I thought if Kai worked out what was going on . . . then he'd tell Selina and shake everything up a bit. That way, Will didn't have to do any of the dirty work. It was all meant to come out organically.'

'Christ, Bonnie, but what about you? Do you not think Selina's going to think you're an absolute fruit loop for coming on this retreat? For staying in her home? If she doesn't think you're mad then she's going to think you're bad. Rubbing her nose in it. I'm not sure what's worse, to be honest.'

'I don't care what she thinks,' Bonnie says. 'I just want to be with Will, and I know it's what he wants too. I'm taking control of my future. That's what you and Dad are always on at me to do, isn't it? And I know that Will will be happy with me and the baby. He wants to be a dad. He said he'd always wanted to be a dad.'

'Well, why didn't he have a baby with Selina then?' I ask.

'She had to have an emergency hysterectomy after Kai was born. She can't have any more children. That's not Will's fault, is it?'

I pull her towards me and we hug, her head resting on my shoulder. She seems so young, so fragile and vulnerable. Even though she puts on this front, this huge bravado, I know deep down she just wants to be loved.

'You should have talked to me before . . . before it got this complicated,' I say. 'Oh, Bonnie, I'm so sorry you thought you couldn't.'

'I'm always letting you guys down. I didn't want you to think I'd messed everything up again.'

'That's just not true! You're amazing, Bon. The most talented chef I know. Quirky, friendly, stylish. You always see the best in every situation. You have so much going for you. Honest.'

We hear a shout from the barn. Bonnie lifts her head.

'What was that?' she says.

I frown. We leave the tent and walk towards the open kitchen doors. The room is empty, but through the doorway I can see something.

Selina's lying on the floor of the hall, sobbing.

'Oh my God,' I say, rushing towards her. As I get closer, I spot the vomit in front of her mouth.

'Are you OK?' I say.

She groans. Her face is wet with sweat and tears.

'What happened?' I say, staring at the vomit.

She doesn't reply, she just closes her eyes and continues to lie there.

'Let me get Will,' I say, looking around at Bonnie, who's standing a few paces behind me.

'I'll get him,' she says, her eyes wide, and then she disappears back through the kitchen.

'Must be something you ate,' I say, crouching beside Selina, but she just carries on sobbing. 'Let me get some tissue to clear this up. Would you like some water?'

'Mmmm,' she mumbles.

In the kitchen, I pluck the roll of kitchen towel from its stand and rummage around in the cupboard under the sink until I find some antibacterial spray. I do the best I can with the mess, and by the time I've finished mopping and wiping, Selina seems to have calmed down a bit. She hauls herself up to a seated position, and slumps over the bottom step of the spiral staircase.

'You look dreadful,' I say. She's incredibly pale – almost yellow – and the whites of her eyes have a pinky-orange tinge to them. 'What happened?'

She takes a sip of the water I hand her.

'I'm sorry,' she says, after a few minutes. 'I had a fight with Kai. I got a bit upset. Then I . . . I felt a bit dizzy and I fell over. I didn't even realise I'd been sick.'

'What was the fight about?' I ask nervously.

'Your sister,' she says. Her voice is a croak but even so I can hear the venom underneath. 'Apparently she's been having an affair with Will. *Apparently* she's carrying his baby.'

'Oh, I—'

'No, I know,' she says, wiping her forehead with the back of her hand. 'It's ridiculous. Kai just said it to hurt me. Anyway, he's gone now. So that's that. I always knew I would lose him eventually. I just didn't think he'd take . . .'

She shakes her head, sips the water again.

'Did I tell you I ran away from home at seventeen? I moved to LA, and I didn't come back for more than twenty years. Apparently it broke my mother's heart. Well, she'd broken mine years before, so it was only fair. But there you are. It's all cycles, isn't it? The cycle of life. And now it's my turn. My turn to experience the pain of losing a child.'

I don't know what to say.

'The thing is,' she says, her voice dropping almost to a whisper, 'I know now, how my mother felt all those years ago. I know what she was dealing with. Trying to keep things together when my dad was a drunk and she couldn't imagine a life without him. We're all just trying our best, aren't we? Mothers. We're all just trying to do our best by our kids but we're doomed from the very start. We'll never be good enough. Nothing we do will ever live up to the high standard we set ourselves. Because we love our kids more than life itself, but we're fallible, because we're human. It's an impossible challenge, and the only option we have is to fail. And so we do. We fail, we beat ourselves up, we promise to try harder and then we fail again. The desperation makes us fail.'

She pauses, gazing out across the driveway.

'But it's not the same for men, is it? They succeed without even trying. They succeed by just being there. Oh, what a good dad he is, he changed his own baby's nappy. And then, just to make it even worse, they get jealous! Jealous of the baby getting all your attention, because deep down that's all they are themselves. Fucking babies.'

She retches, suddenly breathless.

'Sorry,' she says quietly. 'This wasn't what you were expecting when you booked this weekend, was it? Too late now. I've fucked it all up. But I want you to know that I tried really hard. I tried so hard to create this . . . this paradise for pregnant women. I wanted it to be so good, the sort of weekend you'd all go home and tell your friends about. I practically bankrupted us, trying to get it all absolutely perfect . . .'

She coughs. I wonder briefly whether she might actually be drunk. Where the hell is Bonnie, and where is Will?

'Do you want me to get you a cup of tea?' I say, wincing even as I say the words, knowing how inadequate they are.

'I don't feel great,' she says. Her eyes are even more yellow. 'My face feels weird.'

'You haven't been drinking?' I say. 'Sorry to ask, it's just . . . you look a bit green.'

She shakes her head.

'No, I feel . . .' She takes a deep breath. 'I think I just need some fresh air.'

Slowly, she gets to her feet, resting on the banister. The vomit has left a dark smudge on her hoodie.

The hallway clock bongs.

'It's time for our fireside session!' she says. 'I spent so long writing the meditations for this. Come on.'

It's as though the sound of the clock has brought her back to life.

'Are you sure?' I say. 'Don't you think you should talk to Will about what Kai said?'

'No, no, no, it's all planned. I'm not going to let him ruin this one. And Georgia . . . oh God, I forgot all about Georgia. How is she? I need to check on her . . .'

Where the hell are Will and Bonnie?

We're just about to walk back through the kitchen when we hear the sound of a car approaching. We both look through the glass door at the front of the barn. A taxi is pulling up.

'Kai?' Selina says. Her hand flies to her throat; her eyes widen so much they're practically popping. 'I knew it. He can't cope without me. I knew he'd come back.'

We both stand there behind the glass, watching as the taxi door opens, and a figure emerges.

But it's not Kai.

I take a sharp breath in shock at who is standing in the driveway, staring directly at us.

Poppy.

BONNIE

I find Will behind the bathroom block. He's staring out at the field, his hand resting on the plaster on his head.

'What happened to your head?' I say. 'Really?'

He turns in surprise.

'She threw a salt rock at it,' he says. 'I guess I deserved it.'

'God,' I say. 'This morning? When? Why? Did you tell her about us?'

'No,' he says. 'If I had, I wouldn't be standing here with a plaster on my head. I'd be . . . somewhere under there.'

He points to the wood in front of us and gives a morbid chuckle.

'I don't know why you put up with this situation,' I say, squeezing my fists together in frustration. 'It doesn't make any sense. You don't have to, you know. You deserve better than this. You don't owe her anything.'

'If only it was that simple,' he says, looking back at me.

'It is that simple!' I shout, raising my arms. 'You don't have to make it complicated.'

'Kai's left,' he says. 'And he's taken . . . well, let's just say he's taken everything.'

'What?'

'He came to see me, just before the herbal tea session. He knew about us. He'd packed up everything he owns, stuffed it into an old rucksack. Told me he had found somewhere to go, but wouldn't tell me where. I don't even know if it's in this country. He said he never wants to see me or Selina again.'

I frown. I'm so frustrated I could scream. What is it that Will isn't telling me?

I start to cry.

'In a way that's good, isn't it? It means . . .'

'I can't believe I'm actually going to be a father,' he says, gently placing a hand on my stomach. 'It's all I've ever wanted.'

'Well, you are! So please, be honest with me, Will. What's the story?' I say. 'There's clearly something you're all hiding. Is Kai really your son after all? Or . . . or . . . is he ill? Is Selina ill? Cancer?' I tail off. I can't think what else could be making him want to stay somewhere he's clearly so unhappy.

'No, no, nothing like that. It's good that Kai has gone. Hopefully it means . . . it means she'll accept it, when I tell her it's over.'

He holds me and it feels amazing, but my heart is still thumping angrily inside my chest. There's so much that doesn't make sense. What about the weird note? The burning scarecrow? The ring Selina choked on? Who undid Nicky's guy ropes? Was it all down to Kai? And if so, why?

I want to freeze this moment, to push all the fear and unanswered questions away.

'Selina's not well,' I mumble into his chest. 'I'm meant to be coming to get you to tell you.'

'What's the matter with her?'

'I don't know,' I reply. 'We found her lying on the floor in the hallway, and she'd been sick. She was crying.'

'I'm sure it's just her usual attention-seeking,' he says.

'I was meant to come and get you though. I'm sorry. I didn't want to but at the same time . . . she had, you know, actually vomited.'

I feel his body tensing in my arms.

'That's Selina for you,' he mutters bitterly. 'Has to go the whole hog. Loves to put on a show.'

He reaches up, wincing, and pulls off the plaster. Underneath, the wound on his head is much larger than I had imagined. Deeper too, with an oozing orange centre.

'Will,' I say, suddenly afraid. I think of the tiny button of a baby in my stomach, how vulnerable I am, how stupid I've been to put myself in this situation. 'That looks really nasty. You need to get to A&E and get it cleaned up properly. It looks like it might get infected.'

'You're sweet,' he says, sticking the plaster back on. 'But don't worry. It'll be fine.'

'I'm not sweet,' I reply. 'I'm worried about you.'

'You don't need to be worried about me,' he says. 'It's all going to be OK. But you do need to go along with it all. For now. For me. Please. Just go back to the barn, and do what Selina says. We'll get our happy ending, but you have to play along. For just a little bit longer. Please. Trust me.'

I want to shake him.

'You're not making any sense,' I say. 'How can I go back now, and pretend nothing has happened?'

We're interrupted by a call. Nicky is striding towards us, a dark frown across her brow. She's shouting something, waving her hands up and down animatedly, but the wind has suddenly got up again and whips round my ears, carrying her voice away.

'What?' I shout back.

Will moves a few steps away from me.

'It's OK,' I say, stepping back towards him and taking his hand. 'Nicky knows about us.'

'What?' he says. 'How?'

He wrenches his hand free.

'I . . .' The words dry up.

I want to tell him that it doesn't matter. That people are finding out and that it's OK. No one has died and nothing bad is going to happen. Relationships end all the time. People survive.

But I'm too scared. His face. He doesn't look happy.

'Poppy,' Nicky is calling. 'Poppy is back!'

'Oh my God,' I say. Nicky runs the last few paces towards us.

'She's here, she got a cab, she *was* staying in Okehampton after all.'

I let out a breath I didn't even know I had been holding. Will had been telling the truth about dropping her off yesterday afternoon.

'So it was true!' I say.

'What? Of course. I told you,' Will says. He looks even angrier now.

Oh God, what have I done?

'I thought . . . we thought . . .'

'What?'

'I don't know what we thought,' I say. 'I'm sorry. It was all just really strange.'

'It's even more strange now,' Nicky says. 'She seems really cheerful. Excited to be back and looking forward to the fireside meditation. And as for Selina . . .'

She pauses, shooting a look at Will.

My heart is thumping in my ribcage. But as I watch him, his face softens. He takes a breath, then holds out his hands, palms up, towards Nicky.

'Listen, Nicky,' Will says, reaching out an arm. 'I know you must think I'm an awful person, but sometimes these things just happen. I really do love your sister. None of this was planned, I promise. I hope in time we can be friends?'

Nicky's face remains neutral.

He's making an effort with my sister, at least, which is all I wanted, even if it does feel a little forced.

'As I was about to say,' Nicky says, ignoring Will, 'Selina's feeling better. Although she's definitely got some kind of stomach upset. She should probably be sleeping it off but she's determined we go ahead with the session. Listen. She . . . said Kai told her about you two. That you'd been having an affair. But she says she doesn't believe it. She thinks he was just making it up to hurt her.'

'Surely we can't just . . . go ahead with the session now, as though nothing has happened?' I say.

'She seems almost manic,' Nicky says. 'And determined. She really wants the session to go ahead.'

'We should leave now,' I say, to Will. 'This is all such a mess.'

'She was very specific that we should all come to the fire

now,' Nicky says. 'I think, given what you've done to her, it's the least you can do. I've been sent to round you up.'

'What about Georgia though?' I ask, suddenly remembering that the last time we saw her she was complaining about Braxton Hicks, that she had gone to her tent for a lie-down. 'Has anyone checked she's OK?'

GEORGIA

The pain keeps coming, no matter what position I lie in. Every time I get a respite from it, I shift around, but then another wave comes.

I am frozen on the bed, like a beached whale. I can't . . . it can't be happening now. I'm only just eight months pregnant, it's too soon.

I reach for my phone and tap the screen, staring at the photo of me and Brett taken a few months ago, when we were out for dinner. We are both glowing with happiness. But now, he's in a meeting room, far away across the Atlantic ocean, unreachable.

And I'm in deepest darkest Devon.

I start to cry. Whatever happened to third time lucky? This wasn't meant to happen. I was meant to have another four weeks at least, to have time to finish off the nursery. I have a baby shower planned in a fortnight with all my closest friends.

I focus on my breathing. It helps, a little. I try to tell myself that these pains are normal, that it's just my body's way of practising for labour, but even though I've never experienced it before, somehow I know that it's not.

It's not just Braxton Hicks. It's too insistent, too incessant, too regular.

I need to tell someone, but the thought of climbing off the bed and walking even to the next tent feels impossible.

I think of Poppy. Her tragic story. Selina, and her lies. This place is cursed. Why did I come here?

I'm scared.

I'm so very, very scared and alone.

'Georgia?'

I lift my neck and glance at the entrance to my tent. Nicky is there, looking over at me.

'Are you OK?' she says, walking towards the bed.

'No,' I say, tears flooding now in relief. 'Thank God you're here. I think . . . I think the baby is coming. I've been getting these pains, like really bad backache, but they keep coming and they're every few minutes or so . . . but it's too early. I'm only just eight months pregnant! I'm so scared.'

Nicky grabs my hand.

'It's OK,' she says. 'Just breathe. In, out, in, out. Slowly, fill your lungs and out through your mouth.'

She squeezes my fingers. I nod.

'That's brilliant, well done, keep doing that. I'm going to get help.'

'Please don't be too long,' I say. 'I don't want to be on my own. I know it's pathetic but I'm scared.'

'It's not pathetic, and you're not pathetic. It might just be a false alarm still; don't panic. We'll get you to the hospital so they can look you over. I'll be back as soon as I can.'

I stay in the same position on the bed, focusing on my

breathing. I think about all the plans I made, the decisions I took, the way I was going to sit down with Brett as soon as possible and tell him everything. Is this my punishment? Is this karma's way of getting to me for not being upfront with him from the start?

I push the negative thoughts away and continue to focus on my breathing. Miraculously, it seems to work. I feel my heart rate dropping, but the pains still come, feeling more and more like horrendous period cramps each time.

'We're back,' Nicky says, after what feels like ages but can't have been. 'Will's going to drive you to the hospital to get you checked over. Do you think you can get up?'

'Which hospital?'

'Exeter. Don't worry, it's not too far away.'

As I try to sit up on the bed, another wave of pain cripples me.

'God, it hurts so much,' I moan, clutching my stomach.

'Here, take these,' Nicky says, handing me two small white pills and a glass of water. 'Paracetamol. They might take the edge off.'

I swallow them and swing my legs round so that they're hanging off the side of the bed.

'I don't even have a bag of stuff,' I say. 'I had a plan . . . a hospital bag . . .'

'Don't worry about any of that now,' Nicky says. 'It'll all work out fine. The hospital will have everything you need. Let's just go and get you looked at. It's not far.'

'What are you doing?'

We both stare at the entrance to the tent. Selina is standing in the frame.

'Don't move her!' she says, hurrying over. 'If she's in latent labour she needs to rest. Tell me, Georgia, how are you feeling?'

'She's getting really strong contractions, Selina,' Nicky says, standing between us. 'I think it's best if we take her to hospital as Will suggested.'

'Nonsense,' Selina replies. My head begins to ache. I take another sip of water. 'Supporting women through childbirth is literally what I do. And she'll be absolutely fine here.'

'It's too early,' I say, suddenly scared for a different reason. Thinking about what Will told me. I'm at this woman's mercy. Surely she won't actually stop me from trying to leave? 'I'm only just eight months.'

'Exactly,' says Nicky firmly. 'And I think you'll agree that it's best to be on the safe side and get her to a hospital so that she can be examined properly.'

'Are you sure of your dates?' Selina asks, and before I know it she's sitting at the end of the bed, pushing on my bump.

'Ow.'

'It's just you are very big. Is there any possibility you might have got things muddled? That you might be further along than you think? Scans aren't hugely reliable, you know.'

'No,' I say, staring desperately at Nicky. I don't have the strength to push Selina off but I want more than anything for her to leave me alone. 'There's definitely no way. You know why . . . You know why that's not possible!'

'Hmm,' Selina says. There's a glint in her eye, something like excitement. It makes me feel sick with fear. I am utterly helpless. She lifts my jumper, places her ice-cold hands on my naked bump and continues to palpate it. 'The head is definitely engaged. It looks as though it's more than just Braxton Hicks. You might not make it to the hospital in time anyway. Right, let's get things moving. Can you walk? You'd be better off in the house, where it's warmer and we have access to running water . . . Come on.'

She leans over, puts an arm under my armpit and hoists me to my feet. Another surge of pain rattles through me.

'Orgghh,' I gasp. 'Get off me!'

'Look at me, Georgia. Look at me,' she says. Her voice is almost a growl. 'It will be OK. Just breathe and trust in your body. You can do this.'

'What the hell do you think you're doing?' Will shouts. I didn't even hear him come in. It feels stiflingly hot in the tent all of a sudden. Too many bodies in such a confined space. 'Get away from her!'

We all stare at him. I start to cry again. Why did I even come on this stupid weekend? What an idiot I have been. And this is my punishment. Only what I deserve.

'This is nothing to do with you, Will,' Selina snaps at him. Sweat is pouring from her forehead. 'Leave us alone.'

I look from Will to Selina and then back to Will again. Despite the state I'm in, I can see that they're both furious with each other.

'Please,' I whimper. 'I want to go to hospital . . .'

'No,' Selina says. 'Ignore him. Come on, Georgia, you can do this. I'll help you through it. I'll be with you every step of the way.'

'Stop it!' Will roars. In the background, I see Nicky shrink back. 'This isn't a game. You don't have some point to prove here! Leave her alone. She's coming to the hospital with me, Selina, because that's the RIGHT THING TO DO. And this time, we're going to do the right thing . . .'

This time?

Nicky steps forward.

'I agree,' she says, taking my arm and staring directly at Selina. Her voice is calm and steady. 'We can't afford to take any risks. Especially not when the baby is so premature.'

I feel Selina's grip on my torso tighten.

'You're hurting me,' I say to her. She's staring like a zombie at Will, ignoring me completely.

'Selina!' I shout. 'Get off me!'

Suddenly she lets go, sinking to her knees, and I almost drop to the floor myself. Thankfully, Nicky is there to support me. Another contraction comes – because by now I am sure that's what they are – and I try not to scream out with the pain. This is like some kind of nightmare, some horror story, and the only ending I can envisage is me bleeding to death here on the floor of this tent.

'I need to get to the hospital. Now. It's already too late,' I say, my voice low. A visceral certainty fills my previously confused mind. 'The baby will need special care when it's born, because it's going to be too small. I don't want to waste any more time. Please, Will, would you drive me there?'

'Of course,' he says.

I can't bear to look at Selina so instead I allow Nicky and Will to help me walk out of the tent and to the Land Rover. It's only when I'm installed in the front seat – with some difficulty – that I realise I am clutching my mobile phone in my hand.

I stare at it, telling myself that soon – not too soon, but soon – I will be using it to phone Brett and tell him that our baby has been born, safe and well, but a little small. I tell myself this story over and over, until I find that I believe it wholeheartedly. And finally, I begin to calm down.

As Will swings the car round in the driveway, for a brief moment we directly face Selina.

She is standing, like a ghost, one arm outstretched as though reaching for something, the other wrapped tightly round her abdomen, her mouth wide open and slack in a silent scream.

THE FIRESIDE
MEDITATION

POPPY

Poppy is disappointed that she won't have the full audience she wanted now, but of course, Georgia's safety and that of her baby are the most important things. She couldn't bear for Selina to be responsible for yet another baby's death.

Selina is standing in the doorway of the barn, staring straight down the driveway and into the distance. Will's car is long gone.

Poppy walks up to her slowly, and reaches out an arm to touch her shoulder.

It's time she gets what's coming to her.

'Selina,' Poppy says, and Selina's whole body jerks in shock. She turns to look at Poppy. She looks terrible: sweaty and pale.

Selina reaches her hand up to her forehead and screws her eyes up as though she's in pain.

'Are you all right?' Poppy asks, keeping her voice steady.

Selina blinks slowly.

'He shouldn't have taken her,' she says quietly. 'She would have been fine here. It's nearly an hour to Exeter – what if they don't get there in time?'

'I'm sure they'll be fine,' Poppy says, taking her hand. 'Now, do you think perhaps we could do our fireside meditation? I was so looking forward to it . . .'

'You,' she says, staring at Poppy. Poppy can't work out if Selina's drugged or drunk or just in shock. 'You came back.'

'I told you,' Poppy replies, leading her across the barn and in through the kitchen doors. 'I needed a bit of a break. It was all getting quite intense. And you know, I lost my baby last year. So sometimes I find things difficult.'

Selina frowns. It's as though she's not really there. Poppy is tempted to slap her round the face, to bring her back to life, but that wouldn't be appropriate, of course.

Not yet anyway.

All in good time.

Badger has lit the huge metal fire pit. Nicky and Bonnie are sitting on rugs on the grass. They look up with wide eyes as Poppy and Selina approach.

'Poppy,' Nicky says eventually. 'It's good to see you again. We were all . . . rather worried.'

She stares at Poppy's flat stomach.

Bonnie looks pale, even in the light of the flames.

Poppy glances over at Badger. He's staring intently at Selina but then he looks at her and their eyes meet.

Poppy smiles.

Time for the final showdown.

Before coming here, she had no idea how she would feel when she finally met Selina. After building her up in her mind for so long, after hearing so much about her, and reading so much about her online. But when she finally came face to face with her, her overwhelming feeling was one of rage. Rage that Selina had been living here, in this paradise.

But of course, it was all a facade. Like everything else about her, a fake.

Poppy takes a seat on the rug next to Nicky.

'I'm sorry I disappeared like that,' Poppy says. 'I didn't mean to worry anyone.'

Bonnie gives her an uncomfortable smile. Bonnie doesn't like her. She doesn't trust her, but that's OK.

They all sit there in silence, like obedient schoolchildren, looking up at Selina. She is still staring down at the fire, as though in a trance.

'Would you like to start the meditation?' Poppy says. 'We're all really keen.'

'What?' Selina says, looking down at them.

'After all the drama with poor Georgia, I'm sure everyone could do with some regrounding,' Poppy continues. She is quite enjoying her role now. Now that she knows she won't have to play it for much longer, she finds she's more able to keep up the pretence.

'She's gone,' Selina says, before dramatically dropping to her knees on the last remaining blanket. She is still staring into the fire.

'Who's gone?' Bonnie says quietly.

'River,' Selina replies. 'She's gone and she'll never come back.'

Nicky looks over at Poppy.

'River?'

'My baby girl,' Selina says.

'Oh, I am sorry to hear that,' Poppy says, keeping her voice light. 'It's horrible to lose a child. Especially for good.'

Nicky is still staring at her.

'Aren't you feeling well?' Poppy says to Selina.

Selina shakes her head. 'No,' she replies. 'My face ... I've got pins and needles in my face.'

'Perhaps it's the shock,' Poppy says. 'Shock and stress can cause all kinds of strange reactions, can't they? When my baby died, all my fingernails stopped growing.'

She holds up her hands to the light.

'As you can see, they're growing back slowly now, but look, they're all short and split. I had many, many different tests, but the doctors couldn't find a cause. In the end, they put it down to shock and grief. Some people say your hair can turn grey overnight with the stress of grief. Perhaps that will happen to you, now little River's gone. Wouldn't that be strange? Or maybe something else.'

'Poppy,' Nicky says, frowning. 'I think perhaps ...'

'Sorry,' she says, turning to Nicky. 'I know, I'm being a bit strange. But the thing is, I haven't been entirely honest with you all.'

'We know,' Bonnie says. 'About your fake pregnancy. Why did you come here, Poppy? What do you want?'

'All in good time,' Poppy says. She gets to her feet. She glances back towards the barn. Badger is standing there, smoking, watching her.

She takes a deep breath.

'I guess as Selina's not feeling up to it, I should lead the

354

meditation tonight. I think I've picked up a few tips from our sessions. Let's see. Shall I start by telling you all a story?'

Selina nods. Her eyelids are flickering, as though she's about to fall asleep.

'Once upon a time there were two friends. They both got pregnant within a year of one another. One of them, let's call her Jane, started researching things online as soon as she got pregnant. And she decided that she didn't want to go down the conventional route when it came to childbirth – when it came to anything, really.'

Poppy's words are coming out too quickly. She takes a deep breath, makes a conscious effort to slow down.

'And so she decided she'd like to give birth at home. In a birthing pool, with a private midwife by her side. She spent a lot of time – but probably not quite enough – researching until she found who she believed was the right woman. A woman in a nearby village. She seemed friendly, eccentric, but confident. Jane and her midwife became great friends.'

Poppy looks down at Bonnie and Nicky. They are staring at her, frowning.

'They became great friends, but perhaps that was the problem. Suddenly, Jane changed beyond all recognition. She started to believe everything this woman told her. That it was a good idea not to have scans in pregnancy. That after you give birth – at home, without painkillers, of course – you should leave the placenta attached to the baby until it falls off on its own after a few days. She even shared a recipe for preserving the placenta – yes, that's right – in salt and herbs. So that it didn't stink, like the rotting piece of raw meat that it was.'

'I . . .' Nicky says.

'I'm sorry,' Poppy says. 'I know how disgusting it is. But none of this was that important. The thing that really mattered was that this midwife believed that vaccinations were a form of state control. That they were wholly unnecessary, and that in fact they were damaging children. And causing autism, no less. So she persuaded Jane, who by then had had her baby – healthily, luckily – at home, not to bother with any of the vaccinations that the NHS recommends. And so, Jane's baby – a little boy called Sean with bright red hair – well, he never received any of them.

'That was all fine, of course. Except that Jane's friend found her new obsession with all things – let's say, to be polite – *alternative*, rather disturbing. She didn't like the way Jane judged her for using formula milk to feed her own baby, once she was born. And she disagreed with her stance on vaccinations. One day, the two of them had a heated discussion about it, in fact. And they nearly fell out.'

Poppy paces round and round the fire pit as she speaks.

'But you know, we live in a tolerant society, where it's important that we are respectful of people with differing opinions. So Jane's friend decided to live and let live. Sean was Jane's child – it was none of her business how Jane chose to parent him. But then one day, Jane's friend noticed that her own daughter, who by now was just over eleven months old, had a high temperature. And then a rash developed on her feet, which spread within hours to her whole body. She took her daughter to hospital, where she was diagnosed with measles. She had spent the previous week playing with Sean, who had a rash at the time, but Jane dismissed it as eczema. It wasn't. Soon, Sean was also diagnosed with measles. A mild case. He had caught measles because he wasn't vaccinated, and then he'd passed it on to her friend's baby.'

'But why wasn't her baby vaccinated?' Bonnie asks.

'Good question,' she replies. 'I'm glad you've been keeping up. Have you been keeping up, Selina? Forgive me for saying this, but you look like you're about to pass out . . . is this story upsetting you?'

Poppy pokes her on the shoulder but Selina continues staring at the flames.

'The reason the other baby caught measles was because she hadn't yet had her vaccination against it. She was too young. Exactly a month too young. And because she was younger, when she did catch it, she found it harder to fight off. And in the end, her temperature rose to forty degrees. She developed sepsis, then her brain swelled up inside her skull. And then, six days after she was diagnosed, she died.'

Poppy stops. Suddenly, all her previous strength has left her. She feels as though she is floating, a feather in the breeze, the weight of her fury finally lifted.

'Her name was Chloe,' she says. 'And she was my beautiful, precious baby. And this woman . . .'

Poppy rounds on Selina, leaning down to shove her by the shoulders.

'This woman is the reason my daughter died. Because she whispered poison into my stupid friend's ear, telling her all manner of nonsense and conspiracy theories, preying on her gullibility and stupidity, just like she's tried to prey on ours

357

all weekend. And the worst thing of all? She doesn't even feel guilty. She has no regrets. She's still peddling the same dangerous nonsense, to anyone stupid enough to listen. Did you know that measles used to be almost completely eradicated in this country? And now, because of dangerous women like her, and because of stupid women like Jane, in some parts of the country only sixty-six per cent of children have been vaccinated. It used to be ninety-five per cent. Thanks to women like this. I don't think it's unreasonable to call these people murderers, because their actions have led to avoidable deaths. Like the death of my baby, Chloe. And wait until you hear the best thing of all! The most unbelievable, insane thing of all, is that this woman, this woman who calls herself a qualified midwife, holds no qualifications whatsoever. She's a fake, a fraud, a quack, the worst kind of human, taking money from women when they're at their most vulnerable, with absolutely no training or experience to back her up. And here she still is! Running this retreat, this weekend, to whisper her evil in your ears! The reason I came here was to share with you all my story. To stop this woman in her tracks. Because someone needs to stop her, and others like her, before more children die . . .'

Like a wilting plant, Poppy folds over, overcome with exhaustion. She sinks to her knees and stares into the flames herself. She starts to weep for her daughter, and for the sense of relief, that she so hoped she'd feel.

Before she knows it, Nicky is beside her, rubbing her back and pulling her towards her.

'I'm so sorry,' she says, whispering in Poppy's ear. 'I'm so sorry.'

It's all Poppy has ever wanted to hear. But not from her, not from an innocent bystander. From the woman herself.

'I just want her to understand the damage she's done,' Poppy says. 'The pain she's caused. I wanted her to see it, face to face.'

Poppy glances back over at Selina, hoping for something – any kind of reaction – to show that she understands, that she feels remorse for what she did.

But instead of looking back at her, or speaking, Selina simply gets to her feet, and walks away towards the barn.

SELINA

I am not well. I don't know what's wrong with me, but I do know that it's not just the stress of the situation.

I'm really, really ill.

As Poppy paces around me, ranting and raving, I continue to stare at the flames lapping in the fire pit. Part of me wishes I could just fall straight into them, to be extinguished.

Anything to make her stop.

Because I don't see how there's any going back from any of this. River has gone. Kai has gone. Georgia has gone. Poppy is telling everyone what an awful person I am.

Even though that's just her opinion. Not a fact. Just what she thinks.

I know I helped Jane. She had a beautiful home birth. A natural home birth. Everything went exactly how it was meant to, and her son was healthy and happy. He didn't need to go near a hospital. He was born the way nature intended.

The measles was horrible, tragic, but the truth is, it was just bad luck. Sometimes these things happen.

I haven't heard from Jane since it happened. We had become close, but she dropped me after Poppy's baby died. Perhaps she felt guilty about what happened to Poppy's daughter, and couldn't face me. I wish she had reached out though. I would have consoled her, reassured her that it wasn't her fault. That it was exceptionally bad luck for that baby to have died of measles. It's incredibly rare these days.

But none of that matters now. All that matters is that I get some sleep. My face feels numb and tingly, and my chest is tight.

I walk through the kitchen but have to stop short by the table for a few seconds to catch my breath. It feels as though I might faint. I stare down at my hand as it grips the table's edge. My fingertips turn white with the pressure.

'Are you feeling OK?'

I turn my head – an excruciating movement – to see Badger smiling at me.

'No,' I say. 'I don't . . .' I screw up my eyes – suddenly the light in the room is too much. 'I think I'm coming down with something.'

My legs give way from beneath me and then the whole world disappears.

When I open my eyes, I am lying in my bed. Someone is sponging my forehead with something cool.

I can barely see. My eyes feel like they have boulders weighing down on them. As I force them open, it's as though my eyelids are being continuously stung by bees.

'I . . . can't . . . breathe . . .' I say, squinting through the pain. I can just make out Badger's face above me.

'That's because you've been poisoned,' he says, or at least I think he says. His words are woolly and muffled.

'What . . .' I say. He keeps spongeing at my head, but each gentle dab feels like a boot stamp.

'Earlier on,' he says, and despite my confusion and fever I can tell he's speaking very slowly, trying to be as clear as possible. 'I poisoned you.'

I can't respond to that. I must be hallucinating. What is going on? Where am I?

'In about an hour's time, you will die,' he continues. 'At the moment your nervous system is being slowly and systematically destroyed by the toxin you ingested. The feelings you are experiencing right now are all linked to your abnormal heart rhythm, caused by the poison.'

I close my eyes, try to block out his voice, but I see purple sparks behind my eyelids and still his voice drones on.

'It was in the tea you drank,' he is saying. 'I grated some wolfsbane root into it. Looks a bit like horseradish, to the uninitiated. But it's one of the most deadly plants you can grow in an English country garden. The flowers are beautiful. You admired them yourself just last week. They rise tall and majestic. A little like delphiniums, but the most beautiful deep shade of purple. The leaves and flowers are mildly toxic, but it's the roots that are the most deadly.'

I start to splutter. The pressure in my chest is becoming unbearable.

'Please . . . take me . . . hosp . . .'

'What's that? I thought you didn't believe in hospitals. No need for that. And anyway, it's too late, I'm afraid. The damage is done. There's no antidote, even if I was minded to take you to hospital. Just a matter of waiting it out. And then I'll tell

362

everyone. What a tragedy. How you shouldn't use free, unqual-ified labour – the ignorant – to plant your garden. Because they might just plant deadly flowers by mistake, and who knows what might happen . . .'

He slams his fist down on the bed, making the whole thing vibrate. My body convulses with the pain. I try to crane my neck up to see where he is in the room, but it crackles and fizzes with the agony of every movement.

Where are the others? Will is with Georgia, at the hospital. But where are Nicky and Bonnie? And what about Poppy? Do Badger and she know each other?

'Now, you're probably wondering why,' he hisses. 'Why would I do this to you? After all, we're really good pals, aren't we, Selina?'

'Please . . .' is all I can manage in response.

'I mean, we've always got along JUST FINE. But the thing is, I haven't always been honest with you. I came here for reasons you probably won't expect. The truth is, you see, I came here looking for someone. But when I got here, she was nowhere to be seen.'

'Not . . .'

'That's right. Josie. My daughter.'

Josie.

No, no, no. This can't be happening. I try to edge away from him, but I have no strength at all. Surely the others will come soon? Surely they will come and find me?

My stomach turns over and I retch a trail of slime from the side of my mouth. I can't even turn my head, and some of the vomit falls back down my throat, choking me.

My eyes strain against my skull. The pain is indescribable. I just want it to be over.

'Now, I haven't been the best dad over the years, but as you can imagine, I was pretty excited when she got in touch to tell me she was expecting a baby. She told me all about your son, how they'd met while bumming around Europe. She sounded so young, and in love. Just what you want for your daughter, in the prime of her life.'

'I—'

'Don't interrupt, I'm telling you a story. Anyway, she was very complimentary about you – saying what an expert you were in all things pregnancy and childbirth. How they were returning to the farm so that she could give birth here. You know, we're not too dissimilar, you and me. Both believers in alternative lifestyles, and Josie was the same. I was pleased for her, that she was going to get to have a natural birth, as she wanted. She said she'd let me know how it went, so that I could come and visit my grandchild as soon as it was born. I was away on a volunteering project in Borneo at the time, but I arranged to come back as soon as possible. But then . . . then her emails stopped.'

'She . . .'

'I didn't have your address, but I managed to find you online. I couldn't work out what had happened to her, or why she'd cut me off like that. So I thought, I'll turn up, see what's what. And what did I find? Kai. A quivering wreck. Not the man my Josie described in her emails. What had you done to him, Selina?'

He dabs my forehead once again.

His face is so close to mine. I retch.

'I thought perhaps Josie didn't want to see me, that I'd upset her by not offering to come back straight away or something. We used to fall out a lot, you know. She was a feisty one. So I didn't tell him who I was. He had the baby with him, but when I asked him about the mother, he was cagey. Said she'd run off. Now, I knew that my girl wouldn't do something like that. That there was more to it. You were all hiding something, but I couldn't work out what. So I decided to stay, to do a different kind of digging, along with the actual back-breaking digging you set me. And eventually, I wore Kai down. He told me the whole story one night, when I'd given him one too many cans. How you'd taken Josie under your wing and fussed over her, told her how much you loved her, told her you could bring her baby into the world safely. How excited you all were to have a home birth. But when she eventually went into labour, something went wrong. The baby got stuck. And Kai asked you to take her to hospital but you insisted on keeping her here. And after River was born, Josie bled to death.'

'It was what she wanted! She wanted a home birth.'

'Did she want to die though? Is that what you're saying?'

'It was an accident . . .'

'Apparently afterwards you told Kai to be grateful that you'd got the baby out alive, that if you had taken her to hospital, they might both have died. He was in a right state when he told me. A snivelling, snotty mess. Too scared to go to the police, convinced if he did, that social services would take River away. I could see how much you'd manipulated him, used his guilt about his birth and your own operation against him. I mean, he was just a kid, wasn't he?'

365

'No, I—'

'Kai had no idea who I was, of course. I never told him. I hadn't seen Josie for a few years, but I loved her to death. I don't mind admitting to you, Selina, that afterwards, when I was alone in my hut, I cried. Me, a grown man. And the worst thing of all was that Kai said he had no idea where her body was. That he'd been a mess afterwards, and that you had said you'd take care of it.'

I close my eyes again, and visions of that evening swim into my mind. The blood, staining everything . . . Kai screaming louder than the baby.

'What! No! That's not true! It was . . .'

But my throat closes as I gasp for air.

It was Will's idea to bury the body, I want to shout. *I wanted to report it!*

Will had been away that night, staying with Ed. He came home the next morning to find me pacing the kitchen, Josie's body on the floor covered in a blanket. Kai was upstairs at the time. In the end, he didn't leave his bedroom for a week, and then he moved into the pigsties.

I begged Will for help. I was terrified, didn't know what to do. And he was so calm. My hero. Almost as though he was made for this moment. He took me by the shoulders and told me to get it together. Then he took Josie's body out into the woods and buried her.

He said it would ruin us all if it ever got out that she had died on the farm. I was in no fit state to argue; I was in shock.

But I never told Kai that Will was involved . . . I didn't want him to blame Will. They'd never got on very well and I so wanted them to build some kind of relationship.

366

'Apparently you tried to convince Kai that no one would miss Josie. Her mum died a few years ago, she'd been travelling from place to place ever since. You convinced him that if you told the police, then you'd all go to jail for not getting help when she was in labour.'

He pauses. My head throbs.

It was all Will! I want to say, but my throat won't let me. *It was what Will told me to say! I was just doing what he told me to do!*

'I guess this means that you knew you were in the wrong the whole time.'

No!

She wanted the home birth. She was terrified of hospitals, and even when I could see things weren't going to plan, she begged me not to take her.

It wasn't my fault!

'Or is it the case, as Kai was too naive to believe initially, that you actually wanted her to die? That you wanted that baby for yourself? That ever since your emergency hysterectomy – oh yes, I know all about that, how it fostered your hatred of hospitals – you've been desperate to have another child. And how convenient it all was, to have this young girl turn up, fully loaded, about to pop! A ready-made baby without any of the hassle of pregnancy or childbirth! But of course Josie was never going to let you take her baby, was she? Even if she was only eighteen. She would never have given up her baby, so it was much easier, much simpler all round, to allow her to bleed to death on your kitchen floor.'

'No!'

'Well, we'll never know now, will we? That's all right

though, I can make peace with that. Now I know that you'll never be free to do anything like this again. And as for Kai. I don't mind admitting to you that when he told me, well, I felt quite murderous myself. I wanted to wring his scrawny little neck. But then I could see deep down he was just a scared little kid. That he was completely in over his head. That it was all your doing, Selina.'

His eyes bore into mine.

'You know, over the past few months, we've got to know each other. And he's not a bad kid. Just a product of a bad upbringing. I might have messed things up with Josie, but at least I'll get a chance to put things right with Kai. And of course, most importantly of all, my granddaughter.'

'River,' I croak. 'She's mine . . .'

'Not any longer, I'm afraid.'

'It . . . wasn't . . . me . . .' I gulp.

'Tell me where Josie is. Tell me what you did with her!'

He's right in my face now, but I feel strangely at peace because I know that soon he will be gone, and so will I.

I have to fight for every breath.

'The . . . woods. The . . . bluebell woods,' I manage. 'I'm . . . sorry . . .'

'You're not sorry,' he says. 'I've been here for four months, waiting and watching for any evidence that you might be. But you're not. That's OK. That's OK, Selina! Because you're going to be. Very soon. I'd say in less than an hour, you'll take your last breath, and then, right before you die, you'll be the sorriest you've ever been.'

BADGER

That's right, Selina. Take your last breath. Think about what you've done. All the pain you've caused.

You'll never be River's mother now.

They're safe. Staying with my aunt, for the time being, in Okehampton. Then we'll get a place together, the three of us. He's got a bright future ahead of him, that boy. I could see that he had so much love to give, if only he was given the chance. If only someone took the time to see him for what he was, what he has to offer, rather than trying to stuff him into a mould.

He thinks you blame him for the hysterectomy, for not being able to have another baby. He's eaten up with guilt about it.

His birth made you infertile, but even so, Selina, how could you punish a child for that? How could you?

It took a long time to work out how to do it. Which method to use. But then I got talking to Will and he told me about your plan to launch a range of herbal teas. And I thought about my old mate Bill.

He was a good man, Bill. A gardener who died from digging up wolfsbane, touching the root and not washing his hands properly before he ate his dinner. He went into acute cardiac arrest. The autopsy proved it: death by aconite poisoning.

It wasn't too hard to track down wolfsbane. For something so deadly, it's beautiful. It grows in the wild all around here. I planted a small patch, taken from the hedgerow in the lane, right at the back of the wildflower meadow. Didn't want Kai or River to get their hands on it. Or any of the guests, of course.

You're probably wondering how much of a part Kai had to play in all this. Don't worry, I haven't shared my plan with him. He doesn't need that on his conscience, after all. He only wanted me to help him get away, to start a new life with River. And I'm so grateful he told me the truth about what happened to Josie.

I wasn't always the best father to her. But it was hard. She was a scrappy thing. A wild horse that didn't want taming. And certainly not by her dad.

I persuaded Kai to leave earlier, so he wouldn't have to see how you end up. Green-faced and puking as your internal organs slowly disintegrate.

As for Poppy . . .

Well, that was a bit of a turn-up for the books. I had no idea, when she arrived, that she was yet another of your victims. I didn't tell her my plan, either. No one knew. But she did know I wasn't a fan of yours. I saw her coming out of the yoga studio, sobbing, after you'd upset her in her one-to-one session.

I said if it was all getting too much, that she could go and stay with my aunt for the night. That got her out of the way. It means she won't become a suspect if the police really start digging. She wasn't here, so they can't suspect her, despite her strong motive.

I'll be off, shortly. They might think Will's done it. That would serve him right, really. Kai told me he was away that night, but even so. He must have known what you did, and yet he still stayed with you. But even if they do suspect him, it'll be hard to prove. And no one knows about Josie or River, do they? You've been very careful to hide their existence from the world. So no one will ever suspect me. The harmless old farmhand. Useful in his own way, but not worth paying too much attention to.

I know about Josie though. My little girl. And now I know that she's buried out in the woods, discarded like an old pet. That she never got the funeral she deserved.

I can just about bear it, I think.

Knowing that you have paid for your crimes.

And knowing that I have River now.

One day I'll tell her who I really am. Her grandad.

I can make right what I got wrong before.

NICKY

Bonnie and I are pacing around downstairs when we hear Badger come out of Selina's room. He hurries down the staircase.

'I think we need to call an ambulance,' he says.

'What?'

'I don't know what's happened to her, but she was really struggling to breathe and now she's lost consciousness. She was sick again too.'

'Oh my God,' I say.

'Do you have your phone?' he asks. 'God knows where mine's got to.'

'Of course.'

I ring for an ambulance and we rush back upstairs with the phone. I listen as the medical dispatcher on the other end tells me what to do. Selina is lying in the recovery position on the bed.

'Is she still breathing?' I say, rushing towards her, trying to follow the instructions I'm being given.

'Yes,' Badger replies. 'But it's very shallow.'

I place my ear near her mouth. I think I can feel her breath against my cheek, but I don't know for definite.

'I can't tell,' I shout down the phone. 'I think so ... but I can't tell for sure if she's still breathing or not.'

The woman on the end of the phone tells me to wait for the ambulance, to put a hand on Selina's chest to see if it's rising or falling.

'I think so,' I say, 'but it's not ... it's not very regular.'

'The ambulance will be with you as soon as possible,' the woman says. 'Just keep her in that position, and make sure her airways are clear.'

'What on earth could have happened?' I say to Badger, who's standing there, his face pale with shock. I look around for Poppy, but she's disappeared.

'It can't be some kind of reaction to what Poppy said, surely?'

He doesn't respond.

'It makes no sense. I thought she was feeling better.'

'No, she wasn't,' Bonnie says quietly. I hadn't even noticed she was still in the room. 'She started being weird after the tea session, remember? And then she looked awful when Georgia was in labour. Didn't you see the sweat was pouring off her?'

'She must have eaten something dodgy,' I say. 'But even so ...'

There's a banging on the door. Bonnie hurries to let the paramedics in.

'She's in here,' I say, ushering them through to Selina's bedroom. I wonder where Will is – whether he's taken Georgia to the same hospital that Selina will be going to, whether or not I should try to call him and let him know.

We leave the paramedics to it.

'Do you have Will's number?' I ask Badger. 'He should know what's going on.'

'I've already sent him a message,' he says. 'He hasn't replied. I expect he must be with the other lass in the maternity unit – probably got his phone switched off.'

'Oh God, what a mess it all is.'

I look over at Bonnie. She's crying, her arms wrapped around her middle as though trying to give herself a hug.

'It's OK,' I say, pulling her towards me. 'It's going to be OK.'

It feels like the paramedics are in the bedroom for hours. But eventually, they emerge.

They're not carrying Selina.

'Is she OK?' Badger says, his face drawn with concern.

'I'm very sorry. Are you the next of kin?'

Badger shakes his head.

'No, he's . . . he's not here.'

'I'm afraid Selina went into cardiac arrest and we were unable to save her. I'm very sorry. We're not entirely sure what the cause of death was, so the police will be here soon. As this is an unexplained death, there will be an investigation.'

'It must have been something in the tea,' Bonnie says. 'An allergic reaction? Would that make sense? We were . . . we were making these herbal teas earlier . . . oh God! It was Will's idea . . .'

'It's possible that she had a severe allergic reaction to something,' the male paramedic says. 'But we won't be able to say for sure until they do some tests. If you could all just stay here – the police won't be long. Are you all relations?'

Bonnie gives a harsh laugh. Her face is still streaked with tears.

'No,' I say. 'We're guests . . . The woman – Selina – this is her home. She's a yoga teacher, we've been here on a retreat. We don't really know her at all.'

How true those words are.

'I live here,' says Badger. 'Selina's been a very good friend to me. I help out around the place, maintenance and that kind of thing. I can't believe . . . this.'

'And Will? Who's he?'

I don't know if we are being cross-examined or whether they are just trying to be friendly. Do they actually care?

'Will is Selina's partner,' I say, not daring to look at Bonnie. 'But he's had to go to Exeter hospital, as one of the women in our group started having early contractions. We're all pregnant. It was a prenatal yoga retreat.'

The paramedic stares at his feet.

'I'm very sorry,' he says. 'This must be horrible for all of you. Not what you were expecting, I'm sure.'

'No,' I say. 'I can definitely say that nothing about this weekend has been what we expected.'

Three hours later, the police finally leave, followed shortly by Selina's body in a private ambulance. I sit on the sofa in Selina's kitchen, utterly shell-shocked. I called Jon as soon as I could, and he insisted on catching the train down straight away, leaving the boys with his parents, so he could drive Bonnie and me home.

Poppy has disappeared.

'She must have got a cab when we were all upstairs with Selina?' I say.

I didn't know what to tell the police about what had happened with Poppy, so I told them everything. It took more than an hour to go through all the details of this strange weekend. It was all so utterly bizarre.

'You don't think she could have . . .' I begin, staring at Bonnie. I feel absolutely exhausted, both mentally and physically.

'No,' Bonnie replies. 'She wasn't here when we were picking the flowers, was she? She arrived after that, and Selina was already ill.'

'But it just . . . she was so angry. What if she found a way?'

'A way to what? Poison her?'

'I don't know,' I say. 'It's all so strange.'

'I'm sure it was just an accident,' Bonnie says, as though trying to convince herself. The thought occurs to me that Bonnie might be responsible. Surely not? 'Some kind of weird allergic reaction. Maybe she was stung by a bee? And just didn't notice?'

'I've been stung by bees three times and trust me – you notice.'

'Well, something else then. A horsefly.'

'Maybe.'

'And where is Kai? Someone needs to tell him. Oh God, that poor kid . . . you said he had an issue with her,' Bonnie says. 'You don't think . . .'

'No,' I say, although of course I have no idea what Kai was capable of, how deep the resentment of his mother goes. 'No, I'm sure . . .'

'There's still no word from Will,' Bonnie says tearily, glancing down at the phone in her hand.

'He was there the whole time we were doing the tea stuff. He would know, wouldn't he? If she drank something poisonous?'

Of course, I wasn't entirely honest with the police. I neglected to mention the small matter of Bonnie and Will's affair.

'He wouldn't do that,' Bonnie says. 'No way. He's not like that. I promise.'

'Bonnie,' I whisper, 'you hardly know him.'

She stares at me, and lets the tears run down her face.

'No,' she says fiercely. 'He wouldn't.'

'I think your other half is here,' Badger says, appearing in the doorway. 'A cab has just pulled up outside.'

'Thank God,' I mutter, picking up my small suitcase. 'Let's go.'

I open the front door and Jon rushes towards me. I feel an immense sense of safety and relief as I fall into his arms.

'Thank you,' I say. 'Thank you so much for coming to get us.'

'Don't be daft, darling, I wouldn't want you driving after the shock you've had.'

I am so thankful to have him. To have all my boys. I will never take it for granted again.

'Safe journey,' Badger says, smiling as we look back at him. Bonnie hands Jon her suitcase.

'Will you be all right here on your own?' she says sadly to Badger. 'It must have been a huge shock to you too. I know what a great friend to her you were.'

'I'll be fine,' he says, reaching out and squeezing her arm. He has kind eyes. I feel so sorry for him. He doesn't deserve to be alone. 'Lived through worse than this. You take care of yourselves, ladies. And those bumps. Don't you worry about me.'

THE AFTERMATH

BONNIE

The inquest rules that Selina died from acute aconite poisoning.

An accident.

I have to look it up. Monkshood, or wolfsbane, as it's also known, is a really toxic wildflower. A wildflower that was growing in a small patch at the corner of the meadow among the others.

Will swears he doesn't remember planting it.

'It must have self-seeded,' he said, when I plucked up the courage to confront him about it. 'They're common among the hedgerows round here. I would never have planted it ... I would never have let you go out into that meadow to gather flowers if I'd had any idea ...'

I had no choice but to believe him.

After he found out, Will went to the wildflower meadow and set fire to the bottom half of it. I'd been at Nicky's house for the day, and came back to find the patch of land a soggy, blackened mess.

It reminded me of the scarecrow.

I assume Poppy was responsible for that little drama, along with the note I found in the studio and the dead rat.

Who else? I can't really blame her, given what she went through.

Will was sitting next to the patch when I found him, sobbing into his elbow. I put my arms around him, but I didn't know what to say.

He seemed as though he was really upset, but when he looked up, his eyes were dry. The wound on his head was still visible, a permanent reminder of all he had been through. Perhaps it was hard to cry for a woman who had treated him so badly. I would never get to the bottom of their relationship, it seemed.

At night, I have dreams that Poppy did it. Somehow, she magically slipped Selina the poison. But I don't know how she can have done, because we saw her arriving back at the barn, and that was long after we'd picked the herbs.

Either way, the coroner ruled Selina's death a misadventure. No one to blame. Just one of those tragic accidents.

I didn't have Georgia's number to congratulate her on her baby, of course. She left in rather a hurry.

But I found a picture of her new son – Calvin – on her Instagram a few days later. Her American boyfriend was in the photo too, beaming. He's incredibly handsome, in that bland TV-star way. Georgia had a full face of make-up on, which made me laugh. They looked happy. That's the main thing.

I sent her a quick message of congratulations through Instagram, but didn't mention Selina. I have no idea if Georgia found out about her death or not. It was in the papers round here – *Local woman died after accidentally ingesting deadly plant* – but I doubt Georgia would have seen those reports. I don't know if the police ever bothered to follow up with her.

Calvin was premature but healthy, and they got to take him home after a few weeks.

I was pleased for her. It felt like a good omen for us, too.

I have lived here for three weeks now. Our baby is getting bigger and bigger. My face has filled out, and I'm constantly hungry.

I've got everything I ever wanted. Nicky and I have been in touch daily, comparing pregnancy symptoms. The one really good thing to have come out of that dreadful weekend is that we are closer than ever.

But despite that, I can't settle. I feel uneasy being here, as though something isn't right.

I've tried asking Will how he's feeling about everything that's happened, but he won't open up to me. He won't even talk about Selina.

It's just the two of us here now. Badger's moved on – he said his aunt, Mabel, had taken a turn for the worse, that his carefree days were over.

'Time I do my duty and see her through to the end,' he said cheerfully. 'I've got away with it all for too long.'

I thought we might bump into him from time to time in Okehampton, but we never have.

Now everyone's left, Will is like a different man. He's pushing forward with his plan for the cookery school at The Sanctuary. He wants to rename it The View, to run residential cooking weekends here. It's such a great venue, and I have no doubt he'll make a success of it all. He's full of plans, talking more excitedly than he has since I met him.

I'll be honest, it's been a surprise to see how quickly he's got over it all. It's not that I *want* him to mourn Selina for months, but I had expected him to be more upset. Especially about Kai, who we haven't seen since that weekend.

I tried to track him down but had no luck. Will told me he didn't even come to Selina's funeral. He didn't seem bothered about it, said I should put it all behind me.

It seems odd to me that Kai left just before Selina died, but surely, surely, no son could do that to his own mother?

And anyway, the coroner ruled it as an accident.

I'm too scared to bring any of it up with Will in case it upsets him.

After all, his whole family has just vanished, and now it's only me and him here, and the promise of our baby. Almost as though we've simply replaced them.

I've got everything I thought I wanted, but somehow, it's not what I imagined at all. It still feels as though Will's holding me at arm's length. As though there's something he's not telling me.

I can only hope that when the baby arrives, things will be easier.

Perhaps then he'll have some sense of a future, rather than being controlled by the past.

POPPY

Poppy's stomach turns over as she sits in the chair opposite the therapist.

Ant persuaded her to come here, to properly process her grief. And for once, she decided to listen to him.

All her anger seems to have dissipated since that weekend. Faded into something worse, in a way: apathy. Depression.

At least when she was angry, she felt alive.

'When you're ready, why don't you tell me a little bit about how you're feeling today,' the therapist says.

She's a slight woman, in her late fifties, with the kindest face Poppy has ever seen. She is nothing like Selina.

Poppy nods, and tries to find the words. Her mind races.

It might be hard to believe, but she never wanted Selina to die.

When she ran out of her pseudo-counselling session with Selina, her head still sore as she tried desperately not to burst into sobs, she bumped into Badger.

He could see how upset she was, and told her to come with him to the little barn. He said he was good at first aid, that he could take a look at her head.

They sat together, side by side, on a log that he'd fashioned into a bench. Through tears, as he gently parted her hair and examined the wound, Poppy told him her story, about her daughter dying of measles after catching it from her friend. She didn't tell him it was Selina who had persuaded Jane not to have her child vaccinated. That was too risky. But she did tell him that Selina hadn't been sympathetic to her story. That they'd argued about her thoughts on vaccinations.

After what happened to Chloe, Poppy had found out a lot about Selina. And none of it was good.

She was a danger to women. At the time, she tried to explain her findings to Ant but he didn't want to know. He didn't understand her obsession, her need to find someone to blame. They started to fight all the time. Eventually he told her he couldn't cope, that perhaps they should have a break. Chloe's death had driven them apart. Because of Selina, she'd lost everything.

Poppy came to The Sanctuary because she wanted to show her, face to face, what she'd done. The harm and pain she'd caused. And she wanted to warn the others off her, to expose her for what she was: a fraud.

But confronting Selina was more difficult than Poppy had expected. And when Badger found her after her session, Poppy was a mess.

He told Poppy to go and stay with his aunt for the night – 'She's a lonely old girl, she's always grateful for the company' – to get herself together, and to come back the next day when she'd had a good night's sleep.

He said Selina had behaved outrageously towards her, by trying to push her anti-vaccination views on her. He was so kind. Poppy will never forget his kindness and empathy.

Poppy swallows, looking up at the therapist.

How can she explain all that?

'There's so much to say,' she begins. 'I almost don't know where to start . . .'

'One step at a time,' she says, smiling. 'Let's unravel it all one step at a time.'

Poppy nods, thinking of the words she can't quite speak aloud yet.

Maybe one day.

Poppy still has no idea if Selina's death was an accident, as the coroner ruled.

Badger contacted her afterwards to say that he had moved, with his aunt, to Wales, and that Kai was staying with them too, while he looked for work. She thought it was strange that Kai didn't want to live with Will, but perhaps it was all too painful, after losing his mum like that. And Badger and Kai seemed to get on so well.

Poppy never found out what Badger's issue with Selina was, but there's no way he was capable of killing her.

He definitely wasn't.

And after all, why would he want to?

WILL

In the end, things worked out exactly how I wanted. Like they always do.

Born lucky, that's what my brother Ed always says about me.

I mean, I never planned for her to die, but it was certainly the neatest solution.

And I saw Badger do it. Saw him take the aconite root from his pocket and grate it into Selina's mug when her back was turned. I knew what it was. We'd been warned how deadly wolfsbane – its common name – was when I was a kid.

I knew what he was doing.

And I didn't stop him.

I did wonder though. What had Selina done to offend Badger? Say what you like about her, but she could always surprise you. Then I remembered him talking about his daughter, how she'd died. I remembered the way he looked at me when he told me. I hadn't taken it on board at the time, but it was the kind of plot twist you've got to love. Comes straight out of nowhere and bam! Hits you between the eyes. Certainly gets the blood pumping.

Life on a farm is never dull.

And then afterwards, Bonnie told me about Poppy. Her little

performance by the fireside while I was driving Georgia to the hospital and, well, let's just say I was surprised.

If only I'd known about Poppy and Badger's vendettas, I could have saved myself a whole heap of agony. All my elaborate planning. The silly tricks. The burning scarecrow, the dead rat, the note – how ironic that its contents could so easily have been written by Poppy too! – the scarf, the pebbles in the wood . . . putting Josie's ring in her dinner. Letting down the tent – how was I to know Georgia and Nicky had swapped tents? It was Georgia, the journalist, I wanted to frighten. All that shit I'd carefully prepared to ensure the weekend was the perfect disaster from start to finish. Trying desperately to get Selina to crack under the pressure.

I'm most proud of my tearful 'reveal' to Georgia. Acting has always come naturally to me and I really pulled it off. Leaking just enough info about Selina's tricks to set our resident journalist on the right path. To ensure she went away from the weekend determined to do some digging into Selina's background, to reveal all in an exclusive article in the Sunday press.

But in the end, all my hard work was a waste of time. Because what do you know?! Selina had more enemies than I realised.

There are some downsides to how it all worked out though. I'm still amazed the police haven't come for me. After what I told Georgia, she might wonder if I did it.

I didn't, by the way. I've got a strong stomach – burying a body is not a task for the faint-hearted, especially not when it's one as young and beautiful as Josie – but even so, murder. No. That's not something I could do.

389

The irony of it all? Lately I've realised . . . well, don't laugh, but I miss her a bit. Selina. I've been dreaming of her a lot. Wishing I could see her again.

There's a thin line between love and hate.

Bonnie's so young. Sweet. Pretty. Nubile. The sex is great. All that good stuff. But Selina . . . Selina was my match. She was crazy, brave, different, exciting. Bound to lead me into trouble. And I liked that. I liked how much my parents hated her. How unsuitable she was – this half American with her moody teenage son, who wouldn't take any of my shit. Who stood up to me. Punched me when I got annoying.

But then, when Kai turned up after a year abroad with a pregnant girlfriend in tow, Selina finally confessed that she couldn't have any more kids. That was the first time her crazy really pissed me off. The first stab in the back.

It wasn't that I was desperate for children but, well, no one takes away my right to be a father.

And then I came home one night to find my kitchen floor covered in blood, a congealing teenager lying glassy-eyed on the tiles.

And that was when Selina had crossed a line.

It was no good. She had to go. But I knew she wouldn't just let me sling her out. She had her claws in me. I was everything to her. And she was in such a state that night that I'd had to get rid of the body.

In hindsight, I should have just shopped her, then and there, but I'd just come back from a night with Bonnie. It was still early days in our affair and I wasn't thinking straight. And at the time, I thought it might be nice to have Selina owe me one.

But I was an idiot. It left me vulnerable, that body. Preventing the lawful burial of a body is a crime in itself. I knew she could – and would – bring me down if I ever really pissed her off. I had to be cleverer about it.

And then later, of course, there was the small matter of Bonnie's unexpected pregnancy. A ticking time bomb. I couldn't put it off for much longer.

Hence my plans to sabotage the weekend.

My hope was that once the newspaper article ran, revealing Selina as a fake, she'd be scared enough about a potential fraud charge to disappear of her own accord. She had form for that, after all.

I had to be so careful, play it just right. It was exhausting, treading that line all weekend.

But I reckon I would have pulled it off, if more of Selina's past hadn't come back to haunt her.

Anyway, it's a shame how it all ended up, in some ways.

Despite everything, despite the fact that she couldn't make me a father, Selina made me feel alive, in a way no other woman ever has done.

But we'll see how things work out with Bonnie.

Perhaps there's some proper fire in her too, if only I can encourage it to come out.

And she's carrying my baby; that's the most important thing.

Once he's here, I guess we'll see how things go.

ACKNOWLEDGEMENTS

I can't really believe that I'm writing the acknowledgements for my FOURTH published novel. At the risk of gushing, I'd firstly like to say a massive, massive thank you to everyone who has enabled me to continue in the career I love. It's quite something, and it makes me a bit tearful if I think about it too much.

Most importantly – I want to thank the readers of my past three books. I find it very hard to comprehend that strangers have read my words – it's like trying to assimilate that the universe is never-ending; my brain can't quite process it. But it's true, and I am very grateful to you for buying, borrowing and reading my stories.

This novel was really fun for me to write but as always, there's a whole team of people behind the finished product! Thank you to my agent Caroline Hardman, who is loyal and wise and a constant support. It means so much that I'm not doing this job alone. And also the amazing team at Hardman & Swainson – a special thanks to Nicole Etherington for all her behind-the-scenes help.

The team at Quercus is just The Best and I genuinely feel so proud to be one of their authors. Huge thanks to my editor Cassie Browne for her careful and considered editing and for believing in, and sticking by, me. It means a lot. I'd also like to thank Kat Burdon for her invaluable extra pair of eyes on my work. The book is so much better thanks to both of you.

Thank you too to everyone who has worked on this book in the sales, marketing and PR teams at Quercus – Ella Patel, Ellie Nightingale, Dave Murphy, Isobel Smith, Frances Doyle and Sinead White. Often writers don't know just how many people have worked on their novels in some way, but I'm grateful to you all! And especially Lisa Brewster for designing my covers. I feel so proud when I see them all lined up together.

A huge thanks as always to all my wonderful writer friends, but especially to Caroline Hulse, Rebecca Fleet and Nicola Mostyn – you keep me sane. Keep dreaming of St Tropez . . .

And of course, thank you to my friends and family: my mum for beta-reading the whole book in one afternoon, my dad for his enthusiastic plot suggestions and my sister for always championing me. And most importantly of all, to Big Twit and Little Twit for being so proud and supportive – I'm so happy to be in your team.

Finally, I'd like to say that I really hope you have enjoyed reading this book – and I always love to hear your thoughts. So please leave a review if you'd like to. I read them all and find them really helpful when it comes to writing the next novel.

(Apart from the one-word review that just said 'Dumb'. That wasn't much help, although it did make me laugh.)

Charlotte x

PS You can find me on Instagram, Twitter and Facebook – I love hearing from readers so please do come and say hello!